"Not only has Hellmann created a compelling group of believable characters, but the mystery she places them in is likewise plausible and engrossing. *An Image of Death* is highly recommended, even if you don't live in Illinois…"

—David Montgomery, *Chicago Sun-Times*

"A clever blend of thrills and humor…a fresh, new gutsy hero…Hellmann has carved out an enviable place on the local mystery scene…"

—*Chicago Sun-Times*

"As she did in her first two books in this strong series, Hellmann makes sure that images captured on video play an important part in the action. And she balances Foreman's personal life…with her complicated, dangerous frontstory…"

—*Chicago Tribune*

"A chilling subject matter, intriguing psychological suspense, and disturbing Eastern European connections recommends this to most collections…"

—*Library Journal*

A Shot to Die For

"Libby Fischer Hellmann has already joined an elite club: Chicago mystery writers who not only inhabit the environment but also give it a unique flavor…her series continues in fine style…[Ellie]…lights up the page with courage and energy."

—*Chicago Tribune*

"Hellmann reaches the next level with latest mystery novel."

—*Chicago Sun-Times*

"Excellent dialogue, intriguing relationships, and good descriptions… I love Ellie's down-to-earth attitude…a credit to the series."

—*Mystery News*

"The best in the series…the plot has more layers than a Vidalia onion, but Hellmann handles them adroitly…"

—*Mystery Scene*

"Watching the development of this talented author has been a delight…Ellie is endearing, completely believable, and many readers can easily identify with her.

—Aunt Agatha's, Ann Arbor, MI

"This mystery has it all…a thoroughly enjoyable read and as addictive as potato chips."

—Andra Tracy, Out Word Bound Bookstore, Indianapolis, IN

Jump Cut

Books by Libby Fischer Hellmann

The Ellie Foreman Mysteries
An Eye for Murder
A Picture of Guilt
An Image of Death
A Shot to Die For
Jump Cut

Jump Cut

An Ellie Foreman Mystery

Libby Fischer Hellmann

Poisoned Pen Press

Poisoned Pen Press
6962 E. First Ave., Ste. 103
Scottsdale, AZ 85251
www.poisonedpenpress.com
info@poisonedpenpress.com

Printed in the United States of America

*To my mother, ninety-five years young,
and still beautiful, inside and out*

Acknowledgments

I am indebted to a number of people, some of whom did not want to be named. Their expertise in encryption and hacking into corporate systems was fascinating—and disturbing. Thanks also to Fred Rea and Detective Marc. A debt of gratitude to Kevin Smith, a terrific editor; as well as to Jan Gordon, Cara Black, and Kent Krueger, all of whom always tell it like it is. Special thanks, too, to Don Whiteman, who knows something about everything, including drones; and to Eileen Chetti, whose eagle-eyed copy edit picked up issues I never would have. And to the Red Herrings who listened—and critiqued the entire manuscript over the past year. My research took me from one end of the Internet to the other, but I especially want to credit an essay, *Anatomy of the Deep State,* by Mike Lofgren on Bill Moyers.com, which I quote in the book. Finally, I am delighted to once again be working with Poisoned Pen Press. Thanks Rob, Barbara, and Diane.

Chapter One

Tiny clouds of dust exploded whenever the boy kicked the stone down the road. He'd found it two hundred yards back as he skirted the herd of cattle. Flat and round, it looked like a small naan baked by the men in the village, except it was black. That was unusual around these parts; the summer sun bleached everything, including rocks, pasty white. A good omen, he thought, and he made sure to kick with his right foot, to lengthen the trajectory of the stone.

His destination was the madrassa at the village mosque. In a few weeks, he'd be picking cotton in his family's fields, but until the plants blossomed and the bolls split apart, his parents allowed him to attend school. But the boy didn't go very often. Over the past few months the atmosphere at the mosque had changed. Now a palpable energy bounced off the stone walls. Men he didn't know, men with flowing robes and beards, had come to the village, talking urgently about things he didn't understand.

He tried not to take notice. Only nine, he was more interested in playing tag, learning football, and sucking down the sweets his parents allowed him when they traveled into the city of Aksu three hours away. But it was difficult not to listen when the men sat all the boys down and lectured them about joining jihad. In fact, when he told his father about it one evening, his father scowled and put down his pipe.

"These men are not our kind. They speak of matters that do not concern us. They are dangerous. If you are not careful they will

bewitch you. Put you under a spell that will make you leave your home and family and travel across the desert with them."

The boy's eyes grew wide, and he threw his arms around his father. "I will never leave you, Dada," he said. "Or Ana."

His mother kissed the top of his head. "We know that, Yusup." But above his head she and his father exchanged a worried glance. "I have an idea," she said after a moment. "Why don't we go into Aksu tomorrow? All three of us. I have some shopping to do, and afterward we can go to the Internet shop and call your sister."

"On the Skype," his father cut in.

"Yes. The Skype," she repeated. She shook her head. The wonder of the technology still astonished her. "It is like she is in the next room, not halfway around the world." She smiled.

"Our world is changing," Yusup's father said. "Soon, my love, everyone will know about us. And they will come to our aid."

His mother straightened up. "I pray you are right." They exchanged another glance. The boy caught it but didn't know what it meant. He was excited at the prospect of going into town. They were too poor to have their own computer, but he was spellbound by the machines and their power. When he grew up he wanted his own Internet café with all the monitors and printers and Internet connections. He was a curious child, his parents said. Like his sister. To be able to contact anyone on earth at any time, to explore the world whenever he wanted, was the most thrilling activity he could imagine. Already he was anticipating what he would look for tomorrow. His sister always gave him suggestions for places he could search on the Google.

"Of course, we will only go if you have done all your chores," his father said.

So Yusup made sure to feed the goats and cows, sweep the floor, and help Ana in the kitchen. Still, it was early when he finished, and there was nothing to do. Most of his friends were at the madrassa. His parents gave him permission to meet them at the close of instruction. He hoped someone would have a ball.

He kissed his parents good-bye and set out for the madrassa. On his way to the village he passed the stream, flush from the spring thaw. *The stubbles of grass that sprouted on its banks were a stark contrast to the red rocky mountains that hung heavy and silent in the distance. This was his corner of the world, but he wondered what other places looked like. He'd seen pictures of big cities like Beijing and Shanghai. And, of course, the American cities of New York and Chicago, where his sister now lived. He swung his arms and smiled as he kicked the stone. He had much to look forward to: an afternoon of football with friends, and tomorrow a trip into town.*

A few huts indicated he was nearing the village. He quickened his pace and soon the squat buildings of the mosque, the village hall, and the marketplace came into view. He leaned over, picked up the stone, and slipped it into his pocket. As he did, a buzzing sound above pierced the silence. He looked up. He couldn't see anything, but the whining persisted. Sometimes he caught a glint way up in the sky. His father had said those glints were airplanes full of people traveling around the world. He expected to see the sun reflecting off one now and waited. But there was nothing: no reflection, no metallic glitter. Instead, the buzz got louder. Like thousands of wasps hovering inches from his ears.

He started to jog toward the village buildings. Something was wrong. He needed to get inside. Protect himself from the wasps. All at once a hissing sound mixed with a soft thwack overpowered the buzz.

A great white light flashed and obliterated all sight and sound.

Chapter Two

Monday

Before my gangstah-rap neighbor emptied his AK-47 into his buddy, the most exciting thing to happen in our village was the opening of a new grocery store. The store hired a pianist who played Beatles tunes, no doubt to persuade shoppers to part with their money more easily. My neighbor, rapper King Bling, was helping his fans part with their money too, but the shooting ended all that. Once he made bail, he moved and hasn't been heard from since.

And so it goes in my little corner of the North Shore, about twenty miles from downtown Chicago. There are benefits. The King, as he's known to his disciples, gave our cops something to do besides ticket speeders. And the new grocery store gave me the chance to buy prepared dinners so I could dispense with cooking.

Both of which come in handy when I'm producing a video, as was the case now. We didn't finish the shoot until seven. I raced up the expressway toward home, dropped into the store, and was eyeballing a turkey pot roast—the only one left—when my cell trilled. I fished it out of my bag.

"Mom, where did you get the shoes?" I heard chatter and giggles in the background.

"What shoes, Rachel?"

"The ones you gave Jackie." My daughter, Rachel, had successfully, if unbelievably, graduated from college and lived in an apartment in Wrigleyville. Jackie was her roommate. "Everybody thinks they're awesome."

I smiled. I'd bought a pair of shoes online a few weeks earlier. They looked like gray sneakers on a raised three-inch platform. They were adorable, just my style. When I tried them on, however, they were so steeply pitched I knew my middle-aged body would break one of my middle-aged legs in minutes. I'd sighed and given them to Rachel's roommate, who is decades younger but wears my size. "I don't remember. Online someplace." I eyed the pot roast and closed in.

"Did you have a Groupon?"

I wracked my brain. "I think I did. How did you know?"

"You never buy retail. Okay, bye. Oh, wait, Q wants us to take you to dinner."

Q, short for Quentin, is Rachel's boyfriend, and he's lasted longer than her usual flavor-of-the-month guy. They'd been "just friends" in high school but five years later discovered the other person was "pretty cool," as Rachel put it. Apparently it was more serious than I thought, if he was suggesting a meet-up with Mom. That, or else he had perfected the suck-up-to-the-parents routine.

"What a lovely thought," I replied, still eyeing the turkey pot roast, which smelled delicious even from a distance. Unfortunately, another shopper, a man with bushy eyebrows, narrow eyes, and one of those small baskets over his arm, was homing in on it too. I had to move fast.

"Let's talk about it later. I'm getting dinner…ready."

"Oh, Mom, I know you're in the grocery store. I can hear the music."

Busted.

The man with the basket caught me staring at the pot roast. His gaze wandered from me to the food. Back to me. I gave him a steely look. He turned back to the pot roast, shrugged in disdain, and picked up a slab of ribs instead.

I scooped up my dinner. It's the little victories that count.

Chapter Three

Monday–Tuesday

Back home after dinner, I called my father, who was cranky. Then Luke, my boyfriend, who wasn't. After that I called Susan, my closest friend. My daily check-ins complete, I climbed into bed and was soon immersed in a novel about time travel when my cell chirped. A text from Mac, my director and cameraman.

"Call at 6 a.m. Have to light the whole booth."

I sighed and wondered for the umpteenth time if I was getting too old for early morning shoots. We were producing a video for Delcroft Aviation, one of the largest aircraft manufacturers in the world, with huge civilian and military contracts. Headquartered in the Loop, they'd been around for years but had recently updated their corporate communications strategy. Now they wanted to appear "engaged with and interested in" their publics. In the age of Facebook, Twitter, and about a hundred other social media networks, I wondered how much a consultant had been paid to come up with such an obvious strategy. I didn't mind too much, though; the consultant recommended a video about the company, and Delcroft asked me for an RFP. We would feature only Delcroft's consumer aviation side. We were to have nothing to do with their military aircraft, bombers, and drones, which probably accounted for a hefty chunk, if not most, of the corporation's profits.

The video I proposed would be released in "chapters," like a book. A new "chapter" would appear on their website, Facebook, and YouTube once a week over several months. Delcroft would also sponsor a contest in which regular folks could win tickets to the destination of their choice, no strings attached.

Delcroft liked the idea, and we were now shooting one of our final setups, an aviation trade show at McCormick Place, where Delcroft was a major exhibitor.

Mac, prudent as always, was on top of everything.

"I'll bring coffee," I texted back.

The sun winked off the frozen surface of Lake Michigan the next morning as I drove south to McCormick Place. During one of the most brutal Chicago winters in decades, the smudge of purple clouds tinged with pink and gold hinted that the fury of winter might—just might—have peaked. I parked in the overpriced lot, bought half a dozen cups of overpriced coffee, and carried them into the massive exhibit hall.

The crew was setting up lights and shades, and Mac was behind the camera framing shots. MacArthur J. Kendall III owns a production studio in Northbrook. He started out shooting sweet sixteens, bar mitzvahs, and weddings, but parlayed that into corporate videos. We've worked together for nearly twenty years, from the days of two-inch video, to one-inch, three-quarter, and now digital.

Mac's name, salt-and-pepper hair, button-down shirts, and penny loafers scream WASP, but the nasty scar running down his left cheek saves him from total Episcopalian infamy. He tells people he was attacked by a Mexican drug lord and made me swear never to reveal it was from a car accident.

I went up to him. "What do you need me to do?"

"You have the shot list?"

I nodded and pulled it out of the canvas bag that doubles as my purse. We went over it. He gestured to the main area of the Delcroft booth, which featured a large projection screen with the company logo on both sides, and about twenty chairs arranged theater-style.

"What time's the first presentation?"

Teresa Basso Gold, our client contact, had told us to be prepared for a series of short remarks by Delcroft executives touting the company's latest innovations.

I checked my watch. Barely six thirty. "The doors don't open until nine, and Teresa said not to expect anyone until ten. But you can get some establishing shots, if you want."

"Sounds like a plan," Mac said and strolled over to confer with the crew.

Chapter Four

Tuesday

The shoot went smoothly, but there were lots of talking heads, and not many cutaways or B-roll. A lot of video folks don't mind. In fact, jump cuts of people talking, with no cover footage or transitions linking their remarks, are common in our "instant video" society. But I guess I'm a purist.

We did have plenty of video from the manufacturing facilities we'd been to, as well as interiors of the new planes they'd just introduced. Teresa had already sent me some file footage that would help us show the history of the company. Now I suggested she let us fly on one of their new planes to the Bahamas for B-roll; the light would be so much better. After all, it was February in Chicago. She rolled her eyes.

"Well..." I backed off. "There's always Miami..."

She laughed.

I sighed.

A man eyed us as he brushed by and smiled, as if we'd all just shared a joke. He sat in one of the chairs, presumably waiting for the next speaker. He was probably somewhere in his thirties, with piercing eyes, longish black hair, and a slender build. He seemed to be part Asian, part Caucasian, and he reminded me of Keanu Reeves in a pinstriped suit.

Teresa and I exchanged glances. She smiled. "Nice."

I checked her left hand. No wedding ring.

"He's all yours," I said. "I'm off the market."

"Can't do it," she said. "You know what they say about where you eat…"

I shrugged. "Pity." The guy was sexy in an understated but undeniable way.

"You said it."

I liked Teresa.

Producing, when you have a great director like Mac, is easy. I didn't have much to worry about except the script and how we'd edit the footage in post. I drifted around the booth, studying the models of wide-bodied jets. They were three feet in diameter and remarkably accurate, down to the upholstery on the tiny seats. I decided to ask for one of the models once the trade show was over. My boyfriend, Luke, is a pilot. He'd love it. I could picture it on the mantel above the fireplace in his office. Although maybe it should be suspended from the ceiling. I was mulling it over when I was interrupted by Keanu Reeves.

"Pardon me." He smiled politely. "I couldn't help noticing…" He motioned to the crew. "Are you with them?"

I nodded.

"What are you filming?"

"It's a promotional video for Delcroft," I said.

"Promotional?" He tilted his head as if he didn't know what that meant.

Now that we were standing together, I saw that his eyes weren't dark like his hair. In fact, they were sea blue and fringed with dark lashes. Striking.

"We're showing the softer side of Delcroft," I said, stealing the old Sears ad line.

His expression remained blank. He didn't get it. I cleared my throat and stuck out my hand. "Ellie Foreman."

He looked me over. I have long, wavy black hair, which, thanks to my hairdresser, will never contain a strand of gray, and blue-gray eyes, and I can still fit into a size eight, although they keep liberally interpreting the measurements. Still, it didn't appear he was interested in my feminine attributes, which was what I'd figured when he approached.

We shook hands. "I'm Gregory Parks," he said. "Do you work for Delcroft?"

"No. I'm a freelance producer. Delcroft hired me to make this video. Actually, a series of videos," I added.

"Oh." He didn't seem to know what to make of that.

"I used to be in broadcast news." I still feel compelled to tell people that. As if to assure them that while I might be a flak now, I was once a respectable member of the fourth estate. Then again, given the deplorable state of TV news today, it might not have been such a wise decision.

His brow furrowed into a puzzled expression, which was cut short by the trill of his cell. He picked up, and a tender look came over him. He spoke softly in what sounded like Chinese, smiled, then disconnected and pocketed the cell.

His smile brightened, his eyebrows arched, and he looked more interested. I wondered if he'd been talking to a woman. Maybe his girlfriend or wife. I looked for a ring but didn't see one.

Suddenly he was all business again. "What division of Delcroft is making this—this video?"

"Public information." I wondered why he was asking. "What about you?" I asked

"I'm a—a consultant."

The consummate corporate catchall. It could mean anything from janitor to CEO. "That covers a lot of territory."

"My company sent me to research new developments in aviation."

"Oh. What company is that?"

"You wouldn't know it." He smiled, reached inside his jacket pocket, and pulled out a crush-proof box of Marlboros. I'd know the red-and-white logo anywhere. When I smoked, Marlboro was my brand, and the packaging hasn't changed.

I frowned. "Those things can kill you, you know." One of the things I'm most proud of is that I quit twenty years ago.

He colored and reached back into his jacket. "Sorry. I meant to give you this." He withdrew a business card, handed it to me, and put the cigarette box back into his pocket. I dug into my bag and gave him one of mine in return.

I took a look at the card. Just his name, an email, and a phone number.

"And the company?" I asked again.

His color deepened. "Actually—uh—I'm doing some work with Delcroft."

"Really."

He nodded.

"Well, in that case, don't let me keep you. Nice meeting you, Gregory." I dropped his card into my bag and turned away. He'd been pumping me. Checking me out. But he clearly didn't appreciate being pumped in return.

When we broke for lunch at a McCormick Place restaurant, I spotted Gregory again across the room. He waved as if we were best friends. I waved back.

"Who's that?" Mac asked between bites of a supersized twelve-inch hot dog.

"I'm really not sure. At first I thought he was trying to pick me up." I shrugged. "But he wasn't. He was pumping me about Delcroft. But then he said he worked with them."

Mac raised his eyebrows.

"Weird dude." I shrugged.

The rest of the day was a blur of presentations, close-ups of the model planes, and cutaways. By the time we were finished, it was after six.

"Shall I upload the footage to you?" Mac asked.

Now that everything's digital, I no longer need to spend long hours in a dark room hunched over a machine with an editor. I can screen and tag shots on my desktop, then email Mac what I want. Still, I miss the intimacy of the editing room. That's where the magic happens, and if you're lucky enough to have an editor like Hank Chenowsky, who works for Mac, it doesn't feel like work, even when I walk out of a darkened room hours later like a cranky owl blinking in the sunshine.

"You know what? I think I'll come over tomorrow morning and screen it with Hank. Let him know, okay?"

"Good deal," Mac said. "Bring doughnuts."

Chapter Five

Wednesday

I tend to waver between the concepts of free will and destiny, but if ever an individual was destined to become a video editor, it's Hank Chenowsky. He claims he spent his formative years in front of the tube, and I believe him. It gave him an innate understanding of shots, images, and eye candy that make a film—or in our case, a video—more polished and impressive than it has any right to be. I'm not sure where Mac found him—he says he rescued Hank from an after-school computer-programming class—but wherever he's from, Hank's the best editor I've ever worked with.

I dropped the box of doughnuts beside the coffee machine in Mac's studio and opened it. I pulled out a jelly doughnut covered with sugar. After snagging a napkin, I headed down the hall to the third room on the left. The door was open, and I could see Hank already hunched over the console, screening tape.

"For you," I said, placing the doughnut next to a mug half-full of coffee. Hank straightened, inspected the doughnut, and grinned.

"Krishna has revealed himself." He templed his hands.

Thin and gangly, with light blue eyes and long pale hair, Hank's coloring is almost albino, although when I teased him about it once, saying that's what comes from never being out in the sun, he took offense. I learned later that an absence of skin, eye, and hair color is sometimes associated with mental retardation. Hank is as sharp as the sun on a Caribbean beach, but his reaction made me wonder if someone else in his family wasn't.

Now I gazed at him. "Him?"

He looked up, an impish gleam in his eyes. "I am grateful to all gods. Regardless of gender. Especially when they bring jelly doughnuts."

"So I guess that makes me a goddess?"

"The goddess of doughnuts." He bowed his head. "I worship at your altar."

"Jeez. If I bring you chocolate, do I get elevated to supreme goddess?"

He shook his head. "I don't do chocolate. Bad for my skin."

"Ah."

"But…another jelly? Or honey-glazed? That could be worth an entire church."

I smiled and lowered myself into a chair beside him. "Then consider yourself worshipping at the church of Delcroft."

He took a large bite out of the doughnut, followed it with a swig of coffee, and turned back to the console.

Each time I visit Mac's editing room, there is some new piece of equipment I don't understand. Today it was the monitors. There were at least two new ones, each showing something different. Which now made a total of eight. And that didn't include the monitors on the Avid, or whatever new editing system Hank was using. The panel of switches, sliders, and levers on the machines resembled the cockpit of a small plane. It used to look like all the control rooms of the TV stations I worked at, something I understood and felt at home in. Now, though, I was lost.

Hank had already assembled a rough cut of four chapters of the video, and I'd done a rough scratch track of the narration. Once we selected the shots from the trade show, we could easily drop them in. I'd scheduled a meeting the following Monday with Delcroft at which the top executives would, hopefully, approve what we'd done. Then we'd add the professional narration and all the special effects that make our videos a cut above.

Hank and I scrolled through what we'd shot the day before, marked a couple of sound bites from the presenters, and looked for cover footage to make the visuals more interesting. Mac had taped some shots of the model planes on display at the booth, and we decided to do a cross-dissolve from the model to the real thing cruising through the air once we got file footage from Teresa.

We were discussing where to make the dissolve when Mac stuck his head in. "Everything okay?"

I nodded. Like Hank, I'm happy to spend all day in the editing room. I watched as Hank played with the static shot of the model and animated it so it looked like it was flying.

"Nice." I smiled.

Hank smiled too. To create something out of nothing, something we could be proud of, was a form of artistry. Well, at least, skill.

"Foreman," Mac said, "didn't you promise us a trip to the Bahamas? So we could shoot the plane's interior?"

I hesitated. "Um, that's a negative. They didn't go for it."

"Always promising…when are you gonna deliver, Ellie?"

"Teresa seemed slightly more enthusiastic about Miami."

"Yeah, sure."

"Hey…" Hank cut in, "who is this guy?"

"What guy?"

"He's turning up in almost every shot."

I squinted at the monitor. "Oh, him. A consultant or something." I checked my notes. "Gregory Parks."

"Yeah? Well, his name should have been Waldo. Take a look."

Hank had marked the video and rolled through three or four shots. Sure enough, Parks was either hobnobbing with other people, or studying the model planes, or sitting in front of the booth.

"You know, now that I recall, he was pumping me during the shoot."

"About what?"

"Delcroft." I bit my lip. "Keep going."

Hank cued up another shot and pushed "Play." A woman was speaking at the front of the booth, the screen behind her. She was talking about the safety features of the new planes, and the screen showed close-ups of seat belts, fire extinguishers, and defibrillators. When she started in on the automatic pilot system, Mac panned from her to the audience. About a dozen people were listening, including Parks. His expression was so intense I had the sense he was parsing every word. I felt uncomfortable, as if I was eavesdropping on a private conversation.

Mac must have sensed the same thing, because he chose that moment to pan back to the woman. She was clearly avoiding eye contact with Parks, looking everywhere except at him. Although a pleasant smile was pasted on her face, it didn't reach her eyes. She looked worried.

I leaned forward. "They don't look like buddies, do they?"

"No, they don't." Hank leaned back. "Who is she?"

I went back to my notes. "Charlotte Hollander. She's Delcroft's VP and director of engineering. Just moved to Chicago from Utah. Teresa says the woman's a rising star. Could possibly take over the top spot one day. Like the woman at GM."

Mac stroked the scar running down his cheek. He does that when he's surprised. "A woman at Delcroft?"

The three of us studied her image. She was tall, slim, and all business. Probably in her forties. Blond hair in a tight twist. A severe black suit. Dark eyes, and a long pointed nose that made her look sharp. She didn't appear to be wearing a lot of makeup, but she didn't need to. Frown lines on her brow indicated she'd fought more than one battle climbing the corporate ladder. At the same time, a slightly haughty expression said, "Don't mess with me."

Mac frowned. "Engineering, you say?"

I nodded.

"Why was she in Utah?" Hank asked. "Is she Mormon?"

"Hank, your stereotypes are showing," I said.

Mac stroked the scar on his cheek. "I still don't get it. Why would she have to approve the video? We're not dealing with anything close to engineering."

"Maybe to make sure we're not spilling any secrets?"

"Secrets?" Hank made his eyes go wide. "Are you saying a company like Delcroft has secrets?"

"They're the top military contractor in the country," I said. "Fighter jets, drones, all that stuff. In fact, before we got the job, Teresa said she had to do background checks on all of us."

"Now you tell us," Mac said.

"You passed. I was the one they had a problem with."

If it were possible for Mac's eyebrows to arch any higher, they did. I shot him a look. "No worries. We worked it out."

Hank scratched the side of his nose. "That doesn't explain why she's giving the cold shoulder to that guy."

I shrugged. "An ex-boyfriend."

"She doesn't look like the type," Hank said.

"True," I said. "But at first I thought he was trying to pick me up."

"So what do you want to do?"

"Let's just use him once or twice. Lucky for us we're doing serials. Viewers won't remember from week to week."

"You got it."

"Will I need to revise the scratch track before Monday?"

Hank shook his head. "The first four will be ready by Friday."

"Great. You can Dropbox them to me."

"*Sí, señorita.*"

"Wait. So now I'm a Spanish goddess?"

"Just practicing for Miami."

Chapter Six

Wednesday

"If a heart attack doesn't get me, the Medicare paperwork will," my father said that afternoon. "You wouldn't believe the mountain of paper on my desk."

We were in a booth at the kosher-style deli in Skokie that my father loves: a place with black-and-white square tiles on the floor, a giant menu that goes on for eight laminated pages, and a tantalizing aroma of garlic pickles and fresh-baked pumpernickel. Dad always orders the same thing: kreplach soup, corned beef on rye, coffee. He's nothing if not consistent. He's also over ninety, so he's earned the right to be in whatever mood he wants. He continued to grumble.

"You just wouldn't believe it."

"What's the problem, Dad? You've got your Part A and B, your supplemental, and your Part D, right?"

My father leaned across the table. He's never been tall, and age has stooped him. He looks frailer every year, very much like a wizened Ben Kingsley. But his mind is as sharp as a box of tacks, and his heart, which has grown bigger and kinder over the years, makes up for what he's lost in stature. "They send me reports of every doctor's visit, every prescription, every time the home gives me a pill, practically every time I cough, for Christ's sake. Then they tell me how much they're covering, and what they may pay. Then when they actually do pay, they send it all over again. When I die, you're gonna have to dig through the papers just to find my corpse. *Emmes.*"

I sipped my coffee. I'm used to his rants. "So, why don't you just trash them?"

"What…and screw up the environment?" He straightened up. "Plus, who knows? One of those papers might save you a lot of money someday."

I sighed. My father was a lawyer, and he tends to be a hoarder. His case files from fifty years ago are still in my attic. "I can always ask for duplicates," I said.

"Then there will be another mountain of paper to get rid of. I'm saving you the trouble."

I narrowed my eyes. "Since when have you become green?"

"Green?" He looked puzzled. "Oh. That." He lifted his coffee cup. His hand shook, but he didn't spill.

"And anyway"—I reached for a sugar packet—"you're not dying."

"I'm gettin' there."

I don't argue with him anymore. Having reached a certain age myself, I suppose I'm more sensitive to his. Even though there's a steady stream of new acquaintances in his assisted living home, he's lost most of his close friends. He's even outlasted the previous owners of the facility. I keep imagining the new owners slipping arsenic into his food, hoping for his demise so they can double the fees and screw some other old soul. But, as I told Luke, over my dead body.

"And his, it would seem," Luke shot back.

Now, though, I kept my opinion to myself. The waitress, a middle-aged woman with bottle-blond hair and a toothy smile, brought our sandwiches, along with an extra plate of sliced garlic pickles.

"You take good care of us, Shirley," Dad said with a smile.

Shirley winked. "You, Jake. I take care of you."

He beamed. "Will you marry me?"

"Sorry. Been there, done that."

"Haven't we all?" My dad took a bite of his sandwich.

Shirley retreated. As if on cue, a male voice called out, "Well, fancy meeting you here!"

We looked up. Gorgeous blue eyes, silver-streaked hair, a great body. I hadn't seen him in months, so it took an instant to realize it was Barry, my ex-husband and Rachel's father. I'll say one thing for him: he always manages to look incredibly sexy. Another man, presumably his lunch partner, lurked in the background.

"Barry!" I got up and gave him a hug. We've been divorced for more than fifteen years, longer than we were married, and time had conferred an equanimity on our relationship. We'd both moved on. No one was more surprised at that than I.

Barry turned his attention to my father. "Jake..." He reached out his hand. "You don't look a day older."

My father took his hand and covered it with his other. "And you're still full of it..." But Dad was grinning.

Barry didn't miss a beat. "So how have you two been?"

"Fine," I said.

"Terrible," Dad said.

Barry turned to me. "How's Luke?"

"Great." I wanted to change the subject. It's still uncomfortable for me to talk about my new love with the old one. "You look terrific...as usual."

"Thanks..." His smile was just a bit smug, reminding me that he's only too aware of his effect on women. Which he proved during our marriage. Repeatedly.

"You seeing my granddaughter enough?" Dad broke in. He gets right to the point.

"Dad..."

"It's all right, Ellie. I get it," Barry said. He turned back to Dad. "Rachel and I had dinner two nights ago. In Wrigleyville."

"Good. A girl needs her father. No matter what age she is." Dad directed his comment at me.

My cheeks got hot.

Barry nodded. "Well, this was a terrific surprise. Please stay well, both of you. Call me sometime, Ellie. I think we can actually talk to each other now."

I didn't know what we would possibly talk about, but I kept my mouth shut. He backtracked and walked away without introducing the man he was with.

Which of course was the first thing my father asked. "Who was that masked man?"

"No clue, Kemo Sabe. Business associate? Tennis partner? Golf buddy?"

Dad shrugged. "Probably not a bad thing."

"What wasn't?"

"You two splitting up."

I recalled how upset he'd been at first and pasted on my Martha Stewart smile. "It was a good thing."

"Even though what's-his-name isn't Jewish."

"What's-his-name has a name. More important, he makes me happy."

"So when are you getting married?"

I yanked my thumb toward Barry, who was at the counter paying his check. "As Shirley, our wise waitress, said, 'been there, done that.'"

Dad frowned.

"I like the fact we're not with each other all the time. We give each other space."

He snorted. "We didn't need space when I was young. You live together, you live *together*, know what I mean?" He paused. "Then again, I guess I'm getting too old for this world."

I swallowed the sudden lump in my throat. He was supposed to be ageless.

Chapter Seven

Monday

The following Monday, I drove down to the Loop, my laptop on the passenger seat. My treasured Volvo had sputtered out a few years ago, and I was now the proud owner of a Toyota Camry, with Bluetooth, rear-camera vision, and satellite radio. With so many amenities on cars these days, I wondered if it would be possible to move into the car and sell the house. I'm considering it.

I parked in the Delcroft garage, which, curiously, was not underground but occupied the seventh through tenth floors of their building. The garages were patrolled by an armada of security contractors, and I wondered for whom they had been working prior to this gig. Experience has taught me the military-industrial complex is not as big as we think. And that contractors have a tendency to double back.

I slinked past three uniformed guards and shot up to the sixty-fourth floor, which was occupied by the corporate offices. Those offices were as opulent and plush as you would expect from the country's largest military and civilian aircraft provider, with thick padded carpets, oil paintings on the wall, and large glass windows with a spectacular view. On days that weren't overcast, the receptionist insisted she could see all the way up to Evanston.

She led me to the conference room. It contained a huge mahogany table, recessed lighting along the walls, and a blazing halogen light over the table that reminded me of a hospital oper-ating suite. Two dozen chairs ringed the table, and screens hung on all four sides of the room. A sideboard, also mahogany, was set with half a dozen bottled waters, crystal glasses, tiny plates, coffee, and fruit. No bagels or pastries, I noted. Which goes to prove my theory that the higher your rank and salary, the fewer calories you consume.

I was wearing my one designer business suit: black Donna Karan pants with a red jacket. I'd piled my curly black hair on top in a kind of twist, and even put on makeup, which Luke swears makes my gray eyes look like Elizabeth Taylor's. See why I adore this guy?

Feeling very corporate, I greeted Teresa. She was friendly, but her eyes darted around the room, and she nervously ran her tongue around her lips. I smiled, hoping to calm her down, but it didn't have much effect. I was at least ten minutes early, but Charlotte Hollander was already at the table. She gazed at me blankly, then checked her watch and scowled. It was a classic intimidation technique, and Teresa, who was several rungs below Hollander, squirmed. Happily, I didn't have to play that game. I was an outsider. A consultant. I flashed the woman a bright smile.

Hollander seemed puzzled, as if she wasn't sure why I would go out of my way to be pleasant.

Two points.

I stuck out my hand. "Good morning. We met at the trade show. I'm Ellie Foreman."

Her handshake was as limp as overcooked pasta. "Nice to see you again."

I smiled and connected my laptop to the projector, which was at one end of the table. I inserted the flash drive and played with the settings until the titles for the first video flashed on the screen. I paused the laptop.

"I'm very anxious to see what you've done." Hollander smoothed the lapels of her navy blue jacket, even though there wasn't a wrinkle to be seen.

"I am too. I hope you like what we did."

She nodded but wouldn't meet my eyes. Not quite imperious, but close.

Twenty minutes later, the other four executives who needed to approve the videos were in the room, exuding the fake bonhomie that people in ferocious competition with one another do. I was introduced to Dave Foxhall, executive VP of corporate communications, to whom Teresa reported, their chief government lobbyist, who'd flown in from DC, and the deputy chief operating officer. A tall, slim man in his late forties or early fifties, Gary Phillips was way high up at the company. Prematurely gray, he had perfect blue eyes, attractive crow's-feet around them, and an impeccably tailored suit. There was a fourth man, too, older, round, and bald, but Teresa spoke his name and title so quickly I failed to register it.

The men sat at the table, and Teresa made her way to one end. "Good morning, everyone. As we've discussed, one of our key communications objectives is to make our web presence and products more visible, both nationally and globally. To accomplish that, Delcroft is about to join the new world of social media, and these videos are our first 'shots across the bow,' so to speak.

"We want to be perceived as a friendly company—an approachable company—but one that is dedicated to excellence. We're focusing solely on the consumer side, as you know, and we decided to air our first efforts in weekly installments on our website. Like a serial."

I saw nods from most everyone in the room. Phillips, the deputy COO, asked, "Will this be on Facebook, Tweeter, and all the others?"

Teresa nodded. "Yes. The videos will be hosted on our website, but we will get the word out on Facebook, Twitter, YouTube, Pinterest, and more."

"What do you mean 'get the word out'?" the man whose name and title had escaped me asked.

Was he really that clueless? He probably didn't have kids.

Teresa went on. "We'll link to all the social media outlets to drive traffic back to our website, where people can watch the videos, make comments, and ask questions. We've hired a social media manager who will keep track of the hits and comments and even reply when appropriate."

"Reply? What are we replying to?" Phillips asked.

Before Teresa could answer, the lobbyist cut in. "Uh, I think that's a problem. This social media person—who is he?"

"He's a *she*, Harry," Teresa said. "Her name is Naomi Kraft. We hired her about a month ago."

"Which means she doesn't know anything about corporate policy, legal obligations, or congressional work. How can she speak for the company?"

Teresa glanced at Foxhall, her boss, a short blond man with a bristly mustache. He kept his mouth shut.

"If comments involve any of those issues," Teresa said, "we'll get input from your people before we reply. The key is that we must respond, even if we have to tell them it's proprietary information. We want the public to perceive us as one of the 'good guys.' One of the few companies they can trust and respect."

Harry the lobbyist shook his head. "I don't know about this."

Phillips frowned. Teresa was losing control. Why didn't Foxhall back her up? I snuck a glance at him. He was leaning back in his chair and fiddling with a pencil, as if he wanted to be anywhere but the conference room.

"Pardon me," I chimed in with what I hoped was a friendly smile, "but why don't we take a look at the videos? I think many of your concerns will be addressed after you see them."

Teresa threw me a grateful look.

I saw Phillips nod. I stood up, dimmed the room lights, went to my laptop, and hit "Play."

Chapter Eight

Monday

I shouldn't have.

The first installment went well, which I expected. We'd dressed it up with our best shots and some eye-candy effects. I actually saw some smiles and dared to hope everything else would run smoothly too.

The problem surfaced near the end of the second video. Charlotte Hollander's back suddenly straightened, and I saw her scribble something on a notepad. I jerked my head toward the screen. We were in the middle of a sequence we'd filmed at the trade show. Had we done something wrong? Accidentally divulged some proprietary information? I didn't think so, but I jotted down the approximate time code when she'd first reacted.

Then, during the third video, Hollander's mouth fell open and her chest heaved with such a deep breath I was afraid she might explode. I turned toward the screen. We were back at the trade show, specifically the model airplane that dissolved into stock footage of the plane cruising through the sky. Hollander pursed her lips and tried to make eye contact with Foxhall, but he slouched down and practically slid under the table, refusing to look at anyone. Finally in the fourth video, Hollander made more notes.

When the screening was over, I paused the laptop and turned up the lights. The men in the room didn't look annoyed, but I didn't expect them to. Most people don't know the difference between a jump cut and a dissolve and don't really care. They just want to be entertained, and it seemed they were. I saw a couple of appreciative nods, as if the videos had reinforced what a terrific company they had the good fortune to run.

Hollander, though, folded her hands, looked down at her notes, then cleared her throat. The wave of icy fury rolling off her could have frozen Lake Michigan. I knew something bad was going to happen.

"I don't know about the rest of you," she said in a haughty voice, "but I find these videos unacceptable."

The room went silent. My spirits sank. I shot a glance at Teresa. A look of panic unfolded across her face.

Phillips frowned at Hollander. "Why is that, Charlotte?"

"This looks like something my twelve-year-old son could have thrown together. It's a pastiche of amateur photography, editing, and uninspired—in fact, trite—narration. It's—it's"—she waved her hands in the air, searching for the right words—"undignified. If we air these, even on our website, we'll be a laughingstock. And I guarantee we'll take a financial hit."

I think I went into shock at that point, because the rest of her words seemed to come at me from a great distance.

She turned to me. "You"—there was a clear emphasis on the word—"have managed to make us look like a third world company trying to compete with the big boys. This is an abomination."

I heard a few cleared throats and embarrassed rustlings. One man scratched his nose. Another ran a hand through his thinning hair. I looked over at Teresa again. She was staring at me. I knew that stare. Her job and my career were at stake. Immediate triage was necessary.

I took a long cleansing breath and tried to pull myself together. "Ms. Hollander, can you be more specific? We can always make revisions. That's why we're here. What scenes were objectionable?"

She spread her hands. "Everything. I can't believe you'd actually suggest this material is appropriate for a Fortune 500—no, excuse me, a Fortune 100 company."

"GE has done something similar," Teresa said weakly.

"We are not GE."

"I realize that, Ms. Hollander," Teresa went on. "But their approval numbers have shot up. So have their profits. Analysts are beginning to use words like 'admiration' and 'respect' when they write about them. And then there's Richard Branson at Virgin. He tweets, writes blogs, and has an active Instagram account."

"*We* don't make light bulbs, Teresa," Hollander said. "And Richard Branson isn't worth discussing. Delcroft makes fighter jets. Consumer airplanes. Drones. Military aircraft. We are the world leader in aviation. This video makes us look like carnival barkers, cajoling people to go inside the big top. I think the entire project should be scrubbed."

There was more jostling and movement in the room. A heavy blanket of tension was slowly smothering everyone. But my irritation rose. The woman still hadn't mentioned anything specific.

"What if you and I meet with Teresa, Ms. Hollander?" I said. "So we can discuss your specific concerns. As I said, we're happy to make revisions. We want to make sure Delcroft is moving in the right direction. And that you approve."

She stared coldly at me. "I doubt that's possible." She glanced at Teresa's boss. "David, did you approve this?"

He shrugged. Actually shrugged. This from the man who hadn't uttered a word since he'd entered the room.

"Well…," Harry the DC lobbyist chimed in. "I liked it, Charlotte." I wanted to kiss him on the lips. "You have to remember that we're appealing to a younger generation. We want to make sure they know how ubiquitous Delcroft is. A critical part of the fabric of society. As well-known as Cheerios or—well, I hate to say it, but—Richard Branson."

I straightened. Maybe there was a kernel of hope.

Hollander shot him a narrow-eyed look but didn't reply. Was Harry higher up the ladder than she?

At last Phillips, who clearly had been measuring the emotional temperature in the room, took control. "Well, we seem to have some issues about this, Ms. Foreman, but I want to thank you for what you've done. This has been a very—productive meeting. We'll get back to you once we've had a chance to think everything through."

I nodded. I was still dazed, and a monstrous headache was coming on. As the executives left the conference room, I gathered my laptop and cords and stuffed them into my canvas bag. Teresa came over, looking very much like a gutted fish.

"I'm so sorry," I said.

She shook her head. "I didn't see this coming."

"I'll call you later," I said.

"If I still have a job," she replied.

Chapter Nine

Monday Night

I'd consumed most of a bottle of wine by the time Luke showed up that night. I usually don't see him until Thursday, when we spend the weekend together. But I was feeling as battered and bruised and pitiful as an abused puppy, so I called.

When I heard his key in the lock, I jumped up from the sofa and hurried to the door. He'd hardly taken off his coat when I threw myself against him and started to cry.

He wrapped his arms around me and held me, which only made me cry harder. I'd been trying to hold it together, but seeing his face, full of concern, cracked me wide open.

I clung to him. He rocked me from side to side like I used to do with Rachel when she had an "owee." "Whoa, whoa, what happened, sweetheart?"

"I've never been so humiliated in my entire career."

"Tell me."

I shook my head, tears still streaming down.

"It's okay," he said in a soft, gentle voice. "You're okay."

After a minute or so, I calmed down. I raised my face from his sweater and ran my fingers around the spot I'd cried on. "I think I ruined it."

"That's why they have dry cleaners." He smiled and brushed his fingers across my cheek. "Come on, let's go in there…" He pointed to the family room. "I want you to tell me exactly what happened."

I sniffled. He pulled a handkerchief out of his pocket. Luke Sutton is the only man I know besides my father who carries an actual cloth handkerchief. I took it and dabbed at my eyes. Luke wasn't tall, but he was sturdy and strong. His skin was pale and covered with freckles, about which he had to be careful. He wore glasses and had reddish brown hair, what little of it was left, as well as a scruffy gray beard that I had to remind him to groom. But he had the kindest blue eyes east of the Mississippi. My friend Susan describes him as the type of man you can't wait to take home to meet your parents.

Now he led me into the family room and sat me down on the sofa. "So, what happened?"

I explained how Charlotte Hollander had torpedoed the project. "It made no sense. Teresa had said there was a buy-in at the top levels of the company. But she just came at us out of left field, and then the other guy wouldn't say a word, and—"

Luke raised his palms. "Wait. You're going ninety miles an hour. Take a deep breath and start from the beginning."

I did. I went over the history of the project. How excited Teresa was. How her enthusiasm was contagious. How, after I'd unveiled the concept and my proposal, they approved it. How hard we'd worked on the filming and post. "It looks terrific, Luke. Hank was unbelievable."

He frowned. "And you're sure this woman sabotaged it?"

My eyes filled again. "Of course I'm sure. Plus, she was nasty about it. She said her twelve-year-old son could have done a better job. She was out to humiliate me. And Teresa. And she did."

"I don't get it. Who is this woman?"

"Vice president of engineering. She's pretty high on the Delcroft ladder. She might even be CEO one day."

Luke was quiet for a moment. Then: "There had to be a reason she went bat-shit crazy."

"I don't know what it is, but if word gets around, I'll never work in this town again."

"You think you may be just the slightest bit melodramatic?"

I leaned back against the couch. Now that I was calmer, I felt oddly removed from the events. I suppose it's because a human being can endure only so much shame. It might have been self-protection. Then again, it could just have been the wine kicking in. I massaged my temples.

"There had to be a trigger," Luke was saying.

"I don't know. Maybe she doesn't like other women encroaching on her territory."

Luke shook his head. "You don't become VP of engineering doing that. Did something in the video set her off?"

I sniffed again and tipped my head to the side. "Let's see. Everything was great during the first segment. I saw nods and smiles. In fact, I thought they were enjoying it." I paused. "It was good, Luke. No puffery, just, well—you know—sincere. Even a tad self-deprecating."

"Put your personality into it, did you?"

"Stop sweet-talking me." I managed a wan smile.

He grinned. "You got me."

"Hey, can I show it to you? I need an objective opinion."

Chapter Ten

Monday Night

We screened all four episodes. I watched Luke's reactions, but he could be a cipher sometimes. When it was over, I asked impatiently, "Well?"

"I'm no expert in this stuff."

I nodded.

"But I liked it. It was clear, convincing, and warm. And accurate as far as I know." Luke was a pilot. He owned a couple of small planes, and he knew a lot about flying and aviation.

"Not unprofessional?"

"Not at all."

I shrugged. "Then what's the deal? She knows that corporations are marketing themselves to consumers as partners and buddies these days. She understands the benefits of social media."

Luke stood up, went over to my credenza, and took out a bottle of bourbon. He poured himself a shot, then came back to the couch. "It could be one of a million things, Ellie. Delcroft is a huge company. I mean, the frigging CEO advises the president of the United States on technology and national security. Anyone high enough to be in the corporate suite is sitting on top of a cauldron simmering with envious sycophants."

I stared at him.

He checked himself as if I'd just noticed a stain or tear in his shirt. "What is it?"

"What did you just say?"

"That Delcroft is a simmering cauldron of people who all want the top job."

"No. The part about advising the president on technology and national security."

I didn't wait for his response. I slid the video back to the head end and started watching it again. Midway into the second segment was where Hollander had started to have problems. I paused the show, reviewed my notes, and backed up a few seconds. We were in the middle of a fast-paced montage. I advanced slowly. Then I found it. It was only a one-second shot, but there was Gregory Parks, the "consultant" at Delcroft's trade show booth at McCormick Place. He was sitting in the audience listening to Hollander speak. I paused the show.

"This guy. She saw this guy."

"So?"

I told him about how he'd been hanging around the trade show, and the arctic reception Charlotte had given him. "Of course, she's that way with most people, I've discovered."

"So?" Luke repeated.

I fast-forwarded to the next segment and slowed it down. I checked my notes again, found the time code I'd jotted down at the point Hollander got upset. Sure enough, there was another shot of Parks, this time examining the model airplane at the booth.

"This is it! This is why she was so upset. I'd bet my next bottle of wine on it."

Luke leaned forward, hands on his knees. "You don't know that. You just can't make an assumption."

"I think I can. She didn't like the dude. It was clear."

He folded his arms. "Okay, let's say you're right. What can you do about it?"

"Go back and ask her why she hates the guy. Tell her we'll delete every frame of him from the videos. I don't know. Beg."

"Sure, babe. She's certainly going to forgive and forget after what she did to you today."

I straightened up. "Then I'll go over her head."

"Not good."

"Why not?"

"You have no leverage. None at all. This is a company that hires three- and four-star generals when they retire. You're just a grain of sand, comparatively speaking. If you want my advice, I think you should find a new client. There are plenty of other companies in Chicago."

"But—"

"Ellie, if you make trouble for them, they'll make even bigger trouble for you. They probably have your dossier already."

"They do. They did a background check on all of us."

Luke spread his hands. "Well, all it takes is a new report from them about your conduct, your professionalism, maybe even your politics…"

I cut him off. "And I'm screwed."

He nodded.

"That's creepy. You make it sound like we're living in a country like Russia. Or China."

Luke shrugged and drank his bourbon.

We were both quiet for a moment. Then I said, "Well, then, if the mountain won't come to Muhammad…"

"Ellie…" He was quick with his reply. "Don't even think about it. Promise me."

I smiled, leaned over, and kissed him. "You're right, of course."

Chapter Eleven

Tuesday

I was feeling much better the next morning, especially after Luke brought me coffee in bed. I had a few sips, and then we did what we usually do in the morning. And the evening. And afternoons too, if we can. Afterward he went back up to Lake Geneva. I showered and dried my hair.

I was getting dressed when the computer in my guest room, which doubles as my office, chirped to tell me I had an email. I went in cautiously, unsure if I really wanted to read any emails this morning. I sat at my desk.

It was from David Foxhall at Delcroft. Foxhall was the executive VP in charge of corporate communications, the man who hadn't said word one during the meeting yesterday. Still, as Teresa's boss, he was my "official" client contact and had seemed enthusiastic when I proposed the videos. I pressed my lips together and read.

"Good morning, Ellie. After much internal discussion, we've decided not to proceed with the video. We will, of course, compensate you for the entire production, but since we still have issues with the concept, we're going to call off any further production. I hope this doesn't cause too much disruption for you and your crew. We wish you nothing but the best. As I said, please invoice me for the entire project. I'll make sure to expedite payment. Sincerely, David."

There it was. I'd been fired.

My first reaction was relief that Teresa still had a job. My second was less charitable.

"Damn those cowards." I stomped out of my office, went down to the kitchen, and stacked dirty plates and cups in the dishwasher. A minute later, though, my irritation faded, and I marveled at how powerful Hollander must be to have killed the entire project. A minute after that my mood improved even more, and I was grateful that we would be paid for work we didn't have to finish. That would make Mac happy. It might even pay for a long weekend for Luke and me; I entertained visions of flying down to Florida or the Caribbean.

A few seconds later, though, I was infuriated again. I'd been brushed off by a Fortune 100 company. I've been a professional filmmaker for more than twenty-five years, and I fumed as I threw a load of laundry into the washing machine. How dare they? On some level, I probably knew my anger stemmed from those never-ending feelings of insecurity lurking just under the surface. Feelings that were just waiting to wreak havoc on my ego.

During times like these, I'd usually call my friend Susan, and we'd work out our problems with a power walk around the village. But waves of snow flurries outside didn't bode well for a walk, and Susan worked at an art gallery on Tuesdays.

I started pacing around the house. The voices of insecurity mimicked the tone and words of my late mother. "Yes, a B-plus is nice, but where is the A?" or "Sheila got into Vassar. And you're just going to Michigan?" Still, her best role, worthy of an Oscar, had been that of an enabler. "You need to find out who did this to you and why. And fix it."

Chapter Twelve

Tuesday

I found Gregory Parks' number in my bag and punched it in. I wasn't surprised when a ubiquitous female voice recording instructed me to leave a message. Consultants are very busy people.

"Gregory, this is Ellie Foreman. We met at the aviation trade show last week at McCormick Place. I was producing a video for Delcroft. I wonder if you could give me a call."

I left my cell number, disconnected, and wondered what to do. I couldn't bring myself to call Mac with the news. Or commiserate with Teresa. I decided to binge-watch a season of *Homeland*—watching a bipolar CIA agent in trouble always cheers me up—and was just punching "Play" when my phone rang.

I picked up. "Ellie Foreman…"

There was a click on the line that I couldn't figure out. Then a male voice, which sounded like it was coming from a distance. "This is Gregory Parks."

"Mr. Parks, thanks for returning my call." He obviously screened his calls. "I hope you remember me."

"Yes. Yes, I do." He didn't sound impatient. More curious.

"I wonder if you'd be willing to meet with me."

There was a long pause. Then: "Why?"

I cleared my throat. "Well, we're in the middle of our project for Delcroft, and I know how interested and knowledgeable you are in aviation. I thought perhaps you'd like to see the workprint. I have it on a flash drive, which means I can meet you pretty much anyplace. I'd really like your input."

"I'm sorry, but I'm no aviation expert. I don't see how I can help."

I thought about how to proceed. I didn't know this guy, and I didn't know a thing about his relationship to Hollander. I needed to be circumspect.

"Well, Gregory, we met with Charlotte Hollander yesterday and she seemed to react to your presence on our B-roll. I figured that was because—"

He cut in. "What is B-roll and how did I end up in your video?"

"Of course. I'm sorry." I explained how B-roll was cover footage used to set the scene, cover narration, or transition between sound bites. "You did have an"—I searched for the polite words—"active presence at the booth."

"I see."

A wave of noise came over the phone connection. Then it vanished. I frowned. "She had a few—er—concerns about the videos, and I was hoping you might be able to shed some light on her thinking, since you two are obviously acquainted."

"Ms. Foreman, I still—"

"Call me Ellie."

"Yes. Ellie. I still don't see what I can do for you. I hardly know Ms. Hollander. I'm just a simple consultant."

My senses went on alert. Beware of anyone who claims to be an aw-shucks consultant. Especially if he looks like Keanu Reeves.

"I'm just asking for a few minutes of your time. Delcroft is an important player in the Chicago market, and I want to make sure my reputation is—um—A-plus going forward. Ms. Hollander has a lot of influence. Coffee or tea is on me. We could meet at Ann Sather's if you'd like." I snuck that one in. I wanted one of their cinnamon rolls. I *needed* one of their cinnamon rolls.

Parks didn't reply. He was probably wondering what he was going to get out of the meeting. Honestly, the answer was nothing. I was going to pump *him*. So I was surprised when he said, "I'm not downtown. And you live in the suburbs."

"How do you know that?"

There was a slight hesitation. "I—I assumed. At the trade show your director told me he was from Northbrook."

I frowned. Mac wasn't the chatty type. Especially with strangers. Which meant Parks must have been checking me out. But why? This was getting strange. Maybe I should forget about connecting with him. On the other hand, we would be meeting in a public place. Not some hidden back alley.

Then: "I suppose I can take the el in. I have an errand to run downtown anyway. Do you know the station where the Blue and Red Lines intersect?"

Parks must be west of the city if he was taking the Blue Line in. "Yes," I answered. "At Jackson." I hadn't taken the el in years. "As I remember, there's a pedway to get from one line to the other."

"Exactly," he said. "There's a Starbucks in the pedway. I'll meet you there. In two hours."

It wasn't as public a place as I would have liked, but it was better than nothing. "Okay. I'm pretty sure I remember you— I've certainly seen your face enough on the videos. Just in case, though, give me something to recognize you by."

"I'll be wearing a Burberry scarf and black North Face jacket."

How preppy. "Great. I'll look for you at Starbucks."

Chapter Thirteen

Tuesday

I parked at the Linden CTA station in Wilmette, hopped on the Purple Line down to Howard, then transferred to the Red Line for the ride down to the Loop. As we passed Rogers Park, Ravenswood, and Lakeview, bullet-fast glimpses of humanity flashed by. A bungalow with snow on its roof, a sagging porch, a tire swing hanging limp from a bare branch, a kid's tricycle.

I remembered my Lakeview apartment. I was a few years out of college, about the same age as Rachel now. Barry and I had just met, and the spark between us was explosive. We spent as much time as we could getting to know each other's bodies. Winter Sundays were my favorite. A long day and even longer night, our fishermen sweaters, jeans, and boots strewn along the hardwood floor, marking a telltale path to the bedroom.

The train went underground at North and Clybourne, and I caught my reflection in the window. I was smiling. A few minutes later, I got off at Jackson. Mayor Rahm was refurbishing the el stations—funny how he could always find a few million dollars when he wanted to—and the Jackson station had been one of the first upgrades. I started across the pedway. The homeless, who used to designate this spot, along with Lower Wacker, as their overnight accommodations, had vanished. So had the cracked walls and hollow echoes. The once seedy area was well lit, decorated with murals of commuters coming and going, and bursting with trendy shops, including, of course, Starbucks.

I hung around outside. People stopped in, and I watched the swishes and belches of all the machines until I figured I could always have an alternate career as a barista. I checked my watch. Parks was fifteen minutes late. I knew what he'd be wearing, so I decided to walk toward the Blue Line.

It was after lunch, but it wasn't crowded. The bustle of rush hour wouldn't begin for another hour. I followed the signs, walked up a flight of stairs, and wandered toward the Blue Line tracks. It was your average station, two tracks, each going in a different direction, separated by a concrete platform. I saw another set of stairs similar to the one I'd just climbed at the far end of the platform. The lights were dimmer here, or maybe it was just the fluorescent lighting. There was graffiti on the walls, and the slight rancid odor of urine. Remodeling had clearly stopped with the pedway.

I stayed at the foot of the stairs, figuring I would spot him getting off the next train. The train came about five minutes later, but there were so many cars attached—they must have been gearing up for the afternoon rush—that I couldn't see the end of the train. The doors swooshed open, and about two dozen people got off and headed up the stairs. I looked toward the far end of the platform and spotted a few people emerging from the train. I hurried over. Maybe Parks didn't know Starbucks was behind us. I could probably catch him before he finished climbing those stairs. I started to jog.

As I did, I heard a train approaching behind me from the opposite direction. The whoosh of an artificial breeze blew across the platform, and its noise grew from a growl to a roar, finally crashing like thunder as it slowed. It, too, seemed to have a lot of cars attached, which meant it would take longer to come to a full stop. Like the other train, which was just leaving, this train's cars extended beyond my sight line.

All at once, a blur of movement flew across the platform at the far end. A woman screamed. Then a man shouted. The train lurched to a stop, its brakes screeching long and loud, like a wounded animal. A few seconds later, two men raced toward me. Someone else ran up the flight of steps at the far end of the platform.

"Call the police. Get the cops! Right away!" one of the men passing me shouted.

"Oh my God! Oh my God!" the second man cried.

"What happened?" I said.

"Someone threw themselves in front of the train!"

Chapter Fourteen

Tuesday

Everyone's heard about desperate souls ending their lives on the train tracks. I had a distant cousin who did just that. But what was happening now seemed fantastical, like a script from a tragic film or TV movie. Goose bumps covered my arms, but I felt hot at the same time. I had to remind myself I was okay. Alive and unhurt. I hated myself for looking, but I couldn't avoid it, and I hustled to the end of the platform, where a crowd of people had materialized. Where had all these gapers come from? A few people were on their cells, presumably calling the police. But others were already taking pictures and probably posting them online.

I looked around for a Burberry plaid scarf, which Parks had said he was wearing. I didn't see it. I pushed farther into the crowd but was hampered by a woman who had assumed the role of town crier. I used to work in TV news, and I've noticed that people often fall into predetermined roles when tragedy strikes. There's the town crier, who tells everybody else what's going on as if he or she has inside information. There's the Greek chorus, people who listen to the town crier and react with the appropriate horror, sorrow, or fear. Then there are the naysayers, who want nothing to do with the event and barrel through it in an attempt to flee or deny its existence.

I elbowed my way through the crowd, triggering a couple of "Hey, watch it, lady…" comments, but I still didn't see Parks. Unease tightened my stomach. The engineer of the train was now on the platform, having cut the power to the train and third rail. He was staring down where a male, with most of his face hidden, sprawled across the tracks. A portion of his cheek was visible, blackened from electrocution. I couldn't see his face, but when I saw the flap of a beige, black, and red Burberry plaid, I froze.

◇◇◇

A wave of nausea rose to my throat, and I clapped a hand over my mouth.

Someone nearby peered into my eyes. "Are you all right?"

I shook my head. I was about to say something when a loud voice cut in.

"Police. Everyone get back. Give us room."

The crowd parted to let two officers pass. They'd arrived fast; they must have been patrolling the station. The first officer was a woman. She grimaced when she saw the body.

"Shit."

The male officer followed, looked down at Parks, and squeezed his eyes shut. Then he turned to face us. "Time to go, folks. Show's over. But before you do, the sergeant here is gonna need your names and numbers. We'll have someone contact you. Anyone see him jump?"

I was rooted to the platform, trying to process what had happened. A siren shrieked from upstairs. The paramedics had arrived. The cop tried to keep a modicum of order. "Get back. We got a stretcher on the way. Anyone know this man? Anyone see what happened?"

He turned in my direction. My stomach knotted. The officer's eyes narrowed as if he thought I knew something. A wave of guilt washed over me, but I knew from experience that saying anything was going to involve repeating the same thing to different officials for the rest of the day and night. It would also eventually involve Delcroft and Charlotte Hollander. Given my current situation, that would be a disaster. If the company was dragged through the press because of their connection with Parks, and if my name was linked to the mess…I shivered at the repercussions. I felt as guilty as hell, but I kept my mouth shut.

Thankfully, the town crier interceded. "I saw him, Officer."

The cop turned his gaze to her. "You saw him jump?" He pulled out a small notepad. "What's your name?"

"Brenda Huffmann." She was a blowsy woman, with thinning gray hair. I sensed this was the most exciting thing that had ever happened to her and she was determined to make the most of it. "Well, yes. Kind of."

"What does that mean? Where were you?"

"Well, uh…I was down there." She gestured vaguely toward the stairs near me.

"Ma'am, how far away were you?"

Her face reddened. "Well, I was kind of in the middle between the two sets of stairs."

The officer sighed, as if he realized whatever she had to say would be worthless. Still, he made the effort. "Yeah? So what did you see?"

"Well, it was really fast. All of a sudden. First he wasn't there; then he was."

"Where did he come from?"

She glanced around at the remaining gapers, like she was fishing for support. I knew the guy. I should say something. I didn't.

"I—I'm not sure," she said tentatively. "The other train?"

Another man chimed in. "I thought I saw him get off the other train and head for the stairs, but then…"

"What?" The cop asked.

"I—I don't know," the man stammered. "It happened so fast."

I heard a commotion at the top of the steps.

The cop looked up. "Okay, everyone back."

The paramedics trotted down carrying a gurney, a cardiac defibrillator, and a duffel probably full of other equipment. They glanced down at Parks' body.

"Well, I guess we won't be needing that," one of them said, pointing to the defibrillator.

A new, artificially loud voice cut in. "Everyone's gonna have to clear the area. Emergency protocols are now in place. Trains will be delayed for the next few hours. Buses are on their way to take you where you need to go." A self-important-looking man in a CTA uniform came toward us. "Come on, now." He made a shooing motion with his hands. "There's nothing more to see."

The police officer pulled him aside and spoke to him.

The CTA man cleared his throat. "Before you go, please give the officers your name and number. We're going to need to interview you." His sudden use of the proprietary "we" made me want to smile. Almost.

The police officers were joined by four more uniforms and two men in plainclothes. Detectives. This was my last chance to step forward. To tell them what I knew. No. The risk was too great. The guilt I felt for thinking about myself at a time like this intensified, but I knew I might never work in this town again if my name surfaced along with Delcroft's and Hollander's. I also thought about what Susan, Luke, my father, and even Rachel would say. "Don't get involved Ellie—Mom—honey. Nothing good ever happens when you do."

They were right. I'd have to deal with it in purgatory. I turned around, ready to walk away from the scene. The nearby steps were braced by a sturdy concrete buttress wider than several columns, and the reinforcing support was only a few yards from Parks' body. In fact, the structure was thick enough to block the view from where we stood. Which meant that no one, including me, could have seen exactly what had happened when Parks jumped.

I studied the concrete support as I turned to start down to the opposite end of the platform. But I wasn't really watching where I was going, and I accidentally kicked something with my boot. It rattled.

I looked down and spotted a crush-proof box of Marlboro cigarettes. Parks smoked Marlboros! And I was only about six feet from the edge of the platform where he had jumped. I bent over, made sure no one was watching, and slipped the box into my coat pocket. Then I slowly walked away.

Chapter Fifteen

Tuesday

I jiggled the Marlboro box on my way back to the Red Line. Whatever was inside rattled again, a slight tinny sound. Where was the damn train? Finally it rolled into the station. I tapped my foot until the doors opened, hurried in, and snagged a seat. Then I flipped up the lid of the box.

Inside was a flash drive, the kind I use to screen shows for clients. The label said it was sixteen gigs. That's a lot of memory. An average video—at least the ones I produce—runs about thirty minutes, which, depending on the quality of the transfer, is rarely more than four gigs. I frowned. Why would Parks stash a drive like that in a Marlboro box? He *had* mentioned an errand he had to run. Was he planning to deliver it to someone? Had it flown out of his hands when he jumped? What was on it?

I stared out the window but, unlike this morning, paid no attention to the glimpses of Chicago racing by. This day couldn't get any worse. I'd been fired from a job, someone I knew had killed himself, I was nursing a bout of guilt for not coming forward, and now I had a mysterious memory stick, which, for all I knew, contained proprietary or illegal data. What was next?

When I got home I treated myself to a big glass of wine and ran upstairs to my office. I slid the drive into my computer. My Mac politely informed me I was now connected to an external drive and asked whether I wanted to open it. I clicked and saw the familiar blue icon that indicates a folder. There was no name on it, just a series of what looked like random numbers. I clicked, and a bunch of files popped up. There had to be more than fifty. They weren't labeled, though, and I couldn't figure out what app had created them. I clicked on one. A screen popped up that had nothing but a rectangular box and the instruction to "Enter Key."

It was encrypted.

I tried a few of the other files. They were encrypted too. I closed out and clicked "Get Info" on the folder. The folder contained five point five megs. Depending on what was inside, that might or might not be a lot of data. It was impossible to tell.

I sipped my wine and thought about it. Then I copied and dragged the contents of the drive onto my hard drive. I reopened the folder, clicked on a file that directed me to enter my key, and took a screen shot. I emailed it to Mac and asked him what he might know about it, aside from the fact it was encrypted. Then I realized I hadn't told him we'd been fired. I picked up the phone.

Chapter Sixteen

Tuesday

"Where did you get it?" Mac asked on the phone after he saw the screen shot.

"Um, I found it in a Marlboro crush-proof cigarette pack."

"What is this? A setup for a joke about spies?"

"What are you talking about?"

"Oh, come on, Ellie. You've seen it in dozens of movies."

I didn't say anything.

"Where were you when you found it?" I was about to reply when he added, "You know what? Maybe we shouldn't talk about this over the phone."

I bristled. "Oh, come on. You're always worried about stuff like that."

"That's because I know who I'm dealing with."

I sighed dramatically. "There's nothing to worry about, except my wounded ego."

"I'm not sure I like the direction this conversation is taking," he said.

"I'm not liking this entire day." I swirled the wine. I needed more. I walked the glass down to the kitchen and filled it again. "So, do you know anyone who could take a look at it?"

"The flash drive?"

"I'd like to know what's on it."

"Why? It has nothing to do with you."

I hesitated. "Well, um, that may not be the case."

"Okay. Enough bullshit. What's going on?"

I took a breath. "Yesterday and today have been the days from hell. I got an email from Delcroft this morning."

"From?"

"Dave Foxhall, the corporate communications guy."

"Why do I have the feeling I'm not going to like this?"

"Because you're clairvoyant." I told him about the meeting the day before, how angry Charlotte Hollander had been, the cold, humiliating way she'd burned us, and how we'd been fired via email. Then I told him I'd called Gregory Parks. I reminded him who he was. "But here's the punch line," I said. "Are you online?"

"Of course."

"Google his name, or just hop over to the channel seven website."

There was a minute of silence. Then: "Holy shit, Ellie."

I told him what had happened at the Jackson CTA station. How shocked and scared I was. "I'm still shaky." I also told him how I didn't say anything to the police.

He interrupted me. "That's got to be a first. But what about the flash drive?"

"It was an accident. I found the cigarette box near the edge of the platform where he jumped."

"So, let me get this straight. You were there when it happened?"

"I was."

"And you didn't talk to the cops and explain your connection to him."

"I did talk to the cops, but I didn't say I knew him."

Mac went quiet.

"So, I'm wondering if you know anyone who might be able to decrypt the files."

"Why do you care? Just because some guy you barely know jumps off a subway platform doesn't prove the Marlboro box was his. Or that it's any of your business."

"I guess that means no," I said.

"Ellie, you can't mess around with people who work for Delcroft."

"He's a consultant. He's not an employee."

"Yeah, and look what happened to him."

Mac had a point. "I get it, but consider this. What if the drive did belong to Parks? Maybe he stole data from Delcroft. If I can return it, quietly, with no fanfare, maybe we'll get back in their good graces?" I said hopefully.

Mac took a moment to respond. "There's so much wrong with that assumption I don't know where to start. First of all, you can't suck up to a company like Delcroft. You won't win. Second, you have absolutely no proof the flash drive belonged to Parks, or had anything to do with Delcroft. Third—"

"But I'd really like to know what's on that drive. Wouldn't you?"

"Not a chance. You have to drop this, Ellie. You're way above your pay grade. It could get ugly fast."

"Mac, you're scaring me."

"I hope so. Throw the fucking drive in the lake. Go find us a new client instead."

"Let me ask you this. What if it wasn't suicide?"

"Now you think he was murdered?"

"If Delcroft is as powerful as you say, who knows?"

"I have no idea. And neither do you. I'll admit this is probably the craziest thing you've ever been involved in. Wait, I take that back. One of the craziest. But just leave it alone. Like I said, find us another show to produce."

Chapter Seventeen

Wednesday

That night my bed was either too hot or too cold, and I kept kicking off the quilt then retrieving it. My brain was running in circles. Mac was right, of course. I shouldn't get involved. This was a potentially dangerous situation. On the other hand, I had been humiliated professionally. If the drive belonged to Parks, and I was sure that it did, and if it had something to do with Delcroft, and if I returned it to them, maybe I'd be a hero. Or maybe it was so sensitive it was going to get me into deeper trouble.

A lot of ifs, I knew. Still, the temptation to restore my reputation was irresistible. So was my curiosity. What the hell was on that drive? And why was Parks hiding it in a Marlboro box?

At around five I gave up, went downstairs, and brewed a pot of coffee. I waited until eight thirty, then made a call.

"Georgia Davis…"

"Ellie Foreman."

"Hey, Ellie, how are you?"

"In a bit of a jam."

"What else is new?"

I ignored the comment. "How are you doing, Georgia?"

"Terrific."

I knew she was seeing Jimmy Saclarides, Lake Geneva's chief of police and a close friend of Luke's. Our paths hadn't crossed yet, but they would.

"So what can I do for you?"

"I need to decrypt some files on a flash drive, but I don't know anyone who does that. I was hoping you did."

"I might. Are we on the record or off?"

"What do you mean?"

"You heard me."

I thought about it. "Off. Definitely off."

"Okay." I heard soft tapping on a keyboard. "You remember that guy we went to see in Park Ridge who was an expert in enhancing video?"

"Sure. I don't remember his name, but he had a dog. Jericho."

She laughed. "Right. It was Mike Dolan. Well, he has a brother who's an ethical hacker."

"A what?"

"You'll find out. Let me call him and make sure he'll see you."

Behind the white-picket-fence colonials and McMansions of Northbrook is the village's industrial zone. While residents take pride in their well-tended lawns, sculpted landscaping, and tidy exteriors, the industrial section is almost dystopian. Hidden under the spur of the Edens Expressway, it's a collection of one-story structures, Quonset huts, and parking lots. Every once in a while there's a tree. I will admit it's clean—to the point of immaculate. I didn't spot a dead leaf, fast-food wrapper, or bird droppings. Nothing that would lend the area any personality.

I pulled into a parking lot next to a one-story redbrick building. I'd called earlier and Zachariah Dolan said if I was a friend of Davis', I was welcome. I walked around to a concrete path that led to a door with nothing but the building number on it. It was unlocked, and inside was a hall that ran the length of the building. But there was no directory of names in front, and none of the office doors bore nameplates. I checked the note I'd made on the phone. He was in Suite 1505.

The man who answered the door was burly and sported a beard, but his apple-red cheeks said he couldn't have been more than twenty-five. I tried to remember what his brother looked like, but it was so long ago I couldn't figure out if there was a likeness. With dark hair and eyes, Zachariah's hair was long enough to frame his cheeks and blend into his beard.

We shook hands. "Thanks for seeing me, Mr. Dolan, but I've got to ask, what's an ethical hacker?"

He laughed. "It's Zach, and I'm one of the good guys."

I smiled. "I assumed that. Were you once one of the bad ones?"

He grinned. "You could say that."

"So what did it take you to turn from black to white?"

"Confession and three Hail Marys."

I liked him already. He led me from the door into a spartan office with four computers against the walls and a conference table with chairs around it in the center. That seemed to be the only room. He motioned me into a chair. "Actually, it was Mike who helped me see the error of my ways."

"Mike? How is he? And Jericho?"

Zach's smile faded. "Mike's fine, but Jericho has gone to the rainbow bridge."

I hesitated. "I'm so sorry. He was a great dog. Totally devoted to your brother." I cocked my head. "So. Ethical hacking?"

"An ethical hacker is a geek who hacks into his client's system—with their knowledge, of course—to find flaws and loopholes that a nasty hacker might be able to penetrate and exploit."

"That's fascinating," I started but then stopped. "Wait. If guys like you are on the case, why are there still so many hacks? Big ones, too."

He patiently folded his hands, as if he'd been asked that question before. "Lots of reasons. Technology is always changing and evolving. You plug one leak, and another one springs a hole. You have to realize that the black hats on the other side are just as capable and smart as us. Sometimes more. And the IT guys in large corporations are, shall we say, a little territorial."

"How unusual."

He smiled. "They're sure their systems are hack-proof. So they don't bother with guys like us." He shrugged. "Their loss.

Sometimes they come to us afterward with their tail between their legs."

"So you work for large corporations?"

He nodded.

"And you met Georgia through Mike?"

"I do some forensic work too."

"Like your brother."

"Yeah, it's pretty amazing, actually. I get paid to do what I love."

"Lucky dude."

He spread his hands. "So what do you have?"

"A flash drive with encrypted files."

"And you don't have the key."

"Right. I don't know the first thing about encryption." I dug it out of my bag and handed it to him.

He got up and went to one of the computers, inserted it into the USB port, and tried to open it. He stared at the files that appeared, then scratched his beard. "Well, I'll take a look, but I can't promise anything. Encryption is—uh—delicate."

"Really? Well, I'd be grateful for whatever you can do."

"Want to tell me what you know about it? Where it came from? How you got it?"

"Not particularly."

"I figured." He smiled again. "You didn't steal it, did you?"

I hesitated. "No."

"How do you know Georgia?"

"We have a long history. It started with my daughter over ten years ago, when she was a teenager. My daughter, that is. Georgia was still on the force then."

He studied me.

I cleared my throat. "So how much will this cost me?"

"Depends what I find. There is a minimum of three hundred. That's the friends-and-family rate, by the way. I'll get to it in the next couple of days."

"Great."

"You're sure you want to go ahead with this?"

I frowned. Was he trying to warn me off? Did he think three hundred would deter me? I was about to answer when I heard a loud scratching noise and a bark.

Zach rose and headed toward an alcove I hadn't noticed. "You okay with dogs?"

I nodded. He opened a door and a large German shepherd bounded out, his tail wagging furiously. He raced over to me and laid his head in my lap. I petted him on his head and scratched his ears. His tail wagged even faster. "And who is this?"

"Joshua," Zach replied with a twinkle in his eye. "He's my credit manager."

I giggled. "Wait. Joshua...Jericho...and you're Zachariah. What's with all the biblical names?"

He templed his hands as if in prayer. "We're a pious family."

Chapter Eighteen

Wednesday

On the way home from Zach's, my Camry chirped. Now that I have the latest Bluetooth technology, my cell rings through the radio and I can answer it hands-free. It even tells me who's calling. I was expecting a call from Susan, but my car said caller ID had been withheld.

I pressed "Answer."

A woman's voice said, "Hello. Is this Ellie Foreman?"

I knew that voice. "This is she."

"This is Charlotte Hollander."

It's a good thing the call was hands-free. Had I been holding the phone, I would have dropped it on the floor of the car. "Uh—really? What can I do for you?"

She cleared her throat. "I was wondering whether we could meet—for a drink."

"You? And me? Together?"

"I live in Lake Forest, and I know you're up that way as well."

Of course she lived in Lake Forest. It's the most affluent village on the North Shore.

"Why don't we meet at the Happ Inn, say, at five? It's right on my way home."

"I—guess that would be okay. But why—"

She cut me off with a crisp good-bye. "I'll see you there."

I pressed "End Call," my stomach knotting in shock. What did she want? To hammer the final nail in my coffin?

◇◇◇

The Happ Inn is the latest incarnation of a space in Northfield that's gone through so many rebirths over the past twenty years that even Buddha would approve. Now owned by the chef of an upscale restaurant in Highwood. It's a trendy bistro, with enough menu variety to please six-year-olds as well as sixtyish gourmands. Previous versions of the place had been decorated by each owner, but this rendering suited the affluent suburb in which it sat: polished oak booths and tables, private rooms for parties, and pieces of wall art that made puns using the word "Happ." There was even a flat-screen TV, just to remind everyone it was a "HAPPening" place.

I put on a pair of slacks with a silk shirt and applied my makeup carefully. I walked in an appropriate five minutes late and looked for Hollander. She wasn't at the bar, but the hostess came up to me and asked if I was waiting for Ms. Hollander.

"As a matter of fact, I am."

"I'll take you to her." She led the way across the dining room to a private room, which was small and cozy, with brocaded sofas, chairs, and a polished wood coffee table, more like a living room than a restaurant. Hollander was the room's only occupant, and she sat on a sofa, sipping what I thought was a scotch and soda and talking on her cell. She swiveled toward me and motioned me over to the sofa. I sat in the chair next to her. She finished up her conversation with a "Gotta go. I'll call you later." Then she smiled.

This had to be the first time I'd ever seen her smile, and it altered her entire face. Her brow smoothed out, and she suddenly looked softer, even appealing.

"Thank you for coming, Ellie. Especially on such short notice. What are you drinking?"

I debated whether to order scotch too, then thought, *To hell with it. I'm a wine drinker.* "Chardonnay. With ice on the side."

"And I'll take another as well," Hollander said.

The hostess, who'd been hovering, said she'd be back.

"I know you're wondering why I wanted to meet."

"You might say that." I eyed her. She was wearing a soft beige suit that looked like a St. John. It was more feminine and delicate than I'd expected.

"I want to explain." She paused dramatically and finished her scotch. "And apologize for my behavior on Monday."

I inclined my head. Was this the same woman who'd humiliated me in front of Delcroft's top execs? What was I supposed to say? I had no idea, so I said nothing. The hostess brought my wine and another scotch for her.

She didn't seem bothered by my lack of a response. "So first, the explanation." She leaned toward me. "What I'm going to say is top secret. And highly confidential. I know David did a background check on you, so I'm relying on your discretion."

"Of course." I slipped an ice cube into my wineglass and took a sip. She pretended not to notice.

"I know you set up a meeting with Gregory Parks yesterday. I also know it never happened. And I know why."

I stiffened. "If you knew, why didn't you—"

"We'll get to that." She picked up her glass and swirled the contents. The ice cubes tinkled.

"I'm sure your motives were legitimate." She gave a dismissive wave. "And probably had something to do with me. But"—she set the glass down firmly on the table—"you've managed to end up in the middle of something rather nasty."

I took another sip of wine.

She went on. "I'm sure you noticed the Asian cast to our late friend, Mr. Parks."

I nodded, thinking of Keanu Reeves.

"Gregory Parks was a spy for the Chinese government."

Chapter Nineteen

Wednesday

"Holy shit." I couldn't help it. "Parks was a spy?"

She nodded. "The Chinese like to steal our drone technology. Which they copy and produce for half the cost. And then either use it themselves or outsell us in the marketplace."

"But—but how do you—?" I sputtered, sounding like a Fourth of July sparkler losing its hiss. Mac was right. I was *way* above my pay grade. "I thought we had a truce," I said. "They won't steal our stuff, and we won't steal theirs."

"Right," Hollander replied. "If you say so."

She held up a palm. "I'll answer your questions. But first I want to tell you something. I've spent most of the past year out in Utah, designing and putting the finishing touches on a new system."

I thought about the thousands of drones we were using to target ISIS. To hear the military spin it, we'd dropped so many bombs we should have knocked out every terrorist in the Middle East. "What's so special about it?"

She shot me a patronizing smile. "That's a need-to-know situation. But I can tell you our so-called truce with the Chinese is a sham."

I countered, unwilling to let her get away with that. "If it was important enough to cancel a video and now Parks is dead, maybe I do need to know. Especially since, as you say, I've ended up in the middle."

She peered at me with a look that said she was unsure whether to criticize or praise my doggedness. Then she sighed. "You are persuasive. But, remember; anything I tell you going forward is highly classified." She lowered her voice.

Was she actually praising me? Or was it just another tactic to tell me what she wanted me to know?

"It's a counterdrone system. We call it DADES, Delcroft's Air Defense Energy System. Whether an enemy deploys smaller, tactical drones or ones the size of a B-1 bomber, we need a way to protect ourselves. That's what DADES does. And it works anywhere, no matter what the weather or terrain."

"It shoots down drones?"

"It takes control of them. Takes them off course, jams them, shoots them out of the sky. Whatever we want." She smiled confidently. "Actually, the system is almost flawless."

"How so?"

She looked around the room, then lowered her voice even more. "It can be mounted on a plane, a tank, a ship, even a drone itself."

"But how is it almost flawless?"

"Because we're using artificial intelligence. But that's all I can tell you."

It was enough. I swigged the rest of my wine so quickly I missed savoring the oaky smooth taste of good Chardonnay.

"It's not a new idea, of course, but only a few of us know how much success we've had in the trials. So you can imagine my reaction when I saw a man whom I know to be actively trying to acquire the plans for China on your video."

"He said he was a consultant," I said dully.

"They all do." She picked up her glass, which, I noticed, was practically empty. Hollander could put it away better than I.

"Is that why you canceled the video?"

She smiled, but I had the sense it was practiced. "At the time I thought it was better to be safe than sorry. In hindsight, I was rash."

I'll say. But I was polite. "In what way?"

"It did present us with an opportunity."

"An opportunity?" I frowned.

She leaned forward and spoke in a conspiratorial voice. "To exploit the situation. Find out exactly what and how much Parks knew."

Spy on the spy. I squirmed in my seat, suddenly uncomfortable with the conversation. "How did you figure out he was a spy?"

"I can't tell you."

I looked at her. "How did you know he and I were going to meet?"

"How do you think?" Her voice turned prickly, as if her patience was wearing thin.

"You tapped his phone," I said.

She raised her glass in mute acknowledgment. "Would you like another wine?"

I should stay razor-sharp. If Hollander had tapped his phone, she was probably tapping mine, too. I remembered how I'd dismissed Mac's worries about talking on the phone. When would I learn?

A waitress suddenly appeared. "Another round?"

Yes, I should stay razor-sharp. But a distinct sense of unease whispered across my skin. "Sure."

A threesome, two men and a woman, walked in and sat at the other end of the room, where there was a similar arrangement of sofa, chairs, and coffee table. They had clearly already had a few and talked in too-loud voices, sprinkled with too many laughs and giggles. Hollander looked them over but seemed to decide they were no threat. She turned to me.

"You have a daughter, I understand?"

I stopped in mid-motion at the abrupt shift in topic. Where was she going with this?

"I do. She lives downtown." Was she trying to intimidate me? Show me she had dug into my background? Well, two could play this game. "And you have a son."

"He's twelve."

I tried to picture her as a soccer mom. I couldn't. "Was he with you in Utah?"

Her eyes narrowed fractionally, as if I'd ventured into forbidden territory. Then her composure returned. "Yes."

"What kinds of things is he interested in?"

She waved a hand. "Oh, you know, the normal things. Soccer, ham radio, computers."

"Really? My best friend's husband is a ham radio freak. Has been since high school. I would have thought ham radio is too tame a hobby for kids today."

"Oh no. He loves talking to people all over the world."

I nodded. We continued to chat about unrelated things. I leaned back against the upholstered chair cushion and started to relax. The waitress brought us a third round, and I started to feel warm and fuzzy. Charlotte was turning into a person I might even like. That's when she switched gears.

"Now," she said, "I owe you an apology. I am sorry this—this snafu changed your plans and your schedule. I know what it's like to be a single working mother."

What didn't she know about me?

"I want you to know I am going to make it up to you. I'm going to give you a huge video project, much bigger and probably more relevant than those—website videos." She waved her arm.

I straightened up. All was not lost.

"Ellie, would you be amenable to that?"

I smiled for the first time since we met. "Of course."

"Good. Let's set up a meeting for next week."

"Great." I tapped my finger on my wineglass. Maybe Hollander wasn't such a bitch. In fact, I felt a grudging respect for her. It takes guts to make nice with someone you've previously battled. The air cleared and my mood soared. The people at the other end of the room weren't drunk; they were happy. I was no longer persona non grata, and I had another shot at a video. Life was good.

The wine had definitely kicked in. In some dark recess of my brain, I knew I should still be careful of what I said. But before I could stop myself, I blurted out, "You may be right about Parks."

She inclined her head in a much too casual way. "How so?"

For a fleeting moment, I wondered whether I should say anything. Then again, both of us had been drinking hard, and she'd answered all my questions. In fact, I wondered if she'd told me a little too much about DADES and Parks and spies. Still, I leaned forward and whispered, "About his—Parks'—activities."

"What makes you say that?"

"I found something that may have belonged to him."

"What?"

"A flash drive."

Her eyebrows arched. "Really? What's on it?"

"I don't know. The files are encrypted."

She studied me. I couldn't read her expression. But I was beginning to sense that maybe I'd said too much.

"Where did you find it?"

Crap. No way to unspill the milk. "On the subway platform in a cigarette box near the spot he jumped."

She didn't say anything. Then: "Do you still have it?"

I had enough presence to shake my head.

Her expression turned calculating. "That's too bad. We could have used that drive."

"Even though Parks is dead?"

She shrugged. "The information on it is still out there. We need to get it before someone else does."

I shivered. "You're starting to make me think that maybe Parks didn't jump. That maybe someone pushed him."

She leaned toward me and lowered her voice. "That's exactly what worries me. If someone killed him for the flash drive, and they think you have it…"

She let the rest of her sentence trail off.

Chapter Twenty

Friday

The word that best describes Susan Siler is "style." It's part of her DNA. I've never seen her with her strawberry blond hair out of place. Tall and willowy, she wears the perfect outfit for every occasion. Her house is beautifully decorated, and she has a lovely family. She's also a gourmet cook, and she has a calm, wise perspective on life. I've seen her lose her cool only once, when someone outbid her for a Louis XVI chair at an estate auction. Susan is my closest friend, which gives meaning to the adage that opposites attract.

It was unusually mild for late February—blue skies and temperatures in the forties, thanks to a buckle in the jet stream or a high-pressure system or whatever the weather bloviators say to explain a beautiful day—so we decided to walk. Of course, winter in Chicago is relative. Snow, now mottled and dirty, was piled on lawns and curbs, and any hint of spring was weeks away. But we bundled up in hats, scarves, boots, and gloves, and set out from my house.

As we rounded the corner—my house sits on the edge of a cul-de-sac—we approached the Schomers', which, due to Mr. Schomer's stroke and his wife's cancer, was now for sale. They'd lived on the block more than fifty years, and the place needed work. A dirty green pickup was parked out front. Inside were two men in bulky jackets and wool hats pulled low on their foreheads. The man in the driver's seat gave us a penetrating stare, then conspicuously looked away.

"Do we have some abnormality that makes us look strange?" I asked.

"Well, we are walking outside in the middle of winter," Susan said. "And with all this gear, we probably look like Eskimos."

"Eskimos, okay. But the abominable snowman? Did you see that guy's expression?"

"They're workmen." Susan pointed to the "For Sale" sign. "Was there an open house?"

I nodded. "I heard a family with four kids is interested."

"Really."

"The block is turning over. Soon there are going to be tons of kids, and I'll be the crazy old lady at the end of the street." Susan grinned as if she was going to speak.

"Don't you dare," I said.

She laughed. "Okay. But you do have the best Halloween candy in the village. Ben used to say that all the time." Ben is Susan's now twenty-eight-year-old son.

As we passed the pickup, something about the men nagged at me. They were just sitting there, not making any attempt to gather their tools or equipment and proceed to the Schomers' front door. I turned around and took in the license plate. Illinois. I repeated it a few times, then pulled out my cell, opened my Notes app, and entered it.

"What are you doing?"

I shrugged. "Nothing."

Susan narrowed her eyes but let it pass.

During the walk we analyzed the new grocery store inventory—some major brands weren't in stock. Then we considered the recent mayoral primary, which would end in a runoff, despite the fact the election was in Chicago. Then we moved to the global economy, deploring the state of Greece, Portugal, Italy, even poor, sunny Spain.

Twenty minutes later, we realized it was too cold to make our usual three-mile trek around the village, so we turned around and headed back. We were both quiet, the frigid air having sapped our energy.

As we rounded the bend on my street, the pickup was still there. So were the two men.

"That's odd," Susan said. "They must be freezing their butts off."

"And look at that." I jutted my chin.

About thirty yards away, another vehicle, an SUV, with two men inside, was just pulling up.

Susan checked the time on her cell. "Someone is late."

I looked at her. "Huh?"

"Whoever's in charge of these guys."

"Oh."

Suddenly the driver of the pickup gunned the engine, pulled out, and raced off down the street.

It was Susan's turn to frown. "Now, what is that all about?"

I peered at the SUV, took in the plate, and entered it in my Notes app. Susan watched me. "Ellie, what's going on?"

"Nothing." I tried to sound cheery.

"Nope. Not buying it. What aren't you telling me?"

"Really, it's nothing."

Susan pursed her lips and shot me a glance that was puzzled, disappointed, and maybe a little angry all at once. But what could I say? That I'd spent another sleepless night hungover, obsessing about the flash drive and Charlotte Hollander? That I realized the woman bought me drinks, not because of any contrition on her part or the desire to make amends but because she wanted to pump me about the flash drive, which she probably already knew about? That I really didn't like being manipulated and had no desire to produce a video for her even if she plied me with wine and paid me a fortune for the work? And, most important, that given what happened to Parks, I was beginning to be concerned about my own safety?

Chapter Twenty-one

Friday

It was only mid-morning after our short walk. I felt at loose ends, so I went to work out. The place I go is owned by the Glenview Park District, but it's more like a country club than any park district facility. There's a huge gym with every conceivable machine known to torture the human body, a plethora of classes spread out during the day in another huge gym, an Olympic-sized swimming pool, a hot tub, and an indoor running track.

I was just in time for Zumba with Debbie, my favorite instructor. The class helped me forget about everything. Get some good salsa music going, let me swivel my hips, and I'm in Cuba or Latin America, waiting for a gorgeous sunset and the mojito I hope will be coming.

After class I stopped to chat with a woman I know, and we headed out to our cars together. She went in one direction, I in another. I got into my car and pulled out. I headed toward the grocery store.

As I drove up Waukegan Road I realized someone was following me. It wasn't the pickup truck I'd seen earlier, and it wasn't the SUV. It was a battered green Toyota. A chill streaked over me. Now what?

I checked the rear view, but the sun hit the mirror at just the wrong angle, and I couldn't see the driver. Still, I wasn't ready to give up. I tried to get the license plate number, but the glare of the sun in the rear view prevented me. I needed a Plan B. I blew out a breath and made a sudden right turn off the main road. The Toyota followed. I drove a block or two, then turned right again. The Toyota did too. If I kept turning, I knew I'd end up in the middle of a residential neighborhood, not unlike the one in which I lived. I made another turn. So did the Toyota.

I was curious whether the person tailing me had the *chutzpah* to follow me to a dead-end street I knew was coming up. If they did, I would at least get a good look at them and their license plate. I turned left into a cul-de-sac. I drove to the end and waited.

No Toyota. I waited another five minutes.

It didn't come.

It was over. For now.

Chapter Twenty-two

Friday

After I did my shopping at the supermarket and was on the way home, I called Dan O'Malley, the police chief of my village. He and I know each other too well. He took my call right away.

"Ellie! Haven't heard from you in a long time. You must be behaving yourself."

I wasn't sure how to reply, so I let it go. "Congratulations, Dan. I don't think we've talked since you were promoted." He'd been deputy chief for as long as I'd known him.

"Thanks. After twenty years, it feels good. Now, what can I do for you?"

"I was wondering if you could look up the final disposition of a case in Chicago for me."

"Go on."

"A man jumped in front of a subway train the other day, and I was there when it happened." I made sure to phrase it carefully. "I was just wondering if the cause of death has been formally decided. Or will be."

"I heard about that one. Didn't know you were involved."

"I wasn't. I just happened to be there."

"I see," Dan said in a tone that clearly indicated he didn't believe me. He was quiet. Then: "Let me see what I can find out. You wouldn't happen to have the case file number, would you?"

"Sorry."

"I'll call you back. You still at the same number?"

"I am. Thanks a lot." I disconnected.

A message from Zach Dolan was on my voice mail when I got home.

"Hi, Ellie. The work is—well—it's turning out to be more complex than I thought. Whoever encrypted it didn't use Voltage or DataMotion or other software that companies use on their networks. But I'm working on it. Just wanted to give you an update."

I erased the message, wondering what Voltage and DataMotion were, but decided I'd rather check out the "workmen's" license plates I'd punched into my cell. Unfortunately, I didn't have time for either. My father, Rachel and her boyfriend, Q, and Luke were coming for Shabbos dinner, and I had to cook.

My family has handed down a secret brisket recipe for at least forty years that is out-of-this-world delicious. There are probably ten million other people who know about it, but calling it "secret" confers a special sought-after quality. You take a brisket, rub it with dry onion soup mix, baste it with ketchup, then pour a bottle of beer—Heineken works well—over everything. Some chefs insist it must be cooked in a plastic bag. I'm not rigid about that, but I do add carrots, onions, and potatoes during the last hour. Combined with matzo-ball soup, a salad, and my signature apple cobbler, it's a surefire hands-down feast.

That evening Rachel, who more and more resembles my late mother, said the blessing over the candles, cupping the flame with her hands three times, then covering her eyes. Dad always says the Barucha over the challah, and I'm happy to bless the wine.

I dished out matzo-ball soup, which Rachel helped pass. Before we dug in, my father cleared his throat. "Before we eat this wonderful meal my daughter has prepared—"

I cut in. "You haven't tried it yet."

"Be quiet, Ellie," he scolded. "I just want to say these dinners...these occasions with family and friends"—he nodded to Luke and Q—"are what life is all about. I am so grateful to have you all with me. I couldn't ask for a kinder, more generous family." He looked around solemnly, then broke into a grin. "That's all. You may now—what is it you say?—return to your regularly scheduled programming."

As requested, I kept my mouth shut, but I found myself blinking back tears. It wasn't like my father to get sentimental. A bittersweet feeling swept over me. I was grateful my father was still alive and alert, but I was also aware how fragile life is, especially when you're on the "back nine," as Dad often says.

Luke seemed to understand what I was feeling and reached for my hand. I squeezed his in return. With the swell of conversation, the tangy aroma of the brisket, and the clink of spoons in the soup, I wanted to record this moment, keep it in my memory box forever. Apparently, Rachel had the same idea, because she whipped out her cell and snapped a few pictures.

"Oh no. Rachel, please don't upload those to Facebook," I said. "It's a family moment." Her thumbs clicked on her cell. "And my hair looks terrible."

"Too late. They're already up." She grinned as if she'd beat me at checkers. Some things never change.

◇◇◇

We were clearing the table when the phone rang. When I was growing up, my parents used to let it ring. "We should have peace and quiet at least on the Sabbath," my father would say. But as his law practice expanded and clients called with emergencies, the custom lapsed. I never reinstated it. I picked up in the kitchen, expecting it to be O'Malley.

"Ellie, it's Georgia Davis."

"Hey. What's up?"

"I just got a call and thought you should know. Zach Dolan's office? In Northbrook?"

An uneasy feeling roiled my gut. "Yeah?" I said slowly.

"Zach's okay. He wasn't there. But some kind of IED just blew the place up."

Chapter Twenty-three

Friday

Feeling unsteady, I went back into the dining room and told them what had happened. Everyone went quiet. Even the candles, which had almost burned down to their base, flickered, as if alarmed.

Then they all started to talk at once.

"What's going on?" "Who is Dolan?" "What business did you have with him?" "Spill, Mom." Only Q, mercifully, was quiet. He probably didn't want to make waves. He didn't have to. The ones around the table were already cresting.

"Okay, okay." I sat and poured myself a glass of wine. "You remember how Charlotte Hollander fired me from the job at Delcroft? And then the guy I wanted to talk to about her killed himself on the subway? Well, Hollander called me on Wednesday to apologize, sort of. We met for a drink, and she told me the guy who committed suicide was a spy for the Chinese."

Silence. Then my father threw me a stern look. "A spy? What *mishegoss* is this?"

I felt my cheeks get hot. "I don't know, but I found a flash drive on the subway platform that I'm pretty sure was his."

The silence sucked all the air out of the room.

"It was encrypted. So I took it to someone to decrypt."

Luke's eyes went from flat to angry. "Are you crazy?"

"Why are you getting involved?" Rachel said.

"I—I never thought it would be dangerous," I said.

"Delcroft. Number one manufacturer of drones. For all intents and purposes, owned and operated by the United States military. And Chinese spies thrown into the mix." Luke flipped up his hands, a hard expression on his face. "And you didn't think it was dangerous?"

"Wouldn't you want to know what was on it?" Before anyone had a chance to reply, I added, "Well, I did. But now Hollander wants it. She claims it will prove what she's been saying all along."

"About this—this spy?" my father hissed.

I nodded.

"So? You don't owe her a damn thing," Rachel said.

"Rachel!"

"Mom, you don't. She's using you." It's at times like these I'm reminded how much she takes after her father.

"Your daughter's right," Luke said.

I ran a finger around the rim of my glass. "Well, someone may be using *her*. The place that blew up was where I took the drive."

No one said anything.

"So…" I gulped down my wine and looked around. "Shabbat shalom."

Chapter Twenty-four

Friday night

I turned on the ten-o'clock news upstairs. The table was cleared, dishes stacked, guests gone. Luke was watching Netflix in the family room, which was fine with me. I wanted to be alone. I felt like I'd been sandbagged at dinner. I never had the chance to tell them that when I took the drive to Zach, I didn't know a thing about Chinese spies. As a result, I hadn't said much since. Luke wisely left me alone. Happily, there was nothing on the news about the explosion at Zach's place. Yet.

The sportscaster came on, a fresh-faced woman reporter, and the story cut to a star Bulls forward for a sound bite. It could have been a Bears, Sox, even a Cubs player. Whatever the sport, athletes these days seem to talk in a practiced monotone, as if they're reading a grocery list. I keep thinking some TV coach has instructed them to tamp down their emotions, to show what good sports they really are. The problem is they've taken all the passion out of the story.

I got up, went into my office, and booted up my Mac. I was pretty sure someone had hacked into my computer, and the less they saw the better. I made another copy, deleted the contents of Parks' flash drive from my hard drive, and dropped the new copy into my purse. Then I went back to bed. I heard Luke's tread on the stairs and grabbed a book off the nightstand. I pretended to read. He poked his head in, as if trying to ascertain my mood before he came all the way in.

I looked up. "It's okay. I'm not contagious."

He came in and sat on the edge of the bed. He was wearing his reading glasses. "You ready to talk?"

"What more is there to say? Everyone already got their two cents in."

He peered at me over his glasses. "Is it possible you might be playing the victim, just a little?"

"Well, how would you feel if everyone talked to you as if you were a disobedient brat? Including your daughter?"

He didn't reply for a moment. Then: "Well, you're right about one thing. This isn't child's play. Ellie, do you really understand how much danger you could be in?"

I closed the book. The memory of a figure flashing across the subway platform strafed my brain. "So I'll give back the drive and everyone forgets what I said tonight." I snapped my finger. "Problem solved."

"No. Problem not solved. You're on somebody's radar."

"So is everyone in the world, according to Edward Snowden."

I sensed him sigh inwardly. I knew I was being bitchy. And he was so patient with me.

"True, but it's clear someone has taken a special interest in you. Delcroft, the military, NSA…God knows…maybe even the Chinese government. You've got to be careful."

I ran my fingers up and down the spine of the book. "Of course I'm worried. I'll never forget that Parks smashed into that train." I looked up. "And now…well…I'm not convinced it was suicide."

Luke inclined his head, a question on his face.

"In fact, I think someone's tapped my phone."

His spine stiffened. "How do you know?"

"Whoever blew up Dolan's studio knew he had the drive. Dolan and I exchanged a few calls. In fact, he called this morning." I swallowed. "And there's more." I told him about the "workmen" in the cars in front of the house down the street. How one of the cars took off when they saw Susan and me returning from our walk. And how I thought I'd been followed when I went to work out and then to the grocery store.

"Okay." Luke crossed his arms. "I want you to do me a favor."

"What's that?"

"I want you to use your cell, not the house phone, as much as possible from now on."

"My cell? But I thought—"

"There's a pretty good security app that's free. We're going to download it."

"Will it keep me from being hacked?"

"It will make it a lot harder. Here, give me your phone."

I leaned over and fished it out of my bag, and watched as he went to the app store, downloaded something, and installed it. After a minute, he gave it back. "It's really easy to use. Just follow the directions. Oh, and I disabled your GPS and location tracker, too. Don't use them."

"Really?"

He nodded. He wasn't kidding.

I bit my lip, scanned the app, and pressed a few buttons to see what was there. Then I lay back against the pillows, my anger dissipating. "Thanks. I know you're trying to help."

Now he smiled. "And I know you hate to be rescued. But I'm—I don't want anything to happen to you. I love you."

I stroked his cheek and played with his beard. "I'm sorry. I overreacted."

"I know people. I can find out things…"

"About Delcroft? And what they're working on?"

He nodded.

"Is that really necessary? We already have a general idea."

"The more we know, the better positioned we'll be."

"For what?"

He shrugged. "Who knows?"

"Once a Boy Scout…"

He smiled. "That. And something else."

"What's that?"

"As long as I'm around, no one is going to touch a hair on your beautiful head."

How can you argue with that? I opened my arms. They didn't remain empty for long.

Chapter Twenty-five

Saturday

"You sure Zach's okay?" I asked Georgia Davis on the phone the next morning. I gazed out the kitchen window. An inch of new snow covered the sludge of the past few weeks, promising a day of purity and innocence.

"He's fine, Ellie. He left work early. In fact, he was at a movie with his girlfriend when it happened."

"What about his dog?"

"I'm sure he's okay. Zach would have said something."

"Okay."

There was a long pause. Then: "Ellie, what kind of trouble are you in? Do you need help?"

"I—I don't know. But I'd really like to know who was behind the explosion."

"Wouldn't we all. Be prepared, by the way. You're gonna be getting a visit from the cops. Maybe the feds, too."

"That's going to be a barrel of laughs."

"You know you can't—"

I cut her off. "I know. But I don't want to answer their questions."

"Come on, Ellie, this is a felony crime. You know they're going to ask Zach who his clients are. Your name is going to come up."

"Crap."

Another pause. "You sure there's nothing you want to tell me?"

I thought about Delcroft, Hollander, and Parks. Then I imagined Dan O'Malley, the village chief of police, or one of his deputies interviewing them. Especially the deputy COO at the meeting—what was his name?—Phillips. Gary Phillips. By the time they finished, my reputation, and my bank account, would be heading even further south. Not to mention that as soon as someone said, "Chinese spy," the FBI would swoop in. Maybe the CIA, too. And if anything made it into the media, which, of course, it eventually would, Delcroft would take a hit. And all because I was fired from a job and wanted to know why. I buried my head in my hands. What had I done?

I found out an hour later when an unmarked car with a Mars light on top pulled up to the house. Police. A beefy man in a bulky coat climbed out. It wasn't O'Malley, and I didn't know who it was. Then again, a coat and muffler partially hid his face. That wasn't the case with the sports car that pulled up behind him, a silver Spyder, its fender glinting in the sun. Who the hell had the nerve to drive a sports car in winter in Chicago? Suddenly my head jerked up. I knew that car. And its owner.

As if on cue, a lean, lanky man unfolded himself from the driver's seat. He wore jeans, a black leather jacket, and work boots. A pair of gloves and muffler seemed to be his only concession to the season. As he strolled up to the door, I recognized the green ball cap on his head, which bore the white letters "Different Drummer Charter Fishing."

I sucked in a breath. "This morning just gets better and better."

Luke shot me a questioning glance.

The doorbell chimed.

When I opened the door, the man from the unmarked already had his badge out. "Detective Frank Delaney, village police."

"Good morning," I said. He looked me over, then did the same to Luke.

Luke stuck out his hand. "Luke Sutton. A friend of Ms. Foreman's."

Delaney nodded as if he already knew, but the man in the ball cap tilted his head and gave Luke a curious once-over.

"And this is FBI Special Agent Nick LeJeune," Delaney said.

I nodded. "I've had the pleasure."

LeJeune grinned. "Hello, *cher*. It's been a while."

I motioned to the Spyder parked at the curb. "Same car? How many years has it been?"

"Eleven. Just getting broken in." He grinned. "You look exactly the same, *cher*. How's your daughter? She still like fast cars and faster men?" I was reminded how Rachel, at fourteen, had been so enamored of LeJeune and his car that he let her take it for a spin around the block. I shook my head. Had I really been that cavalier?

Now I frowned. "She's good. She's twenty-five."

"She couldn't be. Where is she?"

Delaney shifted his feet. "Do you mind if we continue this inside? It's pretty damn cold."

"Of course." I opened the door wide, and they stepped in. A wave of cold air wafted in with them. I turned back to LeJeune. "Rachel's downtown. Working for a nonprofit. Helping women in transition find jobs."

"How noble." LeJeune nodded. "Like her mother. She single?"

"She is. And don't you dare get within a mile of her."

His smile widened, and he took off his hat.

When I knew him, he had sandy hair threaded with gray. It was mostly gray now. But his eyes were the same penetrating green flecked with black, and he spoke with the same southern lilt, although it sometimes sounded like he was talking around a marble in his mouth. We'd met over ten years ago, when I'd been working on a video about the water-intake cribs on Lake Michigan, which, now that I thought about it, hadn't been finished either. It wasn't that I was fired—9/11 occurred in the middle of the shoot, and the water department prudently decided not to dispense information on how Chicago got its water.

But that wasn't the end of the situation. I'd found evidence, quite by accident, that some bad guys were intent on doing nasty things to the city of Chicago, and LeJeune had been assigned to the case. Come to think of it, the circumstances now were eerily similar to what had happened then.

Luke, who had been very quiet during our exchange, extended his hand to LeJeune. "I'm Luke Sutton."

"Yes. A friend of Ms. Foreman's," LeJeune said. "Well, well." I felt myself color.

Chapter Twenty-six

Saturday

I led the men into the living room and offered coffee, which everyone accepted. As I brought a tray in from the kitchen, I said, "Actually, Nick, I'm surprised to see you."

"Anytime something goes boom, and we don't know what it is, I get the call. You remember."

I handed them mugs of coffee. "So you're still in the antiterrorism division?"

He shrugged. "I go where they tell me."

Delaney sat in my father's old chair, a comfortable wingback that he'd given me when he moved into the assisted living home. "Got to have something soft for my *tuchus* when I'm at your place," Dad had said. Luke and I sat on the sofa. LeJeune stood in front of the fireplace.

"So," Delaney said after taking a sip from his mug. "Before we start, Dan O'Malley wanted me to tell you everything checked out with the subway accident. It's been ruled a suicide."

Luke peered at me. I knew he was wondering what the hell I'd done.

"Please give him my thanks."

"I will." Delaney cleared his throat. "Now. Zach Dolan says you are one of his clients. Want to tell me what he's doing for you?"

Not really, I thought. "I asked him to decrypt a flash drive. I wanted to know what was on it."

"And you got this flash drive how?"

"It's complicated."

LeJeune leaned an elbow on the mantel. "We have all the time in the world."

"I was really hoping I wouldn't have to go into this."

LeJeune answered. "You know better than that, *cher.* The Bureau is here to help our brethren in blue."

"Right." I couldn't avoid the sarcasm in my voice. "What about keeping it out of the media?"

"If there's a leak, it won't be from us."

I took a breath and told them the whole story. The Delcroft job. Being fired. Parks. The subway accident. Delaney nodded at that. Finding the drive. Hollander telling me Parks was a spy for the Chinese. Neither man took notes, but I figured one of them was recording me.

By the time I finished, Delaney leaned forward. "Let's talk about timing. Did you know you were the only new client Zach picked up in the past couple of weeks?"

"He told you who his clients are?"

Delaney and LeJeune exchanged a glance. "We didn't give him much choice," LeJeune said.

"Your gentle persuasion won him over."

"You always were quick, *cher*," LeJeune said.

I was starting to be annoyed with the "*chers*" and his folksy, too familiar southern Creole ways. I knew he was from Cajun country, some parish in eastern Louisiana. I glanced over at Luke. He was trying to stay composed, but his right eye was half-closed. That happened when he's upset.

"Did Dolan get back to you with any results from the drive?" LeJeune asked.

"Not yet. All he said was that it wasn't a common encryption program."

Both Delaney and LeJeune nodded. They already knew.

"Which of course could back up Hollander's notion that Parks was a spy," LeJeune said almost to himself. "Hey, Ellie. Do you have another copy of the drive?"

"Um, no," I lied. I saw the skeptical expression on LeJeune's face and covered it with a question. "What about the explosion itself?" I asked. "Do you have any idea what it was?"

Delaney cleared his throat. "Our bomb and arson teams are on it." He threw me a warning look. "And we'll ask the questions here."

LeJeune rolled his eyes as though he was poking fun at Delaney. "It's already out, Detective. Some kind of IED."

"Any idea what the components were?" Luke asked.

"Don't know yet." LeJeune cocked his head. "Why do you ask?"

Luke shrugged. "I just wondered if they might have been military sourced."

LeJeune's eyes flashed. I stiffened. I hadn't told anyone what Charlotte Hollander had told me over drinks: that Delcroft had a contract with the military to produce a counterdrone system. And that she'd been working on its design for more than a year. Except Luke.

But LeJeune was no dummy. He'd want to know why Luke specifically brought up the military components. To my surprise, though, LeJeune glossed over Luke's question. He must have decided this wasn't the right time or place. Still, I knew he'd be looking into it.

"You were in the air force, weren't you?" LeJeune said. "Did a couple of tours, right? Flying BUFFs."

BUFFs were B-52 Stratofortress planes nicknamed "Big Ugly Fat Fuckers." At one time they carried nukes but now they're mostly cargo planes.

LeJeune had checked Luke out before coming here. Even though I knew he was just doing his job, and doing it well, I was irritated. What right did he have to investigate my boyfriend? I took a breath to steady myself.

"I enlisted," Luke replied. "And yes. I flew missions in Iraq during the First Gulf War."

As if he knew what I was feeling, LeJeune pasted on an angelic smile. "Of course you did. Just wanted to hear it from the horse's mouth."

Luke's eye was almost squeezed shut now.

I crossed my legs, my foot jiggling up and down. "Have you talked to Delcroft yet?"

LeJeune's smile faded. The look he threw me said I was the dumbest fish in the tank.

"I should never have contacted Parks. I was just so angry at being fired. It's all my fault."

"But now you are helping your country," LeJeune said. "Doing the patriotic thing."

"Gee, thanks. I can't wait for my medal. Assuming I live long enough to get it." My foot jiggled even faster. "Look. It's clear someone doesn't want us to find out what's on that drive. What if their next step is to come after me?"

Luke chimed in. "What about protection for her? What can you do?"

"Protection?" Delaney said.

"Her phone has been tapped," Luke added. "And strangers have been casing her house."

"Tell us," Delaney said.

I told him about the fake workmen in front of the empty house. "And someone in a green Toyota was tailing me."

"Describe them."

"I never saw the driver of the Toyota, but I can describe the 'workmen.'" I did, then added, "I can do you one better. I have their license plates."

Delaney's eyebrows rose. LeJeune smiled.

"And I'll give them to you. On one condition."

Delaney straightened. "I know you're friends with Chief O'Malley, but that doesn't entitle you to withhold evidence. You could—"

I cut in. "Once you identify them, you have to tell me who they are."

"I don't know," Delaney said. "I'll have to clear it with the chief."

LeJeune gave Delaney a sidelong glance, then turned to me. "You can look up plates yourself these days, you know."

"I know. But what if they hacked into my computer? They'll know I'm looking for them."

"Which is why she needs protection," Luke said.

"You don't think that's a little far-fetched?" LeJeune said.

"In today's climate?" Luke replied. "No. I don't."

"If protection is warranted, we'll provide it," Delaney said after a long moment.

"Which means that right now it isn't," Luke said. "So we're on our own."

"You look like you can handle yourself. And the lady." LeJeune paused. "You know the drill. Don't say anything on the phone you don't want overheard. Don't drive anywhere you don't want to be followed. We'll be in touch when we know something."

Luke glanced at me, nodding.

I went into the kitchen, returned with the plate numbers, and handed them over.

"Good girl," LeJeune said.

Girl? I bristled. Had he really called me a girl?

He winked as if he knew exactly what he'd done.

Chapter Twenty-seven

Saturday

After they'd gone I cleared the coffee mugs and set them in the kitchen sink. Luke followed me in. "So you want to tell me about this character?"

"There's not much to say. I was working on a video about the water-intake cribs that got canceled because of 9/11. But I had outtakes of a guy—well, like I said, it gets complicated."

"You seem to have a habit of getting fired."

I whirled around, ready for battle.

"Just kidding." He raised his palms. "The Bureau guy has a very high opinion of himself."

"I think he's the kind of person who skates over life's surfaces but has trouble handling the currents underneath."

"I don't have anything to worry about, do I?"

Was Luke jealous? This was a new experience. I dried my hands, went to him, and stroked his cheek. "From LeJeune? The only thing you have to worry about is that he knows the best Creole joints in Chicago."

He leaned in and kissed me. "Still, I am worried. Not about him, but you. This can't go on."

"I get it." I hesitated. "By the way"—I disengaged from his embrace and looked up—"there's something else you should know."

"What?"

"I do have a copy of the flash drive. I made it before I ran the first one over to Dolan."

"Of course you did." He sighed. "And whoever wants it probably knows it. Including LeJeune."

"I had it all on my hard drive, but I deleted it the other night. I decided to keep the copy on me at all times. Just in case."

"Why not put it in your safe-deposit box?"

"I'll think about it."

Luke folded his arms. "You might want to make your mind up soon. By the way, while you're deciding, I'm going to do some due diligence of my own," Luke said. "We're not going to sit around waiting for someone to come after you."

If LeJeune glided through life at his own pace, Luke attacked life head-on. He walked out of the kitchen. A moment later I heard him on his cell.

We piled into Luke's pickup later that afternoon. Luke's father had been a highly successful railroad magnate. He developed the automatic coupler between train cars, which made him a fortune. Luke had inherited all his wealth and could afford—well—a dozen Spyders. But flash wasn't his style. He didn't even want the new Benz pickup; he liked a Dodge Ram. The only concessions he'd made when he bought a new one were comfortable seats, AC, and a GPS, mostly for me.

"Where are we going?"

"You'll find out."

"Oh, I just love secrets."

He shot me a look, but then took a roundabout route across the North Shore, winding around streets, turning sharp corners, and twisting onto side streets, all in a seemingly random pattern.

"You think we're being tailed?" I asked.

He didn't answer, but I was grateful. He wasn't taking anything for granted. We headed north on Route 41 past Lake Forest and Lake Bluff. Eventually we turned east to Great Lakes Naval Station, boot camp for navy recruits and the service's largest training facility. More than eleven hundred buildings sit on sixteen hundred acres, making it a small city unto itself. I figured we were going to meet someone there, but when Luke passed the entrance I was confused.

"We're not going in?"

He shook his head.

Five minutes later we were in downtown Waukegan. Unfortunately, Waukegan, Illinois, is not an example of progressive urban planning. After the affluence of Highland Park, Lake Forest, and Lake Bluff, Waukegan seems like the orphan child left behind. With a hundred thousand people, the city isn't small, but whatever charm it may have had has been gutted by decades of mismanagement and corruption. Now it has a distressed, hardscrabble landscape broken up by a string of chain stores and gas stations.

"Luke, why are we here?" I asked.

Luke studied the rear view as carefully as the windshield. After five minutes circling the block, he pulled up to a place that had to be two steps below a dive bar. A corner tavern, its walls were covered by graffiti in loopy letters, and its windows were probably last washed during the Depression. It didn't even have a name, but a neon sign above the door said "Bar." The letter *r* flickered in the dusky light.

"We could have gone to Solyst's," I said. "Why did we have to come all this way?" Solyst's was a bar in my village, although the new owners recently upgraded the bathrooms to semi-luxurious, so I'm not sure it still qualifies as a dive.

Luke got out of the truck, came around to my side, and opened the door.

"Something tells me I'm not gonna like this," I said.

Chapter Twenty-eight

Saturday

The bar's interior was as shabby as its exterior. Scuffed linoleum floors, a cracked ceiling running the length of the room, and warped, bowed-out paneling. The only saving grace was a cheerful swath of colored Christmas lights high up on the walls, which I guessed was a permanent fixture, since it was nearly March.

Luke craned his neck at the people in the booths lining both sides of the room. His gaze stopped at the back, where a guy in a gray hoodie and a Sox ball cap stared back. As a die-hard Cubs fan, I wasn't sure how I felt about that. His expression was curious, perhaps even suspicious, but when he saw Luke, recognition lit his face, and he smiled brightly.

"That's him." Luke guided me toward the booth. As we approached I spotted a pair of crutches lying on the cushion beside him.

He reached for one of the crutches and attempted to stand.

Luke hurried over. "No. Don't get up." He embraced him. "Hey, man!"

"Hey, man, you!" They exchanged joyful looks that indicated they were thrilled to see each other. Then the man's gaze turned to me.

"This is Ellie?"

I smiled. "Guilty."

"Ellie, this is Artie Hubbard." We shook hands. He had a lean face, a pointed chin, a forehead with deep lines, but soft brown eyes. "He's an old pal."

Hubbard cleared his throat loudly. "It's Commander Hubbard now, pal." He stroked a growth of gray stubble on his chin, which could have been a beard or the result of not shaving for a week.

"Well, I'll be damned. You finally did it, you old geezer," Luke said. He turned to me. "We used to call him Grizzly. Maybe you can see why."

Hubbard patted his chin. "The stubble effect. Supposed to drive women crazy."

I giggled.

"Funny…that's what the other ladies did, too."

I slid into the booth across from him. Luke got in beside me. "You're in the navy?" I asked.

"Great Lakes is my home."

"But Luke was in the air force. How did you meet?"

Luke cut in. "We grew up together in Lake Geneva. We both worked at the old Playboy Club during high school."

I nodded, remembering Luke's history at what was now called the Lodge but at one time was one of the trendiest spots north of Chicago.

"We stayed in touch," Grizzly said.

"You're one of the lucky ones," I replied. "The only other friend of Luke's I've met is Jimmy Saclarides."

Grizzly looked like he wanted to say something, but Luke cut him off. "How's the leg?" Then he grimaced. "Sorry. You know what I mean."

"No worries. There's still some phantom pain, but I live with it." He turned to me. "I lost it in a helicopter accident in Afghanistan."

"You were lucky, bro," Luke said.

"Don't I know it." He paused. "My pilot wasn't." He rubbed his nose as if trying to erase the memory. "Hey, the pizza here isn't bad."

"Then, that's what we'll order," Luke said. "Drafts all around?"

We nodded. Luke went up to the bar to place the order.

I gazed around. "So, why are we meeting here?"

Grizzly smiled. "Because your boyfriend wanted to."

"Luke picked this place?"

"He didn't tell you?"

"Not a word."

"Well…" A jukebox in the corner I hadn't noticed before belted out a Taylor Swift song. "I'm on my last assignment. Base commander's training staff."

"In what?"

"Intelligence." He paused. "And before that, I was director of all source intelligence analysis in Qatar. And before that in Afghanistan."

I was beginning to understand why Luke had brought me here.

Grizzly's next words confirmed it. "I know a lot about drones."

Chapter Twenty-nine

Saturday

Twenty minutes later, I was lifting skinny strings of mozzarella cheese and winding them around a slice of pepperoni pizza before I shoveled it all into my mouth. Which I washed down with a draft. The taste of spicy flavors, milky cheese, and cold beer was addictive. Pizza was my favorite cuisine. And no need for forks or knives.

"I understand you have some questions about counterdrone systems," Grizzly said to me.

I held up a finger while I chewed and swallowed. Then: "I'm not sure if 'question' is the right word. Confession might be more accurate."

"You may confess to me, young lady."

"Thank you, Father." I glanced over at Luke. He nodded. "I was told by a top executive at Delcroft that they've been working on a counterdrone system for over a year. This executive was testing it in Utah. She says the system is flawless."

Grizzly took a swig. "I'm not surprised. Anti-drones use the same technology as drones. All you have to do is reverse engineer them."

"What do you mean?"

"Most of them are controlled by old-fashioned radio signals."

"Radio signals?" I knew a little about radio signals, ironically, because of the case through which I met LeJeune.

"Satellite GPS signals, too."

"Okay."

"As you probably know, the payloads on drones are either cameras and sensors for surveillance or explosives for attacks. Sometimes both. If I wanted to take control of a drone, I'd mimic and boost its radio signal. That way I could feed it misinformation about where to drop the bomb or what to spy on—they call them spoofing attacks—or just shoot it out of the sky if I wanted."

I nodded, pretending I understood a lot more than I did.

"So, whatever system Delcroft is developing would probably have a sensor to detect and triangulate the targeted drone's position. The counterdrone would fly over to it. Once it was within range, the guys on the ground would transmit a signal with new directions. The counterdrone would acknowledge the new input and do whatever it's been ordered to do."

"You make it sound simple."

Grizzly shrugged. "You know, I am curious about something, Ellie. Why is it supposed to be so flawless?"

"Something to do with artificial intelligence."

"Really?"

"Does that surprise you?"

"I suppose it does. Radios and radars used to be built with hardware that could only transmit in certain ways. Today, there's software that can change how they emit from moment to moment. For example, we heard that someone recorded one burst transmission—he didn't say from where—that changed modulation eight times in two seconds. In order to do that, the thinking goes, it has to be controlled by a 'cognitive' computer—ergo, artificial intelligence." He went on. "And if you do that, you've opened the door to all sorts of other things."

"Like what?"

"Hacking into enemy networks. Placing malware on enemy systems."

"NSA-type hacking?"

"You betcha. But from the air. Unmanned. Untraceable. It's pretty amazing. Remember, Delcroft has the most advanced drone systems in the world. Hell, they even make an F-16 drone, and they've come up with a way to control drones from an Apache helicopter. So whatever anti-drone system they've come up with probably takes those issues into account. It's pretty advanced technology. Not a lot of companies have the investment dollars to perfect it. Or make it flawless."

"But Delcroft does?"

"What do you think?"

I took another sip of beer. "So, bottom line, assuming Delcroft has this bigger, better system, there might be 'parties' who want to get their hands on the technology."

"Are you kidding? Of course. We've done a shitload of damage with our drones. Our enemies want to pay us back. Although, like I said, if the engineers of those 'parties' know what they're doing, they might be able to figure out Delcroft's technology on their own. You remember how the Iranians shot down a drone a few years ago?"

I nodded.

"That was a CIA drone." His voice held just a trace of smugness. "The Iranians claimed they jammed the signals, reverse engineered it, forced it to land where they wanted, and lifted all its data."

"Did they?"

"Who knows? Ultimately, it doesn't matter. It's not rocket science."

"Funny."

Luke got up and brought back a fresh pitcher of beer. I pushed the pizza plate toward him. One slice was left. He scooped it up.

"So what's your deal with Delcroft?" Grizzly asked.

Luke and I exchanged glances again. Then Luke said, "Ellie has information that someone connected to Delcroft might be selling this new system to the Chinese government. Or military."

"They're one and the same," Grizzly said. "So that's why you wanted to meet off base. What's the story?"

I looked around. The booth next to us was empty, and there weren't any people close by. Still, I lowered my voice and explained about the video, Parks, the flash drive, Hollander's suspicions, and the IED that blew up Dolan's office.

Grizzly worked on his beer while I talked. When I finished, a tiny layer of foam coated the top of his lip. He wiped the back of his hand across his mouth.

"Good old Delcroft. The military's best friend. They know more about our country's capabilities than your average brigadier general or admiral."

"So if Delcroft is building a supersecret counterdrone system, people would know about it?"

"By 'people,' I assume you mean our enemies?" Grizzly asked.

I nodded.

"It's hard to keep that kind of thing secret for long." He wrapped his hands around his empty beer glass. "By the way, most of the counterdrone tests for the military happen at the navy's Point Mugu, near China Lake. That's in California, not Utah."

"Are you saying Hollander lied about where she was working?"

"Maybe."

"Why?"

"Because she can."

I thought it over. "Wait a minute. If she lied about Utah, could she be lying about the artificial intelligence part of it, too?"

"It's possible. Remember, our enemies aren't stupid. They can take advantage of our technology and push it out fast. In some ways we're still playing catch-up. It pays to lie. Confuse the situation. Make the enemy think we know or have more than we really do."

My head was spinning. "Jesus. This is worse than going through the looking glass. Who do you trust?"

"No one."

"But this is our country's security we're talking about."

It was Grizzly's turn to glance around. "Let's blow this pop stand. Take me for a ride in your pickup."

I frowned, but Luke promptly got up and went to the bar to pay.

Grizzly picked up his crutches and grinned. "I need to hang out with rich guys more often."

Chapter Thirty

Saturday

The three of us crammed into the front seat of Luke's pickup and threw Grizzly's crutches into the bed. Grizzly's forehead puckered; he looked like he wanted to say something. Luke was about to turn over the engine but unexpectedly stopped as if he'd received a telepathic message. He opened the driver's side door and jumped down.

"Don't touch anything," he said.

We watched as he walked slowly around the pickup, peeked underneath the body, then opened the hood and peered in. Apparently satisfied nothing was wrong, he returned to the cab and hoisted himself up. Then he turned off the GPS. Grizzly's forehead smoothed out.

"Was that really necessary?" I asked.

Luke and Grizzly exchanged glances. "It was."

"I don't like this," I said.

"Join the club." Luke keyed the engine and we pulled out.

"Why'd we leave the bar?"

"Because I didn't want anyone to hear me," Grizzly said.

"And that's because…"

"Look. This may be my last assignment, but I'm still in the navy. We're not supposed to have opinions that—uh—well, we're not supposed to have opinions at all."

"What kind of opinions?"

"You asked me who did I trust, and I told you no one."

"So?"

"Luke," Grizzly said. "Turn on the radio."

As soon as the Stones belted out "Brown Sugar" on the classic rock station, he spoke. "Ellie...DOD is a fucking wormhole. The left hand never knows—or trusts—what the right hand is doing."

"But you're part of it."

His tone was patient, not irritated. "You know that picture of the galaxy with zillions of stars and the arrow that says 'You are here'?"

I nodded.

"Well that's what it's like to work in Defense. I mean, think about it. The country has seventeen intelligence agencies, and most of them are connected to DOD. Then, a couple of years ago, the Pentagon says the military needs its own team of spies to get human intelligence. There was no debate in Congress. No public announcement or explanation. But a few months later there's something called the Defense Clandestine Service."

"Number eighteen?"

He nodded.

I was feeling the buzz from the alcohol and the carbs. "You're pretty cynical. Maybe even paranoid."

"A career in military intelligence does that." He pulled out a cigarette and matches from a crumpled pack. "Fucking oxymoron." He rolled down the window, struck a match, and touched the flame to the cigarette. He took a long drag and blew it out. "But you know something? It doesn't make a coon's bit of difference what I think. Or you. Or our friend Luke over there."

"How come?"

"Because we live in the Deep State."

"Okay." I hesitated. "What is the Deep State?"

"It's the government behind the one on either end of Pennsylvania Avenue. A state within a state."

"Now you're a conspiracy theorist?"

"No. I'm a realist."

"That's nothing new. Eisenhower warned us about the military-industrial complex sixty years ago."

"But this one has new, more powerful members. Everyone is focused on national security, so we're talking not only the Pentagon, but State, Homeland Security, the CIA, and Justice. Even Treasury. As well as major corporations with the same agenda."

"And Congress?"

"Nope. All they do is rubber-stamp what the Deep State does. But here's the thing. Everything the state does is secret. Classified. It's a surveillance state run amok. And, more and more, it's run by the private sector. Banks, Wall Street, and your buddies at Delcroft, for example."

"What do you mean?"

"Weapons suppliers. Private contractors, digital types like the old Blackwater crowd, ethical and nonethical hackers. They all work *with* the government now. Closer than ever."

I thought of Dolan and cleared my throat.

"About seventy percent of America's intelligence budget goes to the private sector. To root out terrorism and protect the country."

"That much?"

He tried to smile, but it looked like a scowl. "Yeah. Which, in practice, means that the CEO of Delcroft advises the president on technology and national security probably as often as the Joint Chiefs. Add to that the fact that most retired admirals and generals end up on the boards of companies like Delcroft. In fact, most big corporations have their *own* intel operations today. And they share information. On a scale that would shock even Edward Snowden." He took another drag. "Did you know that the government is starting to protect companies like Delcroft and Google and AT&T from privacy lawsuits in return for their data?"

I shook my head. "What about the subpoenas and things they need to get at that data?"

Grizzly's laugh was hollow. "Gone with the wind."

"But doesn't it take a long time to find specific data and transmit it?"

"If you think a fraction of a second is a long time." He paused. "Look, I love my country. I lost my fucking leg because of it. But I don't recognize it anymore."

Luke cut in. "So, you're saying they could be looking into Ellie right now?"

"You bet they are. Delcroft, the FBI, probably this new DCS too." He crossed his arms. "But you already knew that, didn't you?"

I slumped against the back of the seat in the pickup.

Chapter Thirty-one

Saturday

We dropped Grizzly at the entrance gate of Great Lakes—he'd taken a cab up—and headed south. Neither of us talked. I was trying to internalize everything Grizzly had said. I'd faced threats before, but there was usually an individual or group on the other side. People with names and faces whom I knew were not my friends. But this was an entirely new script. Who was after me? How many of them were there? And who wanted the flash drive?

Charlotte Hollander was the only person outside of my family, Zach, Luke, and Grizzly, whom I'd told about the drive. But whoever was tapping my phone, if it wasn't Hollander, also knew since I'd called Dolan about it from home. So there was Hollander, Dolan, Luke, the phone tapper, and now Grizzly. Whom did Hollander tell? And whom did they tell? The number of people who knew about Parks and his flash drive, and the fact I had it, had possibly increased exponentially by now.

But why? What was on it? If Parks really was a spy, had he hacked into Delcroft's system and stolen the plans? Hollander had been pretty antsy to get the drive back, and she was Delcroft's queen bee of drones. But was she behind the phone tap? She'd told me over drinks that she'd tapped Parks' phone. Why not mine, too? Or had she run it up the chain of command? Grizzly had said most companies had their own intel departments now, and he'd also said Delcroft and the military were practically married to each other. Did that mean the NSA had hacked into my computer? And if they had, where did it stop? Were they also tracking Rachel? Or my father? I shivered.

"Luke," I said. "I want to give the drive back. I don't want to be involved anymore."

He flicked his gaze from the road to me. "I agree."

"So what should I do?"

"Call Hollander in the morning. Drop it off at her house."

"Somehow that sounds too simple. What if it's a trap?"

Luke didn't reply.

I swallowed. We passed a sign that said we were entering Lake Forest. I sucked in a breath. "I have a better idea."

"I'd like to get home."

"Hollander lives in Lake Forest. Let's drop it off now."

"Why? Do you have the drive with you?"

"You know the answer to that. Please. Pull over." I fished my cell out of my pocket.

Luke didn't stop, but he did slow down. "It's not gonna work. Someone with her security clearance won't be listed. You're not going to find her unless she wants you to."

I jiggled my foot again; I'd been doing that a lot recently. Then I sat up. "I know how to find it. Please."

Luke's brows knitted, but he turned off Green Bay Road onto a side street and stopped the pickup. I fished my cell out of my pocket and called Susan.

Thankfully, she picked up. "Hey, Ellie. What's happening?"

"I'm in a hurry, and I need a favor. You know people whose kids go to Lake Forest Middle School, don't you?"

"Sure. Jim and Carol Milgram's kids."

Susan knows everyone. "They'd have a student directory, right?"

"Yes…" Susan stretched the word into three syllables, which meant she wasn't sure she wanted to go any further.

"I need an address and phone, if it's listed, for a twelve-year-old boy whose last name is Hollander."

"Ellie…"

I cut her off. "Please, Susan. It's important."

Chapter Thirty-two

Saturday

We pulled up to 1642 Greenview Place twenty minutes later. The first surprise was how modest the house was, more like a New England cottage than a Lake Forest mansion. A white brick home at the end of a short driveway, it had dormer windows, a red painted door, and an attached garage. Tidy trimmed hedges edged the front, and a big oak sprawled on one side. A spruce stood on the other, brushing against the roof of the garage. Not exactly the home I'd expected the queen bee of drones would occupy.

The second surprise was how empty it looked. The lights in front were on, and there was a light over the garage, but I didn't see any lights inside. A thick, soupy fog had descended, which made the house look even more dark and deserted.

"I don't like this, Ellie," Luke said. "Let's go."

"It's Saturday night. Maybe she's out to dinner. Or went away for the weekend."

"Well, you can't just leave it on her doorstep." He paused. "In fact, don't even think of getting out to sniff around."

"Why not?"

"First off, there have got to be surveillance cameras all around the place. There's probably a silent alarm to call the authorities, too, which might or might not be the local cops. In fact"—he

revved the engine and pulled out from the curb—"hold on." He
rolled to the end of the block, about fifty yards from the house,
turned the corner, and parked.

I smiled.

"This still doesn't mean you're getting out."

"Why not? I have a hoodie." I reached behind my neck and
flapped the hood of my sweatshirt.

"Ellie…what happened to the woman who was scared shitless ten minutes ago?"

"That's why we're here. Let me just make sure she's not home.
One minute, no longer." He killed the engine and squeezed his
eyes shut in exasperation. "You don't have to come," I added.

"Oh, yes, I do."

I shrugged out of my coat so the hoodie would hide my face
and we slid out of the pickup.

"You've got exactly one minute," Luke said, pulling a flashlight out of the glove compartment. "Listen…," he added. "If
you spot a camera, don't, for God's sake, look into it. And no
talking. Not one word. If you need to get my attention, wave.
If that doesn't work, bark like a dog."

"Seriously?" When he nodded, I said under my breath, "I'm
better at catcalls."

I wasn't sure if he heard me, but he shot me a look, so I
lowered my head in a silent apology.

We walked back to the house and stopped at the edge of the
driveway.

I pulled my hoodie over my face as far as it would go and
pushed my hair back. Luke turned his jacket inside out to avoid
revealing the North Face logo on the front and pulled his hood
over his head. We examined the front of the house. Nothing
looked out of the ordinary.

I headed for the garage. On one side was a window. I peeked
in. A car was parked inside. A full-sized sedan, it looked like
an updated version of a Volvo, which I used to own, but I'm
notoriously bad at identifying cars. Luke followed me over and
turned on the flashlight. Whatever model it was, it sat in the

middle of the garage, and the light from the flashlight glinted off the front bumper. Maybe she was out for the evening. Dinner, likely. With friends who'd picked her up.

Luke backed away and ran his flashlight up and down and across the garage door. I didn't notice anything, but he zeroed in on something, and I heard a sharp intake of breath.

"What?" I whispered.

"He raised a finger to his lips, pointed to the door, and aimed the flashlight at the door.

I looked. A black *X* had been scrawled in magic marker near the middle of the garage door, which was painted white.

"Someone's been here, Ellie." He whispered. "Someone who wants another person to make sure they see this."

I frowned. "Are you saying someone is spying on Hollander? Besides us?"

He nodded. "We really need to get out of here. Now. And no more talking."

I raised my index finger. "I'll be careful," I mouthed and went back to the curb where the mailbox stood. That was the third surprise. The mailbox was crammed with what looked like three or four days of accumulated mail. I motioned to Luke and pointed. He nodded. I held up my palms. He shrugged. Maybe she'd taken her son away for a long weekend. Door County. Or Michigan.

Luke checked his watch and made a circular motion with his index finger, meaning I should hurry. I held up my palm and trotted around to the back of the house, determined to make a full circuit. Maybe in the back we'd see a light on inside. Not that it would make me feel better, but at least I'd know someone was there. Cloudy wisps of fog hampered our view. But I was able to make out that the land in back extended farther than the land in front. There must have been an acre of property, most of it surrounded by an eight-foot wooden fence that hid a patio from prying eyes. So much for a modest home.

Bushes and evergreen shrubs were planted in front of the fence, at least on three sides. The cold air sharpened the aroma of pine and spruce. I found a gate on the side facing the house. It was locked, but not with a normal latch or padlock. A numeric keypad was attached to one side. Luke pointed to it, as if to say, "I told you so." I squinted and looked through a crack between two slats of fencing. I saw a good-sized swimming pool covered for winter. And what had to be a grill, also covered, although the fog might have been playing tricks on my eyes.

I turned around, deflated, ready to leave. I'd learned nothing new about Charlotte Hollander, except that she wasn't home and had a nice car and a swimming pool. Luke yanked his thumb toward the front, and we started back around the house. Suddenly, a pair of headlights swam into view, and an SUV cruised down the street and stopped at Hollander's house. Whoever was driving killed the engine. A second pair of headlights followed. The doors to the vehicles slid open. Luke and I exchanged panicked looks and dove into the bushes.

Chapter Thirty-three

Saturday

Although yews are evergreens, they tend to look threadbare in winter. I crouched behind two and hoped like hell no one would see me. Despite the fog, I had a view of the sidewalk in front of Hollander's house, but my sight line was limited. Fog muffles sounds as well, so it was hard to hear. I thought I heard the click of car doors closing. Footsteps crunched on the few remaining snowy patches of ground. But no voices called out, and I heard no conversation. Only the persistent bark of a dog a few houses away—at least I hoped it was a dog and not a coyote. Whatever it was, apparently it realized that "human" scents had invaded its turf.

As my eyes adjusted to the dark, three figures that appeared blacker than the night around them materialized, heading toward us from the front of the house. I tried not to move, but it was cold, and my only outerwear was the hoodie. I shivered, afraid my quivering would somehow translate to the yews. I tried not to breathe either. Little clouds of vapor coming from the bushes would not be a good idea.

The three figures clustered at the side of the house, and then, like those videos of dividing cells you see on *Nova*, they split apart. One of the figures headed across the yard toward the garage. But the other two came our way. My heart slammed against my chest, and my pulse raced so fast I felt dizzy. I tried to tell myself to hold on.

As the two figures skirted the oak tree, their indistinct shapes sharpened and resolved into men in dark-colored clothing. Both had solid builds, even bulkier because of quilted jackets, wool hats, and thick boots. For one frightening moment, the angle as they strode across the yard made me think they'd spotted us, but at the last second they cut toward the gate. They seemed to be doing the same thing Luke and I had been: casing Hollander's house.

When they reached the gate in the fence, they stopped. They were fewer than twenty feet away. Their backs were toward me, and the odor of stale cigars wafted over.

All of a sudden a bright light crashed through the dark. My breath caught. One of the men had snapped on one of those ultrabright halogen flashlights. Thankfully, the man aimed the light toward the house, but how long would that last? I ducked down further and tried to shrink into a ball.

The beam danced across the back door of Hollander's house, played over the windows, then rose to the second story and swept back the other way. *God, please don't let him shine the light this way.* I had a feeling Luke was mentally saying the same prayer.

But the light did turn in our direction. It darted from left to right across the fence about five feet above the bushes behind which we were hiding. In a few seconds they would find us. I couldn't breathe. One of the men let his gaze drift from side to side. He was going to point the flashlight our way. I bit my tongue. We were doomed.

Without warning the dog started barking again. It sounded closer than before. Was its owner taking it for a walk? I know a dog's sense of smell is five hundred times more powerful than humans'. It had to be scenting the men…and us.

The men must have thought the same thing because they jerked their heads up. I heard a growl followed by a "What the fuck?"

"Let's go!" the other man said. Both men jogged back to the side of the house they'd come from. A moment later they were out of sight. The dog was still barking; in fact, its howls were coming faster and were higher pitched. The men were actually closer to it now than they had been in the back.

A man's voice cut in. "Barney, settle down! It's just the fog."

I was about to take a relieved breath when I felt a tap on my shoulder. I nearly jumped out of my skin. I whipped around.

Luke.

"C'mon," he whispered. "Let's get out of here. Now."

He emerged from behind a nearby shrub and started to run. I followed. Instead of heading to the garage or the front of the house, he took off in the opposite direction. We ran farther back along the fence line. In thirty yards, the side of the fence ended and made a ninety degree angle. We found ourselves at the property line of Hollander's neighbor. A fence cordoned off their yard too—this was Lake Forest, after all.

But behind both fences was a small passage, bordered by the fences on one side and a stand of evergreens on the other. There was just enough room to squeeze through. Empty beer bottles, trash, and dead tree branches that landscapers had failed to remove littered the area, making it a small dump. I wondered if the homeowners even knew it was there. Given the cigarette butts and fast-food wrappers, their kids did. But none of that mattered.

Luke and I ran through the passage, which extended to the end of the block. Then we turned left. We were about to race to the pickup when Luke froze. I was behind him and nearly stumbled into him. He shook his head. I regained my balance and looked. One of the men from the SUV was lurking by the pickup, a revolver in his hand.

I whimpered and covered my mouth with my hand. Luke shot me a fierce look that clearly meant "Shut up." I cowered behind him, wondering what the hell we were supposed to do now. We couldn't go back. We couldn't go forward. We were trapped. Why hadn't I listened to Luke in the first place?

Slowly Luke backtracked into the yard of the house on the corner. I followed. The man with the gun shifted his feet and looked both ways but didn't appear to see us. Suddenly the dog started to bark. In short, low-pitched growls.

"Barney!" A voice said. "Stop that. Everything's okay."

But Barney kept barking, and the dog and its owner emerged from the fog directly in front of us on the sidewalk. I squeezed my eyes shut; we were going to be discovered. Luckily, though, the man with the revolver saw them too, hurriedly slipped the gun into his waistband, and took off around the corner in the direction of the car.

Barney's owner stopped, and the dog, instead of barking, began to whine. It was scenting us. Thank God a human's sense of smell is so much weaker than a dog's. Barney's owner looked around, pulled the leash tighter, and murmured, "I don't know who that was, but I don't think I want to know. Let's go home."

We waited until it was quiet, and I dared to take a breath. Luke clicked the key fob and the doors to the pickup opened. We ran over and flung ourselves inside. I grabbed my jacket and threw it over my shoulders, then rubbed my hands together. Luke started the car and started to pull out, which was when we hit our next surprise.

Greenview Place had no outlet. Like my street, it ended in a cul-de-sac.

"Shit…shit…shit," I said.

"You can say that again," Luke said.

We would have to drive past Hollander's house on our way out. "The men casing her house are going to see us. They were heading toward the front, remember?"

"Maybe not," Luke said. "Let's wait."

"And make ourselves a target?"

"We're around the corner. Just hang on."

We waited for what seemed like an eternity. The dog and its owner made their way back to their house. Barney was a Rottweiler. Its barking had subsided, but it was still alert. Five more minutes passed. Barney was back inside. A minute later all three men appeared in front of Hollander's house. The fog and the dark made it difficult to see, but it seemed as if they had discovered the mailbox full of letters. Especially after one of the men turned his palms up and shrugged.

Finally, they returned to the back of the house. Luke started the engine, and we turned onto Greenview and sped out the way we'd come. As we passed Hollander's house, I checked out the SUV parked in front. It looked familiar. My gaze went to the license plates. My stomach lurched. The SUV was the same one that had been outside my house.

Chapter Thirty-four

Sunday

When Luke and I got home, we tumbled into bed, both of us exhausted. I didn't even try to make sense of what had happened in Lake Forest. Like Scarlett, I'd think about it tomorrow.

After breakfast the next morning, Luke said, "I think I should stay here for a few days."

"I thought you had a meeting up in Lake Geneva tomorrow."

"I do, but given what happened last night, I'm going to reschedule it."

"That's not necessary. I'll be all right. I'll put on my big-girl pants."

"I don't know."

I walked him to the door. "Luke…I can survive without you for a day or two. Really." Still, I stayed in his arms longer than usual, fear and loneliness already setting in. I felt like Janis Joplin; he was taking a little piece of my heart with him.

"You know something?" he said.

I shook my head.

"I think I'll come back Tuesday."

I looked up at him. How could he read my mind like that? "That would be wonderful."

"In the meantime, I want you to call or at least text twice a day so I know you're safe." I nodded. "And do *not* use your landline, unless it's just to order a pizza. Use your cell. The encryption app I uploaded is pretty secure. But just to be certain, be sure you block your caller ID." I nodded again. "And don't use your computer, either."

"Unless it's to order a pizza," I said.

He grinned. "I love you, Ellie Foreman."

"Me too you." I gave him a smile and a fierce hug.

After he left, I decided to trace the license plate of the SUV that had staked out my house and materialized at Hollander's the previous night. Despite the risk of someone finding out that's what I was doing, I had to know. In fact, I should have done it days before, but every time it crossed my mind, something else seemed to require my immediate attention. I trudged upstairs to my office and went online. Several websites proclaimed they could identify every license plate in every state of the country. But when I entered "W80-6939," a plate from Illinois, they suddenly wanted money, and I knew better than to give them my credit card number.

I sighed, got up, and called Georgia Davis on my cell. As a former cop and now a PI, she had better resources than mortals like me. She called me back ten minutes later. There was no record of the plate. Not in Illinois, or anywhere else.

"What does that mean?" I asked.

"It could mean a lot of things. With no registration, it could be a stolen car. Or someone who wants to fly under the radar."

"The SUV looked like it was well maintained."

"How do you know? You said there was a dense fog."

She didn't miss anything. "That's true. Tell me something, Georgia. Could an unregistered vehicle like that be used by corporate security people? Or intelligence operatives?"

A long silence followed. "Ellie, what exactly are you involved in?"

"I really can't—I wish I could—I just need an answer."

Another silence. Then: "Let me put it this way. If I was working for the FBI or the CIA or one of the ABCs, I'd do one of two things. Either use a dummy corporation to register the car, or have it registered in so many overlapping jurisdictions you'd never find out who it belonged to."

"But it would be registered."

"Listen. You know how the mayor keeps getting all those tickets?"

The mayor of Chicago's motorcade was well-known for running red lights and driving well over the speed limit.

"Well, he'd have even bigger problems if his cars weren't up-to-date with tags and insurance."

"So the SUV I'm talking about was probably stolen?"

"I didn't say that."

"You're confusing me."

"I don't mean to. But a lot of so-called private security consultants do fly under the radar. Who knows what equipment they have or how they got it?"

"So you're saying—"

She cut me off. "I'm saying that just because the SUV isn't registered doesn't mean a whole hell of a lot." Another pause. "Are you sure there's nothing you want to tell me?"

I heaved a breath. "I never thought I'd be saying this, but sometimes I wish I wasn't a video producer. I just seem to keep running into problems that turn out to be—well—dangerous."

"How dangerous"?

"I'll tell you. But it's all off the record, okay?"

She laughed. "It always is."

I told her about Gregory Parks, Delcroft, and Charlotte Hollander. When I got to Parks' subway accident, she cut in.

"I heard about that. People I know aren't convinced it was a suicide."

"Yeah, well, they have a point. He could have been pushed. Delcroft thought he was a spy for the Chinese government."

"Holy shit!" She paused. "Does the flash drive you called me about have something to do with all this?"

"Uh-huh."

She let out an exasperated breath. "Ellie. These people do not screw around. What can I do?"

"Nothing at the moment. But I'll let you know."

Chapter Thirty-five

Monday

Monday dawned with one of those crystal-blue Chicago skies that says spring is imminent and it's time to pack away one's winter clothes. I didn't; when you live in Chicago, you know better. I brewed a pot of coffee and waited impatiently until eight-thirty, when I could start making business calls. The first was to Charlotte Hollander. I still wanted to get rid of the flash drive and extricate myself from everything having to do with Delcroft—video or no video. It was time to withdraw into white-picket-fence land.

But I didn't get the chance. My call went to voice mail. I left a message for her to call me.

A minute later my phone rang. I picked up, fully expecting Hollander to be on the other end. She wasn't.

"Hi, Ellie. Zach Dolan."

"Zach! Are you okay? I was shocked to hear about the explosion at your office. What happened?"

"That's why I'm calling. We're fine. Joshua and me. We weren't there when it happened."

"I heard. Still, it's got to be devastating."

"It's all right. I'm working out of my brother's house until the insurance adjusters cut a check. He sends his regards. Hey, do you want to meet for a cup of coffee?"

"You have news?"

"We haven't had coffee in a while," he said.

I got it. "Sure. Coffee would be great. I have something for you anyway."

He didn't answer, but we arranged to meet in thirty minutes at the Starbucks closest to my house. I arrived first and parked in the lot. I was just climbing out of my car when Zach pulled up in a Beemer. Clearly ethical hacking had its rewards.

He slid down the window and motioned for me to get in. Joshua occupied most of the backseat. I hadn't realized how large he was. And how wolfish he looked, though he was a shepherd. Thankfully, his tail was wagging furiously.

I hopped in. Zach pulled away.

"Why the change in plans?"

"You know our phones are tapped."

"I figured that's why we're meeting."

"Exactly," he said. "And they think we're going to that Starbucks, right?" He yanked a thumb behind him. When I nodded, he added, "Well, let's just make it a little more difficult for them."

"There's a Dunkin' Donuts a block away," I said hopefully.

"I think we should just walk around somewhere. It's safer."

I swallowed my disappointment. I didn't need the calories anyway. I dug into my pocket and pulled out another flash drive. "I made another copy before I gave it to you. So here you go."

"Thanks. But there's something I haven't told you," he went on. "About the drive."

"I want to tell you something too," I said. "Things are getting out of control. Like us having to meet in person. And people following me. Then I found out there's an executive at Delcroft who knows I have it. In fact, the explosion at your office may be connected to it."

"Is the executive's name C. Hollander?"

My jaw hit the floor of the car. "Charlotte Hollander. How did you know?"

He turned down a side street off Willow Road that bordered a park. With the mild weather, lots of little people had converged on the slide and swings, releasing excited screams, the kind children make from the sheer joy of being alive.

"Let's take Joshua for a walk," he said. He shoved the drive into his pocket, opened the glove compartment, and took out a leash.

We climbed out of the car and Dolan put the dog on the leash. We started walking toward the park.

"I don't know if this is going to make a difference, but before the explosion, I started playing around with the drive."

"And?"

"You know what metadata is, right?"

"Data about the data."

"Right. So, a lot of systems include logs of who emailed who, when, sometimes even the subject. As a user, you wouldn't normally see them, but they end up in a file. And, if you know what you're doing you can extract them."

I halted on the sidewalk. "And you found the log?"

"I did. In fact I made a printout of it. I'll give it to you, although you might not be able to read it. It's in—well, it's in computerese."

I inclined my head. "What did the log say?"

"It looks like three people were communicating regularly. Almost every day. Most have cc's on them."

"Who were the three? No, wait. It's got to be Parks and Hollander. But who's the third?"

"A General Gao," Zach said.

Joshua took that moment to sniff a pile of leaves and twigs on the ground. Then he issued a whine.

"Damn straight, Joshua." I looked at Dolan. "Who is General Gao?"

"I Googled him. He's a big shot in the Chinese military. Like a five-star general. Or higher."

I rubbed a hand across my forehead. "This doesn't sound right."

"Look him up. But don't do it from home. Go to the library, okay?"

I couldn't help the quiver that rolled through me. My phone was hacked. My computer, too. What was next? "You don't have any content from the correspondence, though?"

"Not yet. I haven't been able to crack the encryption. It's probably a Chinese system. But I'll keep trying." We turned, making a circle around the playground.

"So what do you make of it?" I blurted out.

He shrugged. "That's your job."

I thought about it. Hollander had told me Gregory Parks was a spy. But she'd been in daily communication with this so-called spy, as well as a general in the Chinese military. Instead of clearing things up, Hollander's behavior was making everything murkier.

Joshua barked as if on cue. I jumped. A poodle on a leash held by a woman who looked like she was on her way to Nordstrom strolled by.

Zach looked over. "You sure you want me to go ahead with this?"

I gulped. "I don't know."

Our village library occupies only three rooms, one of which includes five computers that were all in use, so I waited. Eventually I presented my library card. Then I sat at one of the computers and Googled "General Gao," confident in my relative privacy. Libraries, bless them, set their computers to delete everything a user has done once they log off, including their search history.

Zach was right. Gao was a hotshot. He was one of only eleven men on China's Central Military Commission, which essentially ran the army. The commission made all the senior appointments and supervised troop deployments and arms spending. Unfortunately, there wasn't much about General Gao the man. He was in his fifties, young by Chinese standards. He had been raised in Shanghai but studied at Oxford. Which meant he was educated and spoke English. It didn't say what he studied, but I suspected it had something to do with aeronautics.

There was one image of a young Gao grinning in a racing shell, brandishing a paddle. He must have been on crew at

Oxford. But aside from a 1994 group photo of about two dozen Chinese officers in front of a palatial building, I couldn't find anything recent. I made notes on my iPhone, printed out the two images, and logged out.

Chapter Thirty-six

Monday

As I got back into my car, I tried piecing things together.

If Parks was a spy for the Chinese, why was Hollander trading daily emails with him? As well as a Chinese general? Was she trying to entrap Parks and Gao? Extract proof they were spies? Or was she part of the ring herself? Either way, this did not give me a warm and fuzzy feeling.

Which reminded me. I pulled over to the curb and called Hollander's office again.

This time a woman answered. "I'm sorry. She's not here."

"When do you expect her?"

"I really don't know." Her voice was brusque.

"Will she be in today at all?"

"Who did you say you were?" The voice turned suspicious.

"Sorry to bother you." I hung up. Where was Hollander? Still on a long weekend? I didn't know, but I wasn't going to turn over the drive to anyone except her. And I certainly wasn't going to mail it or messenger it downtown if she wasn't around.

After meeting with Grizzly, I was on the lookout for a tail whenever I drove, and coming home from the library, I found one. It wasn't a battered green Toyota, it wasn't a pickup truck, and it wasn't an SUV. This time it was a nondescript beige car, the kind of four-door sedan that looks almost institutional. Still, the fact that anyone was shadowing me gave me the creeps and made me intensely aware that any privacy I might be entitled to was a myth. Was this the way covert agents felt? If so, I'd make a lousy one.

I peered into the rear view, which, I realized, was now becoming my only tool to confront the surveillance. A man was driving, and a second person whose gender I couldn't determine occupied the passenger seat. The driver had a ball cap pulled low, blocking his face, and the other person wore a wool hat, also low across his or her forehead. Friends or foes?

Irritation shot through me. I was tired of being a target, the mouse with whom someone's cat could toy. I couldn't live my life in fear. At the next stop sign I considered mustering my courage. I would put my car in park, climb out, and approach the driver's side door. I could play cop as well as the next guy. I would demand they tell me who the hell they were and why they were following me.

Then I reconsidered. What if they had a weapon lying on the front seat? What if they lowered their window and shot me point-blank? That is the precise reason my attitude toward cops, whom in my younger days I was apt to call "pigs," had changed. I knew now that cops put their lives in jeopardy every time they made a traffic stop, and I respected their courage. The erstwhile pigs had become "pals," and I didn't have their guts.

So I gritted my teeth and tried to get a license plate number. Naturally, there was no plate in front. I accelerated and raced the rest of the way home, hoping my "pals" weren't out ticketing speeders today. The warmth of the day did nothing to dispel the chill that came over me. Thank God Luke was coming back soon.

Chapter Thirty-seven

Monday

Gary Phillips, Delcroft's deputy chief operating officer, loved his corner office on the sixty-fourth floor of Delcroft's Loop office building. The eastern window framed a magnificent view of Lake Michigan, and it was high enough that low-hanging diaphanous clouds occasionally hugged his window. Phillips had flown F-16s during the First Gulf War, and like most pilots, he loved the solitude and power of flying, the sense that he was the only human in the sky, both servant and master of his own fate. But after the war Delcroft lured him away from McDonnell Douglas, and he spent most of his time at a desk. Now, though, with the problems Delcroft was facing, he wished he could fly back into the clouds.

He was lamenting the pile of Monday morning messages and decisions to make when his office door flew open and Delcroft's chief of security, Warren Stokes, barged in. There had been no intercom warning from Gena, Phillips' executive assistant.

Phillips looked up from his desk. He didn't like Stokes, but the ex-Agency guy had been forced on him by Delcroft's CEO, Brian Riordan, to whom Phillips reported. Delcroft thought they had a secure system in place, Riordan said, but their contacts in the military persuaded them that the escalating concern about corporate espionage, particularly by offshore hackers, made people like Stokes a necessity. He had a clean record, Riordan added. Phillips, himself a member of the Ivy League old boy's network, had no choice. The days of handshake deals and honor codes were long gone.

Stocky, with ruddy cheeks, a buzz cut, and a web of tiny spider veins on his nose, Stokes looked like he'd be more comfortable in a bar than in Phillips' office. As the man pulled up a chair to the edge of his desk, Phillips noted his denim shirt and khakis. You'd think with all the money Delcroft was shelling out to him, he could afford a suit.

Phillips sighed, pulled the plug out of his desk phone, and switched off his cell, as he'd been instructed. Only then did he let his temper show.

"Okay. Tell me what the hell is happening around here. Ever since Hollander saw that video I'm hearing strange things."

Stokes replied in an even voice. "I talked to Hollander. She was concerned about Gregory Parks when he showed up in the video."

"Parks...Parks...why do I know that name?"

"I'm sure you remember. He was the guy in the video that Hollander went bat-shit crazy over. The guy who—supposedly—jumped off the subway platform last week."

"Yes. I remember." Phillips cleared his throat. "But what does 'supposedly' mean?"

"It means that Parks turned out to be a huge security risk. I had to neutralize the threat."

Stokes had had a thirty-year career at the CIA, with postings in Eastern Europe, Afghanistan, and Iraq. But, according to the CEO, he'd exited the Agency several years earlier. He went on to create his own security firm and, apparently, had become highly successful. He now operated a mini-CIA, staffed with more than fifty former intelligence operatives from the Agency, the Bureau, Secret Service, even Blackwater. The company was known for getting results fast. Which was both a blessing and a problem.

"Wait a minute, Stokes," Phillips said. "Are you saying you had something to do with his death?"

Stokes didn't answer, but his smug expression told Phillips what he needed to know.

"Goddammit, Stokes. This is not something we do at Delcroft."

"You didn't. I did."

"Yeah, but I sure as hell didn't authorize you to push the guy off a subway platform."

"I don't hear anyone saying you did."

"Stokes. Listen to me. Assassination is not part of our mission statement."

Stokes leaned forward, his expression flat. "My charter is to do what I deem necessary to protect the security and safety of the largest and most important defense contractor in the world. Parks was a ticking time bomb. You can't trust the Chinese. They're polite to your face, but behind your back, they're just waiting to screw you. They're worse than the Russians."

Christ. They weren't even speaking the same language. Phillips massaged his temples.

"Look," Stokes added. "I know this is not your area. That's why Riordan hired me." He looked Phillips in the eye. "Parks was a problem. And now we have a bigger one."

The faint stench of cigar smoke wafted over Phillips. Stokes had probably lit one up before coming in because he knew Phillips hated them.

"What's that?"

"Hollander."

Phillips bent his head. "Charlotte? What's going on?"

"She's gone. Disappeared. Not here."

"What are you telling me?" Phillips straightened his spine. "You didn't—"

Stokes cut him off. "Relax, pal. All I did was stake out her house over the weekend. Her mailbox was overflowing. No lights on. And her car hadn't been used in days. She's outta here."

"Maybe she went on vacation. You talk with her people?"

"Didn't have to." He folded his arms. "I checked her computer."

The security measures put in place by CEO Riordan were excessive. Especially when someone like Stokes was implementing them. If Riordan knew Stokes had killed Parks, he'd explode. Stokes was acting like a third-rate hit man. Even if he had worked at the Agency. What did they call them—cleaners? Phillips decided to talk to Riordan. This had to stop. He folded his hands on his desk. "Is there anyone here you're *not* bugging?"

Stokes pretended to smile. Phillips guessed the man didn't like him very much either. "My team accessed Hollander's computer and phone. There were four calls to a number that turned out to be Parks' cell."

"From Hollander?" Phillips asked. "Are you sure?"

Stokes nodded. "She was desperate to reach him. Even left him a voice message. When my guys checked out her hard drive, we think we know why."

Phillips gazed at him.

"All her correspondence was encrypted."

Phillips shrugged. "So is mine. Everyone's is. You were the one who made us do it."

"In her case, she's using a program we didn't approve."

Phillips thought for a minute. "That might have been a wise decision on her part. She deals with extremely sensitive information."

Stokes crossed his arms.

"Did you decrypt the files?"

"A buddy of mine is working on it. But we got lucky with the logs, and we've been able to extract a few headers. You know, the "froms" and "tos." Other metadata as well, which—"

Phillips cut him off. He'd been through a full day of training on computer security at the CEO's order. "And?"

"There were half a dozen or more emails sent to someone named Gao Zhi Peng. Want to take a guess what nationality he is?"

Phillips, knowing he was being patronized, let out an irritated breath. "So he's Chinese."

"A general in the Chinese army. There are also three-way emails between Parks, Hollander, and Gao."

"Your conclusion?"

"We're still investigating, sir." Stokes emphasized the last word. "Anything I say would be purely hypothetical."

Phillips felt his patience slip away. "What do you think is going on? Hypothetically?"

Stokes unfolded his arms. "Well, your director of engineering might be selling DADES to the Chinese, using Parks as a middleman."

"That's a goddamn huge assumption."

Stokes inclined his head. "Why not cash in her chips? Get ready for retirement?"

"Charlotte? No way. Her father was in the military. A four-star general. She enlisted when she was eighteen. The army paid for her engineering degree."

"Look, Phillips. I've seen this more times than you know. Someone isn't getting their due, their credit, their promotion. So they sell out. Bottom line, it's all about the money. I'll wager the Chinese are paying her a shitload more than Delcroft."

Phillips plucked one of the cuffs of his shirt.

Stokes smiled again. "Look at it this way. Now you have a reason to get rid of her. She's your only real competition for the top spot."

"This is not how I wanted to run the company."

"You're not," Stokes said. "Running the company. Yet."

Chapter Thirty-eight

Monday

The two men exchanged cold glances.

"Over the weekend I went into her computer again. She's wiped the entire drive. Everything's gone. On both her office computer and her Mac at home."

"Her Mac? At home? You broke into her house?" When Stokes didn't reply, Phillips' gut twisted. Great. Now he could add breaking and entering to Stokes' felonies. He gazed out the window. What wouldn't he give to be in the air? Hell, he'd even take his old Cessna, which he'd traded up for a private jet. Reluctantly, he refocused on Stokes.

"I can't believe it. Everything was going her way. DADES, the success and accolades that come with it. She's not a traitor."

Stokes paused for a long moment. Then: "I have two words for you. Aldrich Ames. He's serving a life sentence with no parole. Snowden will too...if they ever get him back."

It was Phillips' turn to cross his arms. "How do I know you're telling me the truth?"

"Because I interviewed her. Before Parks was—had his accident. She tried to convince me she knew Parks was a spy and she was trying to expose him." He shifted. "But she claimed Parks was extorting her, threatening to blow her sky-high if she didn't come through with more about DADES." Stokes paused. "Then she told me something else."

"What?"

Stokes licked his lips. "She said there was a flash drive involved. That Parks told her he had proof she *was* selling the system to the Chinese. She figures he must have copied all the emails between them and the general—"

"Gao?"

Stokes nodded.

"Christ. This just gets better and better. What was Parks doing for us anyway?"

"He was a 'consultant' to Hollander."

Phillips tapped his fingers on his desk. He didn't like where the conversation was headed.

Stokes cleared his throat. "Actually there is one piece of good news. Hollander called me the day after we talked. Before she split. She had drinks with the woman who produced the video."

"Why the hell did she do that?"

"Because on the day he died, Parks was on his way to meet the woman. Hollander says he gave the drive to her."

"Foreman, right?" When Stokes nodded, Phillips asked, "Why her?"

"We're still trying to figure that out. But Hollander asked if there was any way I could get it. She said it would exonerate her."

"And you thought the best way to get it was to kill Parks?"

"That's not the reason he was eliminated. I told you; I was protecting the company. Hollander, too, for that matter. At least at that point."

"And now you want to kill Foreman? No way. This has gone far enough."

"All we want is the drive."

"Sure you do." Phillips shook his head. "What a cluster fuck." He was quiet for a moment. "What about Hollander's son? Where is he?"

"He's with his father. In Ohio."

"Do they know where she is?"

"From what I can tell, no. At least that's what the son's been texting his friends."

Was there anyone Stokes wasn't hacking? Phillips let out a sigh. "You don't think she—"

"Killed herself? Not a chance."

"How can you be sure? Maybe she knew you were on to her and felt the walls closing in—"

Stokes cut him off. "No."

"And you know this because…"

"There's too much money involved. The woman got the hell out of Dodge. Probably stashed millions in the Caymans. She's on some tropical island now with no extradition, laughing it up." Stokes paused. "But there's only one way to know for sure."

"And that is?"

"The flash drive should have a record of all their emails."

"I still don't understand why you couldn't get what you needed from Hollander's computer."

"Like I said, it was a system we've never seen before. In fact, we called in our brothers to help. It's probably Chinese. Or Russian. The Russkies are still the best hackers in the world."

But Phillips wasn't interested in the Russians' hacking proficiency. "Brothers? You mean the NSA?" When Stokes didn't answer, he said, "Christ. Who else knows about this shit storm?"

Stokes shrugged. "NSA has been 'keeping tabs' on Delcroft for years. They've got eyes on all your phones and computers. Doesn't matter whether it's Turbine, Gumfish, or Foggy Bottom; they get whatever they want whenever they want. They know what Hollander's been up to. And they share that intel with whoever they want: DOD, NSC, the White House."

"Delcroft has leverage at DOD. I think it's time for me to go to the CEO."

"Let me get the drive before you do."

Phillips was uneasy at the thought of any kind of alliance with Stokes, no matter how unlikely. "You realize this conversation makes me an accessory to about six felonies."

Stokes smiled. "Yeah, but if we can nail Hollander and Gao before too much intel changes hands, Delcroft comes up smelling like a rose."

"This is crazy, Stokes. You're tampering with the reputation— hell, the future of the company."

"With all due respect, sir, you didn't hire me. Your boss did. But hey, you don't want me to do this? I'll back off. Of course, I'll have to write a report detailing everything, including your objections, to the CEO and board of directors."

Phillips straightened up and gazed at Stokes. "I don't like threats, Stokes. You might want to reconsider. How are you going to explain to Riordan that you murdered one of our consultants?"

Stokes almost smiled. "Good point." He stood, pushed his chair back to its original position, and strode to the door. "Checkmate." He opened the door and pushed through. "I'll keep you posted."

Phillips had no illusions Stokes would follow through—the man was a loose cannon. No wonder the Agency had let him go. He looked out the window again, but this time the view was lost on him. It was time for Phillips to protect himself. Find a good criminal lawyer before the shit hit the fan.

Chapter Thirty-nine

Tuesday

I called Hollander again on my cell the next morning. This time I heard a couple of clicks, which indicated the call was being automatically transferred. A woman's voice picked up. "Human Resources."

I straightened up. "Uh, I was trying to reach Charlotte Hollander."

There was a long pause. "Who is this?"

So far I hadn't left my name when I called. But this was a direct question, hard to avoid. And I didn't want to hang up until I got some answers. I sucked in a breath. "This is Ellie Foreman."

"Well, Ms. Foreman, Ms. Hollander has been transferred."

"Really? She never said anything to me."

"May I ask what your business was with her?"

I faltered for an instant, then decided I could tell the truth. Or part of it. "I'm a video producer, and we scheduled a meeting to discuss an upcoming project. Can you tell me how to get in touch with her?"

"I'm afraid that information is classified."

Classified? Neat trick. "But she specifically requested me to call her this week."

"I'm sorry. I will note that you called."

Now there would be a record of my call. "Thanks." This time I did hang up before I could get in more trouble.

I pulled out my vacuum cleaner, cleanser, and a sponge. I stacked all the dirty plates and utensils in the dishwasher, wiped the counters. I changed the sheets on the bed, then went to work on the bathrooms. I've always believed that the physical activity of cleaning, organizing, and putting things into their proper place has a similar effect on my thinking. I didn't much care whether it was real or a placebo. I needed clarity.

I doubted Hollander had been "transferred." That happened to mid-level managers, not senior corporate executives. They were the ones who ordered transfers for others. In this instance "transfer" was corporate-speak for the fact that she was gone. But why? And why now?

I came up with two scenarios. The first was that Hollander was doing exactly what she said. Gregory Parks had somehow stolen her DADES system and was selling it to the Chinese. She discovered it, and in her effort to expose him, some greater threat came down. It could have been the Chinese. They weren't known to honor the milk of human kindness. They could have tried to harm her. Or her son. That reminded me. I should try to find him. Maybe he'd know where his mother had gone.

The second scenario was more troubling. She could be in league with Parks. She could be selling to the Chinese, specifically General Gao, and using Parks as a middleman. Delcroft—or some other entity—found out about it, and she had to flee to escape a life sentence for treason.

Either way, that would explain why people were casing her house over the weekend. Who happened to be the same people staking out my house earlier. The question was what I was going to do about it.

Chapter Forty

Tuesday

Rachel had the afternoon off and came to the house to do her laundry. It just happened to be the day our neighborhood diner serves vegetable soup. This is no ordinary vegetable soup; people from all over the North Shore flock to the place to fill up. We'd been going since Barry and I bought the house more than twenty years earlier. I'm still not sure why it's so good, but I've narrowed it down to the broth. I've tried to duplicate it at home more than once, but I've never been able to match it, and the owners, a brother and sister from Greece, won't say a word. They know a good thing when they have it.

Chicago was on the cusp of spring. Early March is a month of hope even though the weather is still lousy. The gradual return of longer daylight hours tends to dull the sharp edge of the Hawk's claws. Rachel stayed home, but I was under strict orders to bring back a quart of soup for her to take downtown.

I picked up Dad and we drove to the diner. Once we were inside and seated, he rubbed his palms back and forth against each other. "Hubba, hubba," he said. Whenever he does that, I know he's in a good mood. "Do you realize this spring is gonna be the ninety-fourth one I've seen?"

"I do. Should we plan something special for your birthday?"

His birthday was in October, but when you're ninety-four, who cares when you celebrate?

"Lemme see. I can't play golf anymore, the arthritis has crippled my hands, and I can't sit on an airplane for more than an hour. What does that leave?"

"You still have every brain cell you were born with. And you play a mean game of poker." I thought about it. "Think you could make it to Vegas? It's only a two-hour flight."

He shook his head. "No Vegas. But one of those casino boats—now, that's a different kettle of fish."

"Consider it done." I picked up the large laminated menu, which was a useless exercise, since I always order the same thing.

"What's going on with you? You find out who bombed your friend's office? Everything okay at home? I've been worried."

"We're working on it. It seems as if—"

I stopped when the waitress approached with her pad. This was the same waitress who used to bring over a high chair for Rachel when she was a baby. Clearly, the Greek owners treated their staff well.

"Hi, Jen."

"Hiya, Ellie. Lemme guess. Two vegetable soups, a Greek salad chopped, and a western omelet for the gentleman."

"Pretty good. Plus a quart of soup to take home."

"For your daughter."

I spread my hands. "You've got our number."

"You're predictable."

"That bad? Next time I'll order something shocking."

She eyed me over her pad. "It'll take more than a chicken salad sandwich to shock me."

I sat back. "How did you know that's what I was thinking?"

She tapped her forehead and headed into the kitchen.

I snuck a look out the window. "I should start seeing Fouad soon." Fouad was the man who helped me take care of my garden and my spirit. "I'm sure I saw shoots of daffodils in the front."

My father nodded.

"You and he never really bonded until he rescued me up in Lake Forest." Fouad had shot a man seconds before that man killed me.

"There's a reason for that."

"Dad, he saved my life."

"I know. And I will be forever in his debt. Even though he's Muslim."

I tilted my head. "Seriously? Aren't you too old for intolerance?"

"It's not Fouad. He's a decent man. A good man. Like I said, I will always be grateful to him."

"You realize, of course, that's what they say, or used to say, about Jews? You know, the 'one of my closest friends is Jewish' cliché? When you talk about Fouad that way, you're no better than they are."

He spread his hands. "If I was fifty years younger, sweetheart, I'd argue with you. But now, as I approach my ninety-fifth year, I'll just say you can't teach an old Jew new tricks. Our people have been at odds with Muslims for centuries. And these days their voices are louder. And more dangerous. You can't deny it. Hell, you were in the middle of it yourself."

He was right. I thought back to the time I met LeJeune. It had developed into a situation that involved radical Islam. "You can't hold that against Fouad."

"Did I say I did?"

"No, just all the other Muslims in the world."

Our soup arrived. I decided to leave the conversation where it was.

Chapter Forty-one

Tuesday

It's heartwarming to see one's daughter take responsibility for herself. Even if there's an ulterior motive. By the time we got back from the diner, Rachel's laundry was neatly folded and stacked near the door. Sure, she could have done it downtown, and she mostly does, but even my father knew the reason she was here.

"Wanted your mom to spring for some soup, eh?"

"Not true, Opa. I wanted to see Mom. And you," she added quickly.

Dad's eyes narrowed. "Nice try."

Rachel's eyes widened in mock innocence.

"Never try to con a con." He laughed.

"Or a poker player," I added. "Especially on vegetable soup day."

Rachel threw up her hands. "Okay, okay."

I handed her the carton of soup. Dad looked pleased with himself. "You taking off now?"

"I guess. Unless you want to take me shopping. I was thinking of—"

"It was great to see you too," I said.

She smiled ruefully and turned to Dad. "It was worth a shot."

Dad nodded.

"Oh, I almost forgot. Someone came to see you while you were out."

I stiffened, our banter forgotten. "Who?"

"A woman. Young. Well, around my age. Maybe a couple of years older."

Not Hollander. "What did she want?"

"She wanted to talk to you. I told her you'd be back in an hour, but she said she couldn't wait."

"Does this woman have a name?"

"She didn't say."

"Did you ask?"

"What do you think? Of course. She said it wasn't important. But it was strange. I got the feeling it was, you know?"

"Can you describe her?"

Rachel furrowed her brow. "Small. Delicate. Pretty. Chin-length black hair. Oh, and Asian. At least partly."

On the way home after dropping off Dad, I worried a hand through my hair. I usually get Jehovah's Witnesses on my doorstep once a year, as well as neighborhood kids selling candy, flowers, and lemonade. But whoever had shown up while we were at lunch wasn't either, and the fact that I was now getting visits from strangers filled me with unease.

There was no way I could figure out who'd come to the house, although the fact that she was Asian made me think it might have something to do with Gregory Parks, maybe General Gao. But I didn't want anything more to do with spies, espionage, or the Chinese. Thankfully, Luke would be back tonight.

I parked in the garage and went inside, determined to have a normal afternoon. But a minute later I started to wander around, trying to puzzle out what had happened to Charlotte Hollander. Who orchestrated the explosion at Dolan's office. And what was on the flash drive.

Finally I had an idea. I was about to go online to Google it, then remembered Luke and Dolan's warning. I'd already tracked the SUV online. I shouldn't be taking another risk. Instead I drove down to the library and found the number for Lake Forest Middle School, the school Charlotte Hollander's son attended. I tried to remember his name; Susan had told me when she found the address.

Kevin. That was it.

I got back in my car, fished out my cell, and called the school.

"Lake Forest Middle School. This is Marie. How can I help you?"

I mentally crossed my fingers. "Hello. This is Kevin Hollander's father's secretary calling."

"Oh, hello." Marie didn't sound surprised; in fact, her tone implied she might even have expected the call.

"We were just wondering about Kevin's attendance over the past few days. Is he all right?"

"Um…" Marie sounded confused. "I'm not sure what you mean."

I started to feel uncomfortable. "Well, with all the recent changes, Mr. Hollander wanted to check up on him."

Marie hesitated. Then: "I don't know your name, but—"

"I'm sorry. It's Susan. Susan—um—Wheeler." *Forgive me, Susan.*

"Perhaps you're both a little confused. We sent Kevin's transcripts to his new school in Columbus yesterday. I thought I left a message for Mr. Hollander at his office."

Sent the transcripts? To his new school? Backtrack, Ellie. Fast.

Happily, Marie saved me. "Kevin's last day was Friday."

"Um…oh no. I just looked at the note from Mr. Hollander. It's dated a week ago. I apologize. I am such a flake. I don't know how I got so turned around."

"Oh, that's all right. Happens all the time."

"Please…" My voice turned into an appeal. "Don't tell Mr. Hollander about this. He might fire me. I am so embarrassed."

"No problem, Susan. Glad I could straighten it out. Have a good day."

Chapter Forty-two

Tuesday

Kevin's move was both good news and bad news. Good news because Hollander hadn't taken him with her wherever she'd gone; bad news because it implied she'd been planning to flee. Something was very wrong, and I suspected Gregory Parks' death on the subway tracks had triggered it. But that left me in an awkward position. What should I do with the flash drive? Return it to Hollander's boss? Delcroft's Human Resources Department? Gary Phillips? And what should I say when I did? I would only be getting myself in deeper.

My cell buzzed. I picked it up. The caller ID was blocked.

"Ms. Foreman?" The caller had a gravelly voice. Probably smoked two packs a day.

"Who's calling?"

"This is Warren Stokes. I work for Delcroft. I'd like to pay you a visit."

What was going on? "I haven't run into you before. What is your position at Delcroft?"

A slight hesitation followed. "I worked with Charlotte Hollander, and we've been reviewing the videos you produced for her. We think there's a lot of good material in them, and I want to talk about how we can revive the project."

Surprise temporarily had me at a loss for words. After everything that had happened, now they wanted to resurrect the videos? Then I smiled. There was something very satisfying about coming full circle. Still, I replied cautiously. "I'm open to discussion."

"Good, good," Stokes said. "May I come to your house, say, in two hours?"

Suddenly I was leery. "My house? You don't want me to come downtown?"

"I was just trying to make it more convenient for you."

No way was I letting a stranger, Delcroft employee or not, into my house. Who was this guy, anyway?

"What did you say your name was?"

"Warren Stokes."

"And your title?"

"Head of security for Delcroft."

"Security? What's your connection to the video?"

"I'd rather explain that in person."

A red alert buzzed in my head. I replied cautiously. "Well, I'm sure you'll understand that I'd rather meet you someplace public. Do you know Solyst's? It's a pub in Northfield."

"I can find it," he said, but his tone indicated he wasn't happy about it.

"Great." I checked my watch. It was three now. "How is five?"

Solyst's used to be a dive bar. Then the owner sold it, and the new owners remodeled the restrooms, bought a bunch of flat-screen TVs, and expanded the menu. Now it's a semi-dive, and one of my favorite haunts. I arrived early and nursed a glass of wine at the bar.

At five pm sharp, the throaty sound of a car engine outside hummed. I peeked through the glass doors of the bar. Then I blinked to make sure of what I was seeing. The same SUV I'd seen twice now, staking out my house and at Hollander's the other night, was pulling into the parking lot. The SUV that couldn't be found on any of Georgia's databases. I seriously contemplated an immediate departure. But we were in a public place. If he tried anything at all, I would have plenty of help.

A stocky man got out of the SUV. He disappeared from view for a few moments, then reappeared and pushed through the door. He wore a ball cap and was dressed in chinos, a heavy sweater, and a bomber jacket, as if he'd once been in the military. He appeared to be in his sixties. I was sitting on a stool near the entrance.

"Warren Stokes?" I called out.

He nodded and studied me, as if assessing whether I was a threat. I was dressed in sweats, sweater, and boots, and I thought I saw a trace of relief on his face as he took me in. Meanwhile I assessed him. His eyes were hooded and pale; maybe gray, maybe blue, but definitely not friendly. A tiny spiderweb of veins ran down his nose.

"You're Ellie Foreman?"

I nodded, mentally debating how much to tell him. The people who'd been staking out Hollander's house worked for Delcroft. Which meant Delcroft was spying on their own people. And me. I decided I'd had enough.

"So tell me something, Mr. Stokes. Why were you staking out my house in your SUV last week?"

Chapter Forty-three

Tuesday

To his credit, Stokes didn't deny it. "It wasn't me; it was someone on my team." He turned to the bartender, who was hovering nearby. "Whatever you have on draft," he said. The bartender motioned to an array of spigots a few feet away, all with colorful logos.

Stokes looked them over. "Pale Ale will do."

The bartender nodded his approval.

I changed the subject. "If you needed to check up on me, you should have contacted me directly."

"We were still doing recon on the terrain."

Team? Recon? Terrain? Was this how security chiefs spoke in the hallowed corporate corridors now? "This isn't about reviving the videos, is it?"

The bartender brought Stokes a frosted mug of Pale Ale. Stokes shook his head grudgingly. "No. I'll get to the point. We know you 'retrieved' a flash drive from Gregory Parks the day he died."

"And you know this how?"

"That doesn't matter." His pale eyes turned steely. He took a swig of his ale.

"It does to me."

He went quiet for a moment. Had he not expected to be challenged? Did he expect me to capitulate like a "good girl"?

He rubbed his nose and broke eye contact. "Charlotte Hollander told me."

He was lying. Or at least not telling me the entire truth. "Are you the ones who've been bugging my phone? And hacking into my computer?"

He looked surprised. "No. Is there a reason I should be?"

That response appeared to be genuine, but everybody lies when it comes to protecting their interests. "By the way, what happened to Hollander? She seems to have disappeared."

He turned it back on me. "Why do you care?"

I gave him the same answer I'd given the HR official, which, if he was a decent security person, he already knew. "The video of course. We were planning to resurrect it. Now I'm told she was transferred."

He cleared his throat. "That's right."

"Where?"

"Sorry. That's on a need-to-know basis."

"Seriously? Do you really think the world cares about one executive at one company?"

"You'd be surprised." He took a long pull on his ale. "Back to the drive. Hollander told us you had it. We need it."

But I wasn't ready to talk about the drive. "You blew up Dolan's office, didn't you?"

"I can't comment about that."

"What are you, ex-CIA or something?"

"Or something."

"Look, Mr. Stokes, or whatever your name is, I've had enough of whatever cat-and-mouse game you're playing. We're done here." I swiveled away from him, about to slide off my stool and leave.

"We're not done, Ms. Foreman."

"Yes. We are. I left a message for Hollander telling her I would give the drive back to her. And that's who I'll give it to."

"You don't understand. She's gone. And she's not coming back."

I froze. "Is she dead?"

"Not that I'm aware of."

I let out a breath. "Well, then, exactly what *are* you aware of?"

"Look." He leaned toward me and slid his hands down to his knees, an aggressive position for someone on a barstool. "I'm trying to do this the nice way. But if you don't cooperate, you'll force me to take other measures."

"Look, Stokes. I don't like threats." I mimicked his body language and tone. "I don't owe you anything. Two hours ago I didn't know you existed. You say you work at Delcroft, but I don't know that for sure. I may not have the information you do, but I'm not an idiot. If you really are from Delcroft, you already have the conversations and emails." Even I knew that corporate emails were subject to eavesdropping by employees' superiors.

He colored from the neck up. More of a slow burn than an explosion. But I was on a roll. "I have an idea of what's on that drive. Or could be. But until I'm sure it will get to the right people, I'm not handing it over to anyone."

"You might want to reconsider that. Your life could become unpleasant."

I swigged the last of my wine. "If anything happens to me, anything at all, I'll know who's responsible. And I'll make sure other people know too."

He kept his mouth shut. He was probably wondering how he'd screwed this up. But I didn't know if I was right either. I didn't want the drive, but something about this guy irritated the hell out of me. I just couldn't give it to him. I wanted to tell him I knew he was at Hollander's last weekend, behaving like a common thief. Then again, Luke and I were there too.

He levered himself off the stool and pulled his ball cap farther down his forehead. "This was not a smart move on your part." His voice was laced with acid.

I rose too, opened my bag, and pulled out my wallet. "It may not be. But I have nothing to hide. What about you?"

He wouldn't meet my eyes.

I threw a ten on the bar. He'd have to pay for his own drink. "By the way, it would be nice of you to call off your dogs. The ones that are tailing me, tapping my phone, and hacking my computer." I didn't believe him when he'd denied it. "Or perhaps I should call your CEO. Brian Riordan, right?"

He surprised me with his reply. "Miss Foreman, it wasn't us hacking into your comms. But you can be damn sure it *will* be going forward."

Chapter Forty-four

Tuesday

I drove home, astonished at my *chutzpah*. Where had my courage come from? True, Stokes was arrogant and aggressive, the type I instantly dislike. But his cold belligerence had teased out something similar in me. Did he have that effect on others too? Maybe he cultivated it, counted on the fact that he'd rile people up so much they'd say or do something reckless. No. I was giving him too much credit. He couldn't be that Machiavellian. And while I realized there might be consequences later, I was proud of my gutsy conduct.

Until Luke arrived. While I heated up the lasagna I'd picked up earlier, I told him about my meeting with Stokes.

"So you basically told him to fuck off," Luke said.

"I couldn't help it. He's the kind of creep you want to punch in the nose."

Luke ran a hand through his hair, which didn't take long. He was mostly bald. "Tell me his name again?"

"Warren Stokes. Said he's head of security for Delcroft. He tempted me with the possibility of reviving the videos when he called." I plated the lasagna and set it down on the table. "But at the meeting he zeroed in on the flash drive."

Luke didn't say anything for a moment. Then he sighed. "Okay. I'm not going to tell you what a stupid thing you did.

Or dangerous. Particularly with Hollander gone. And the reason I'm not going to tell you that is because I have a feeling you already know."

"Actually, I don't. It didn't feel stupid when it was happening. It felt—I don't know—like the right thing to do. I mean, what choice did I have? I couldn't let him walk all over me."

"Except now you've pissed off Delcroft's head of security."

"What's he going to do? He's already tapped my phone, hacked into my computers, planted a bomb. For all we know, he could have had something to do with Hollander's disappearance." I opened the fridge, pulled out a beer, popped the tab, and set it down in front of Luke. "I asked him if Hollander was dead, by the way."

"What did he say?"

"He said not that he was aware of."

Luke ignored his beer. "What happened to the frightened woman who just wanted to give the drive back to Hollander?"

I took a swig of his beer. "I think I'm just tired of being pushed around. Look, I get that he's not a good guy. I know what I'm getting myself into. But I need to see this through. At least until we know what happened to Hollander."

Luke reached for his cell and punched in numbers. "Who are you calling?"

He shook his head. A few seconds later he said, "Griz? Luke here."

I took another pull on Luke's beer. He obviously thought I'd overplayed my hand. I wondered if he was right.

While Luke was on the phone, I went out to fetch the mail, which I usually do only once every few days. In years past, it was because of bills that I could barely pay. Now I get most of my bills online, but stacks of junk mail still clog the box. I was standing over the recycling bin tossing the flyers, pseudo-news weeklies, and coupon sheets when I came across a white business envelope with my name on it. It bore no postmark or return address. Someone had delivered it by hand.

I dumped the rest of the junk mail, closed the recycling lid, and tore open the envelope. No salutation and no signature. Just a typewritten note:

> *Please meet me Wednesday at 1 pm at the Dragon Inn North restaurant.*
>
> *I have information about Gregory Parks.*

Chapter Forty-five

Wednesday

The Dragon Inn North is one of the best Chinese restaurants on the North Shore. My ex, Barry, used to say it's because it serves Mandarin food instead of Cantonese. No greasy egg foo young or General Tso's chicken fried in dough so thick it could choke you. Instead, the menu is filled with delicately spiced dishes like ginger shrimp and Mongolian beef.

It used to occupy a small room in the old Belden Stratford hotel, where, my father had told me, Benny Goodman's sister lived. Dad could have been a groupie for the King of Swing; he knew all sorts of arcane details about his life. The restaurant's success in the city had encouraged them to open a North Shore branch. The place is extremely popular, especially on Christmas Day, when lots of Jewish families, and even some exhausted Christians, show up for dinner.

I didn't tell Luke where I was going. I knew he'd disapprove. In fact, I debated going at all. It would entangle me even more with Delcroft. And with Parks' death, Hollander's disappearance, and Stokes' threats, it was getting riskier by the day. But the possibility of finding out more about Parks was irresistible. It might help me figure out what to do with the flash drive.

I arrived at the Waukegan Road location and pushed through the ornate door, festooned with a dragon, of course, in gold leaf.

The owner, whom I knew, stood in the coatroom talking on her cell in Chinese. Always well dressed, with a strand of pearls around her neck, she gave me a casual wave but didn't seem anxious to end her call. Which meant she probably wasn't the person who'd sent me the note.

I sat in the reception area, where I had a view of the dining room. Lunch, even on a weekday, was robust, and the clanking of silverware, the gurgle of water being poured into glasses, and the pleasant aromas of spices and tea were comforting.

Ten long minutes later, I wondered if the note had been a ruse. I pulled out my cell to check for emails or texts. Nothing. I dropped my phone back into my bag. I was getting hungrier by the second and was on the verge of ordering some ginger shrimp to take home, when a young Asian woman wearing an apron hurried out from the kitchen. Her hair was pinned back underneath a hairnet, but a big hank had escaped. She tucked it behind her ear as she approached.

I stood up.

"You are Ellie Foreman?" A thick accent made her *r*'s sound like *l*'s.

I nodded.

"This for you." She pulled out an envelope from her apron pocket, handed it to me, then disappeared back into the kitchen.

What was going on? Time seemed to stop. I looked around. The owner, still on the phone, seemed to be watching me, and a couple of the waiters in the dining room craned their necks. Was everyone in on the secret except me? Or was it just my imagination?

"Hi there." The owner finally ended her conversation and laid her cell on the counter. "You want to order something?" As if someone had released the "Pause" button on a video, motion began again. The owner smiled, waiters went back to their work, and I realized the paranoia had been in my head.

"I'm sorry." I zipped up my jacket. "I forgot about an appointment. I'll be back."

Outside, I studied the thin envelope. There was no name on it, but it had been licked closed. I opened it. Inside was a single sheet of paper and another typewritten note.

Come to the Baha'i Temple at 2 pm. Make sure no one is following.

Chapter Forty-six

Wednesday

Someone was running me through an obstacle course. These messages and out-of-the-way meets were the stuff of B-movie melodrama and spy games. I ought to pick up my marbles and go home. At least call Luke and tell him where I was. In the face of the unknown, even curiosity had its limits.

Instead, I drove east toward Sheridan Road.

I couldn't object to the new meeting place. The Baha'i Temple, one of only seven in the world, is a magnificent structure with an airy, almost ethereal atmosphere. The interior walls are cladded with both white cement and quartz, which capture and bathe everything in dazzling light. The temple's ceiling soars 140 feet, and the dome is designed with intricate symmetrical shapes that lie between intersecting lines. Amid such beauty and tranquility, it would be hard *not* to have a spiritual experience. I parked and went inside, practically tiptoeing around the sanctuary. A few tourists snapped photos; a couple of small kids, clearly not enamored with their surroundings, whined about going back to their hotel to watch Disney movies.

I don't completely understand the Baha'i faith. It seems like an anything-goes Buddhism with few rituals and rules. Which makes it more appealing than other religions, including my own with its 613 mitzvahs. I think you can even have "dual citizenship," so to speak, embracing both the religion in which you were raised as well as the Baha'i faith.

No chairs were set up, so I sat on a marble window seat. Five minutes went by; it was after two. Meditation or not, I was annoyed. I'd give it another five minutes. I stared at the dome, counting down the seconds.

The light tap of footsteps echoed across the marble floor. I looked toward the sound. A young woman who looked half-Asian and half-Caucasian cut across from the opposite side of the temple. Petite and very slim, she seemed to glide rather than walk. Her hair was chin length, her eyes a piercing black. Although she was wearing a parka, jeans, and work boots, she exuded an air of delicacy. This had to be the woman who'd come to the house.

I folded my arms. This waif had been ordering me around the North Shore? We'd see about that.

When she spoke, her voice was light and feathery, with no trace of an accent. "Thank you for coming. I am sorry to make you go through so many hoops before we met. But I had to be sure we weren't being followed. And that you were alone. I am Grace Qasimi."

"I assume you're the person who came to my house yesterday?"

She nodded.

"How did you find me?"

"I found your business card among Gregory's things. After he was...after he died."

I recalled how we'd traded cards when we were shooting the trade show. Was that only a few weeks ago?

She pointed to the window seat. When we both sat down, she lowered her voice. "He said you were consulting with Delcroft. Like him."

"Well, not exactly." I unfolded my arms. I should at least hear her out. "So what's so important that you had to leave notes all over the North Shore?"

A frown crossed her face, as if she was irritated I felt the need to ask. But then she must have thought better of it, because her expression relaxed. "Gregory and I—well, he was my fiancé." She held up her left hand so I could see a diamond engagement ring. "I…I can't take it off. I just, well…" She stared at the ring and twisted it. Then she looked up at me.

"I'm so sorry…"

Her eyes filled and she blinked rapidly, as if struggling to suppress her emotions. My voice trailed off. I got the feeling that she wanted me to know they weren't just living together like so many young people today. That they had formally pledged themselves to each other. It probably was a family tradition. And now she felt like a widow.

"For your loss." I finished.

She swallowed, then nodded as though she was tired of hearing such bland, insignificant words.

"What can I do for you?"

"I'm afraid…In fact, I am desperate."

"Why? Are you in danger?"

"I think so."

"Why?"

"Because I know the truth about Gregory."

I stiffened. "What truth?"

She lowered her voice. "Gregory said he was going to meet with you the day he died. Where the Blue and Red Line intersect."

"That's right."

She looked at me with a wide, unflinching gaze. "Gregory would never kill himself. Never. He was pushed. I know it."

There it was.

"Were you there?" she asked after a pause.

I nodded.

"What do you think?"

I chose my words carefully. "I wouldn't be surprised. Especially after Delcroft said he was spying for the Chinese."

"But…" She bit her lip. "You see, that's only part of it." She looked around the temple, a cautious expression unfolding across her face. Her voice quieted to a whisper. "I'm here because

Gregory said of all the people he'd come in contact with, you seemed like the only normal person."

I consider myself your average garden-variety neurotic, but thinking about Delcroft's high-strung executives, security chiefs, and surveillance teams, Parks was probably right.

"And because you work in video," she went on, "you have contacts. With the news media."

I started to tell her that wasn't the case anymore, but she kept going. "I want to restore Gregory's reputation. His honor. Expose his murder. What they are saying about him is untrue."

"So he wasn't a spy?"

She let a long moment pass. "I suppose he was," she finally said. "But he was a double agent."

Chapter Forty-seven

Wednesday

"Have you heard of the Uyghurs?" Grace pronounced it "Weegers."

It took me a moment to close my wide-open mouth. A double agent? What the hell was going on now? I shook my head.

"They're an ethnic group in China. There are about ten million of us, including Gregory and myself. Most of us live in the Xinjiang Uyghur Autonomous Region. It's in south-western China in a desert called the Tarim Basin. It borders more than half a dozen other countries, by the way, including Russia, Mongolia, Afghanistan, Pakistan, India, even Tibet. But most Uyghurs are descended from Turks, and because of that, they often look more Caucasian than Asian. Like Gregory," she said wistfully.

Keanu Reeves. I ran my tongue around my lips. How had I never heard of the Uyghurs?

"And"—she hesitated—"we are Muslims. In fact, we are the second-largest Muslim population in China."

"Oh."

"The Uyghurs have struggled for independence for years. China won't allow it, of course, and the government has gone out of its way to discriminate against us."

"How?"

"Forced abortions, sterilizations. They refuse to let our children go to school. They put restrictions on food. Some Uyghurs have been—how do you say—kicked out of their homes. And then they put us in prison—on trumped-up charges." She gazed around the temple, as if seeing her homeland through a gauzy curtain of time. "But we have survived. And we have organized demonstrations. Most have been peaceful, but there have been some confrontations with the police."

"That explains why I've never heard of you," I said. "China having such a free press and all."

The corners of her lips moved up, as if I'd scored a point. "Now the Chinese government claims we are terrorists."

"Because you are Muslims."

She ran a hand through her hair, as if she was struggling with what to say next. "Well, frankly, a few Uyghurs are—or were—militant. So China and the US listed them as terrorists back in 2002."

"In the wake of 9/11," I said.

She nodded. "But you see, it was only a tiny percentage of Uyghurs. It is true that China has seen more terrorist attacks recently. But when the government claims that the Uyghurs are responsible, well, that is a lie. They say we are under the influence of Islamic fundamentalists with ties to al-Qaeda and ISIS. They even say we have weapons of mass destruction."

"How unusual," I said. "They must have graduated from the Dick Cheney school of diplomacy."

She almost smiled. Then she gazed around. The family with the whiny kids had disappeared. Only one man remained, and he seemed to be in no hurry to leave. I eyed him.

So did Grace. She took my arm. "Let's walk."

We strolled out of the sanctuary and went down a staircase to the lower level. Ahead of us was a tiny theater where a film about the history of the Baha'i faith was playing. She led me inside, and we sat. We were the only ones there.

Grace went on, speaking just above a whisper. "The important thing to understand is that most Uyghurs are willing to maintain their ties to China, if they would just grant us more autonomy. The truth is that the few incidents that have occurred were motivated by the government's repression, not by terrorism."

I gazed up at the film, which was showcasing the Baha'i temples around the world. There were only six or seven, and Chicago's was certainly the most beautiful. "Grace," I whispered, "what does this have to do with Delcroft?"

"I'm getting to that. As I said, China can't send in the army to kill us, so they send in drones instead. There have been dozens of drone strikes in the area. My brother was killed in one just recently. He was only nine years old."

"I'm so sorry."

She shrugged. "They target madrassas and mosques. China says it is all part of the war on terror. This is why Gregory wanted the anti-drone technology."

"For the Uyghurs, not the Chinese government?"

"Actually, for both."

Chapter Forty-eight

Wednesday

I frowned, about to say, "I don't get it," when the man who'd been loitering in the temple poked his head into the tiny theater. When he saw us, he casually entered and sat in the back row. Grace went rigid, and her eyes grew wide. I motioned for her to get up. Together, just as casually, we walked out.

"We should go outside," I said.

Grace nodded.

I was surprised at how calm I was. Was I getting used to being tailed? As long as no one approached me, I suppose I was. We climbed the stairs back to the main level. I zipped up my parka, and Grace wound a wool scarf around her neck. Together we exited the temple.

"Who do you think he works for?" I yanked a thumb back toward the building.

"I do not know. But they are closing in. I am afraid."

"Maybe you should leave. Get out of Dodge."

Her forehead creased.

"It's an American expression," I said. "It means get away. Leave Chicago."

She didn't reply but steered me toward a battered green Toyota. I sucked in a breath. "You!"

She looked over, clearly surprised by my exclamation.

"You're the one who's been following me all over the North Shore!"

She shrugged, as if tailing me was something she did every day, like brushing her teeth. "I had to make sure you were someone I could trust."

"Do you know how much you scared me? I was ready to call the cops on you!"

She almost smiled. "Now you know what we live with every minute of every day."

I guess I'd asked for that.

"So." I tried to remember where we'd left off. "You were saying Gregory wanted Delcroft's technology for the Uyghurs *and* the Chinese."

"Yes. He wanted it for us so we could defend ourselves from China's drone strikes. But we have no plans to launch them. We don't have the resources. Or the inclination. So, you see, he did not care if the Chinese had the system as well. It's a defensive weapon. Of course China would want to protect itself."

The temperature was dropping. I wrapped my arms across my chest.

"Come," Grace said. "We will sit in my car."

I followed her. Once we were inside, she said, "But you see, the real reason China will never give us autonomy is not because they think we're terrorists. It's because the Tarim Basin is full of oil. Lots of it. In fact, the government is building a pipeline through the area right now."

I sighed. "And the arm bone is connected to the thigh bone."

"What?"

"Another American expression. It always comes back to oil, doesn't it?"

She shot me a puzzled look.

"How to get it. How to protect it."

She didn't say anything.

"And Gregory was tasked with getting the technology."

"He discovered Delcroft was working on a new system and that Hollander was the brains behind it. What he didn't expect was that she was willing to sell it to General Gao under the table. Gregory became their intermediary."

Finally, some clarity. I crossed my ankles. If Grace was telling the truth, Hollander wasn't trying to expose Parks to General Gao. Her explanations to Delcroft—and me—about trying to catch a spy were lies. She was conspiring against her country. She was a traitor.

But why? I gazed through the windshield. She'd been a military brat, I knew; her father had been a high-ranking general. What had turned her against her country? Was it her father? A dysfunctional relationship? Or was it greed? I wondered how much the Chinese were paying her. It had to be millions. Maybe more. I was making mental calculations when Grace spoke.

"It was only after negotiations were under way with her that Gregory realized how useful the technology would be for us."

"So he was working for the Chinese government when he 'consulted' with Delcroft."

She nodded. "Yes, but Gregory did not think Gao, or his superiors, knew he is—or was—a Uyghur activist too. But I am not so sure."

"Do you think the Chinese are behind his death?"

"That I do not know. But he was working with Gao and Hollander at the same time he was working for us."

"Where would the Uyghurs get the money and resources to build a sophisticated anti-drone system?"

"Gregory said he knew sources to tap," she said. "He kept saying the enemy of my enemy is my friend."

"Here? In the US?"

"I do not know."

"But then he was killed."

She bit her lip. "That's why I came to you. It is time to expose everything. Let the public decide who are the guilty parties."

I raised my hands and held them out. "Whoa. Hold on, Grace. I'm grateful to know the whole story, but I can't get involved. Jihadi terrorists…drone strikes…Chinese politics… This is way out of my league."

Her voice turned soft, almost seductive. "But, you see, you already are involved."

I scowled. Then I got it. "The flash drive."

She nodded again.

"But if it is ever decrypted, it will reveal Hollander's collusion with Gregory and Gao. Nothing about the Uyghurs' predicament. Or what Delcroft knew and when they knew it."

"It will be enough. We will show the media the drone blast sites. And the pipeline construction. China will be exposed for its duplicity and repression."

I didn't want to tell her she was being naïve. That even if she did get to the media, they probably wouldn't do anything about it. I changed the subject.

"Tell me something, Grace. Who was Gregory planning to give the flash drive to? When we talked he said he had an errand to run downtown. I assume it had to do with the drive."

Grace's forehead creased in a frown. "I'm not sure. It could have been his Uyghur contact at the consulate downtown. Or it could have been his Chinese military contact, who's at the consulate as well." She smiled. "He often wondered if they knew he was playing them against each other. 'If they only knew,' he would say. And then he would laugh."

"Are you sure they didn't know about each other? And that Gregory was a double?"

She looked at me, concern flooding across her face. "Why?"

"Nothing." I didn't want to alarm her that she might be the only other person, aside from Parks himself, who knew the truth about what he was up to.

Chapter Forty-nine

Wednesday

I climbed out of Grace's car and walked around the back, my boots making a quiet swoosh on the ground. After a moment I went back to her side.

Grace rolled down her window and shot me a cool gaze. "You are not going to help me."

"It's not that. Someone has hacked into my computer and tapped my phone. I'm being followed. I'm pretty sure it's Delcroft, but if it isn't, and I tried to contact the media on your behalf, I'm sure I would be stopped."

"My phone and computers, and Gregory's, too, were hacked," she said. "But I cannot allow that to stop me."

"That's not all, Grace. Aside from the flash drive, you don't have concrete proof. You can't expect the media or government to act on what is essentially little more than conjecture. It doesn't happen that way." I didn't add that even I wasn't sure I bought the whole story. I'd just met the woman. Why should I trust her? Especially with so many double-dealing people in the mix?

If she really was Gregory's fiancée, her pro-Uyghur, anti-China politics would work against her. I'd given up on a black-and-white world long ago and had learned to live in the gray. But Grace was still young. She still thought she could change the world.

I glanced back at the temple. Our tail would be emerging soon. "We need to go."

"Go online. Look up the Uyghurs. You'll see."

"I don't disbelieve you. I just don't know what I can do."

She shook her head, as if she realized she'd wasted precious time.

"Look…," I tried to mollify her. "Let's talk again in a few days. How can I get in touch with you?"

She shook her head again. "You can't. I will contact you."

"Okay. By the way, how did you and Gregory get out of China?"

"Gregory came five years ago. He was, of course, an only child, and his parents were killed in a train derailment. That's when he started to work for the government. He learned English, and they sent him here. I was already here. My parents saw there was no future for me in the basin. They helped me escape to Pakistan ten years ago and I eventually made it here."

"Your parents are still back in China?"

She nodded.

I thought back to my former boyfriend, David Linden. His mother had escaped Nazi Germany and met her husband, Kurt, here. Kurt had been the sole survivor of his family.

"There's something else you should know." She keyed the engine. It started up right away. Toyotas. "Gregory was afraid we would run out of time. China hacks into everything. All over the world. That's one of the reasons I came to see you. I do not know how much more time I have."

She closed the driver's side window, pulled away from the curb, and drove east to Sheridan Road.

I trudged to my Camry, mulling over her warning. If the Chinese knew what Grace knew, and were able to connect Gregory to me…

I pulled my jacket more closely around me.

Chapter Fifty

Wednesday

Instead of heading home, I drove to the library. Melissa, the head librarian, was behind the desk stacking returned books on a rolling cart. "We're seeing a lot of you these days."

"Libraries are my favorite places," I said, trying to appear cheerful.

She arched an eyebrow. "Computer on the fritz again?"

"Busted." I gave her a rueful smile.

I went online and searched for everything I could find about the Uyghurs, their history, and the rise of radical Islam in that part of the world. I pulled up more than I expected, including several short videos. One showed a group of police officers, and what looked like a Chinese SWAT team, swarming a car at a checkpoint. Another showed a car erupting into flames somewhere in Beijing. A third showed a group of demonstrators fleeing from police in riot gear. Another video revealed close-ups of women with bruises on their arms and faces, as well as shots of Uyghurs in various poses and settings, most of them with that curious mix of Asian and Caucasian features.

Then I Googled "drone strikes on Uyghurs." The first article to come up, dated 2012, reported a drone strike that killed a Uyghur jihadi terrorist in eastern Turkistan, part of Uyghur territory. Except the strike came from a US drone, not a Chinese one. The US justified the attack by saying the jihadi was a known member of al-Qaeda. Why was I not surprised? The drones had probably been made by Delcroft.

Another article described a stealth drone manufactured by the Chinese that could be used aggressively. The Chinese claimed they were being used solely for surveillance on terrorists.

Sure.

There were also sporadic reports of explosions that were never explained, as well as people dying or disappearing in the desert that makes up most of the Tamir Basin.

A fifth video, this one on YouTube, claimed to be a drone attack in the Uyghur desert. The silent explosion, seen from above, sent clouds of dust and rocks flying and caused an eruption of flames that ate whatever had been there before. It looked like one of those scenes from *Homeland* when Carrie Mathison ordered drone strikes for the CIA. Finally, a CNN video news report claimed that the market for armed drones, led by Israel and the US, had mushroomed over the past few years and was worth more than twenty billion dollars.

So far everything Grace had told me was checking out.

Chapter Fifty-one

Thursday

Zach Dolan called my cell early the next morning. He sounded excited and asked me to meet him at Starbucks so we could go for a drive. When he pulled into the parking lot, I hopped in. Cadaverous black circles underlined his eyes, and he looked like he hadn't slept all night. Despite that, he was beaming.

"Well?" I asked as he pushed into traffic.

He unzipped his down vest, pulled out an eight-by-ten brown envelope, and slid it toward me. "I cracked it."

"The encryption? Really?"

He nodded. "One of the toughest jobs I've ever done. But I finally got it."

"How?"

"Let me try to break it down for you. Basically, there were several different types of encryption used. On the US end they were using a single-pass method. I finally found the decryption key on the Darknet. But the Chinese encryption was tough. I was afraid it was double-encrypted, which would have made it impossible to decode, but I connected with a Chinese hacker, and he got me the key."

"I don't understand." Now for the final test of whether Grace Qasimi was telling the truth "So?"

"I printed out everything." He placed his hand on the envelope. "I don't need to tell you this is highly confidential shit. If anyone finds out you have it, we're both screwed."

"Maybe I shouldn't take it," I said. Then I stopped. What the hell was I thinking? This was the reason I was involved in the mess in the first place.

"Just so you know, I didn't make a copy of anything. I put the second drive you gave me after the explosion in with the printouts. I don't want to hear about this ever again." He shot me a penetrating look. "Are we clear?"

"Crystal."

He pushed the envelope toward me. I picked it up. It was thick.

I was about to open the clasp when he raised his hand.

"Don't open it here."

I nodded and slipped the package into my lap. "How much do I owe you?"

"We said three hundred, right?"

"But that was before they blew up your office."

He looked over. "I should have known when that went down that I shouldn't go any further."

"But you couldn't help yourself, could you?"

He sighed. "That's about the size of it."

"Should I write you a check?"

"Not on your life. This is a cash-only deal."

"You be careful, Zach."

"You too, Ellie."

◇◇◇

After Zach dropped me off, I rushed home, as if the envelope was on fire and I had to put it out. Luke's pickup wasn't in the garage; nor was it parked at the curb. Still I called out once I was inside.

"Luke? You home?"

No answer.

It was better that way. I carried the envelope gingerly up to my office, closed the door, and pulled down the shades. I opened the clasp and pulled out what was inside. There must have been a sheaf of more than fifty papers.

The first dozen or so sheets were copies of three-way emails between Hollander, Gao, and Parks. I started reading. It felt like a film was unfolding in front of me. At the beginning there were emails of introduction in which everyone said how honored they were to meet the others. That was followed by lots of praise and compliments about each person's respective position within his or her organization. And how kind Gregory Parks was to put them together.

Kindness, my foot. Parks was being paid for the connection, probably by both sides. Chances were he was making a killing. I caught myself and grimaced at my choice of words.

Then the conversation moved into more substantive areas. Parks brought up the system, although he didn't mention the words "anti-drone" or "DADES." He explained that Hollander had been working on little else during the past two years. Gao responded with effusive praise. Parks followed up by saying that Hollander was the only person in the entire world who knew the system inside out, and that her knowledge might be helpful to General Gao, who emphatically agreed. Parks took the conversation further by proposing that the two meet; he understood they might have mutually beneficial needs.

When I read the next batch of emails, I gasped. They *had* met! Six months earlier, all three had flown to the Bahamas for a long weekend. That must have been where the deal was struck, because there was nothing in the emails prior to the trip or afterward that mentioned dollars or contracts or exactly who was getting what.

In fact, the nature of the emails changed significantly after that. The three-way emails between Hollander, Parks, and Gao ended; instead, everything went through Parks. It made sense—both Hollander and Gao had to protect themselves as much as possible. I wondered if Hollander had deleted the earlier emails from her computer—I was sure she had. General Gao undoubtedly had as well.

Fortunately for me, though, my flash drive came from Parks, which contained all the emails that had been exchanged between the three since the beginning. I was able to read the ones from Hollander to Parks, but the ones from Parks to Gao were in Chinese, and I had no idea what they said. Maybe Grace would translate them. Then I reconsidered. I was reading about treason. The fewer people involved, the better.

The final batch of emails from Hollander to Parks were businesslike. Most had to do with delivery timetables, components, and specs. One email from Hollander acknowledged receipt of a deposit. I suspected that might be the most incriminating email. There were also diagrams and charts and schematics attached to some of the correspondence. Again, I had no idea what I was looking at, and probably wouldn't, even if I had a degree in engineering. There were also emails listing reputable suppliers and discussions about who could formulate the parts, especially the electronics, although Hollander told Parks she expected Gao would have his own.

Which would be much cheaper, I thought. The Chinese were known to steal American technology, copy it, and sell it for half the price.

I skimmed the emails between Parks and Gao. While I couldn't understand them, I did notice that Parks had forwarded the attachments from Hollander. I eyed a few of them; they appeared to be the same documents she'd sent to Parks from her end.

Everything from Hollander's side was sent from her personal email, Char24@comcast.net. And nothing from Gao's email address indicated he worked for the Chinese government. Still, if Hollander sent them from work, even from her personal account, there was probably a record of them on the Delcroft computer system, and I was sure Stokes was trying to decrypt them too. But Stokes didn't have what I had, which was the correspondence from Parks to Gao. Which made what I had even more valuable. In fact, now that Parks was dead, I might be the only person who had the full story.

Now I knew why Hollander was desperate to get Parks' flash drive. Stokes, too, even though there didn't seem to be any love lost between the two of them. Hollander needed to destroy the drive, and Stokes—well, I wasn't sure what he wanted to do with the emails, but he couldn't do anything until he had them in his possession. The enormity of what I held in my hands swept over me, and I let out a shaky breath. There might as well have been a huge target on my back. I went into my bathroom, swallowed a Xanax, and tried to figure out what to do.

Chapter Fifty-two

Thursday

I checked the time; it was nearly noon. Luke, wherever he was, would be back soon. Before he could persuade me otherwise, I slid the papers back into the envelope, jumped into my car, and raced over to the place we used to call Kinko's. I printed out a copy of everything, made sure the pages were collated, and drove over to my bank, which was just up the street. I ran in, waited impatiently as they led me to my safe-deposit box, and stashed the originals.

Luke was pawing through leftovers in the fridge when I got home.

I kissed him. "Where have you been?" I asked.

"I've been talking to Grizzly. I need to discuss something with you."

"I have something to discuss with you, too."

He bent his head sideways and closed the refrigerator door. "Okay. You go first."

"Sit." He did. "Dolan cracked the encryption on the drive."

He leaned forward and clasped his hands together. "And?"

"Take a look." I fished out the copies from my bag. "Take your time."

As he started reading, I went to the refrigerator and pulled out a Diet Snapple. I came back to the table and waited. He didn't say anything, and his face had that slight frown that comes from intense concentration. Occasionally his eyebrows arched, and once, he looked up at me in amazement. Finally he got to the last batch, which were in Chinese.

"Holy shit. This is incredible."

I nodded. "But that's only part of it."

"What are you saying, Ellie?"

"Care to take a short drive?"

"Thanks for coming back to the party," Melissa said when we walked into the library.

"We just can't stay away," I shot back. "For the Perle Mesta of the Dewey Decimal System, you throw a hell of a bash."

"How gratifying," she said. "Since she's been dead for forty years." She motioned us toward the computers.

We signed in and sat at one of the terminals. I went online to Google the articles and videos I'd seen yesterday. The video of the car exploding into flames in Beijing was there, but it was much shorter. It showed a clear jump cut in the progression of the video. First the car was rolling along; then it was already on fire. Someone had edited it! I tried to recall what had been there when I saw it yesterday. I think it was a sign that identified Beijing as the location.

I frowned. "Something's wrong."

"What?" Luke asked

"This video has been edited since I saw it yesterday. Yesterday, I could tell the exploding car was in Beijing. Today it doesn't identify where the explosion is. See the jump cut?" I replayed the video so Luke could see it.

Luke stroked his beard. "Are you sure?"

"I'm sure." Then I tried to pull up the SWAT team closing in on the checkpoint someplace in China. It was gone altogether. In its place was one of those benign statements that said, "We're sorry, but this video has been removed by the copyright owners."

"What is going on?" I asked.

"You're the video expert."

I rubbed the back of my neck, then gestured to him. "Come with me."

Luke got up and followed me out the front door. We sat on a waist-high wall that surrounded the parking lot. I lowered my voice.

"There's something else you need to know."

I filled him in on my meeting with Grace Qasimi and what she'd told me about Parks and the Uyghurs. How Parks had been a double agent.

Luke's eyes narrowed. "Uyghurs...aren't they the Muslims in China?"

"Exactly. Remember the video of the car bursting into flames? The Chinese government alleges the Uyghurs are terrorists. That burning car was supposed to be a terrorist act."

"But?"

"Grace says the Uyghurs aren't terrorists. That they're victims of persecution."

"Like the Palestinians."

I tensed. We'd had many conversations about Israel and Palestine. Not with Dad around, of course—he wore his politics on his sleeve. Luke, it turned out, was more sympathetic to the Palestinian situation. I could see both sides of the issue, but being Jewish, I usually refrained from entering that political minefield.

"Let's stick with the Uyghurs, shall we?"

We went back in to the library computer. I clicked on some of the articles I'd read the day before. Two or three that had been the most critical of China bore those "404" error messages, meaning the link was broken and the article was no longer online.

Chapter Fifty-three

Thursday

"Some of the videos and articles aren't here," I said in a surprised whisper.

"You sure?"

"I'm sure. Someone must have removed them over the past twenty-four hours."

Luke shot me a disbelieving look. "Come on, Ellie. Are you saying they're gone because you were screening them?"

"I don't know. I just know they were here yesterday." I clicked onto Wikipedia and started reading. "My God! There was a whole paragraph about alleged Chinese discrimination against the Uyghurs. It's gone too." I turned to him. "I swear to God it was here yesterday. Melissa can vouch for me. I told her about it."

Luke swiveled around and glanced at Melissa, who gave him a tiny wave. Then he turned back to the screen and skimmed the article. When he was done he leaned back and folded his arms. "So. A stranger runs you around the North Shore. You meet with her, and she tells you Parks was a double agent working for the Uyghurs. Then she fills your head with BS about persecution and suffering, and you come to the library to verify her story."

I nodded.

"Yesterday it seemed to check out. But now some of that 'verification' has disappeared."

"You sound like you don't believe me."

"I don't know what to think. Anyone can change a Wikipedia article. Whenever they want."

"I know."

"So who edited the article? And why now?"

"Everyone knows the Chinese are the best hackers in the world," I said quietly. It wasn't my best comeback. "Next to the Russians," I added.

"It doesn't take a hacker to change a Wikipedia article," he said. "The woman you met with yesterday could have done it herself."

"But why? Grace wants the world to know about the plight of the Uyghurs."

"Maybe she doesn't."

"No. I don't buy that."

"Why not? We still have no idea who's on first. Hollander, Delcroft, Parks, the Uyghur woman, the Agency guy—"

"Stokes."

"Whoever. All of them have an agenda," he went on. "And by asking questions and talking to people, and especially by getting that flash drive decrypted, you're screwing them up." He tapped a finger on his lip. "Even if the Uyghurs' claims of persecution are true, it's not a state secret." Luke went on. "It's also no secret that the Chinese and US are working together to fight terrorism in that part of the world."

"So you think the Chinese had something to do with this—this disinformation?"

"Look, Ellie. I don't know who's behind it, and I don't care. But I do care about you. And Rachel." He paused. "Meanwhile, the shit is getting deeper and deeper. Which is why we're going to disappear for a while."

"What—and not follow through on the flash drive? We have to."

"No. We don't. Or should I say, *you* don't. Believe me, if Dolan figured out the encryption, so will Delcroft."

"But I'm the only one who has the whole chain of communications. From both sides."

"You don't think Delcroft, or someone else, was hacking Parks' email?"

I kept my mouth shut. He had a point.

"But, okay. Let's assume you're right. And that flash drive is the only proof of Hollander's treason. What do you think Delcroft will do when they find out their chief engineer betrayed them? You think they're going to thank you and give you a medal?"

"Luke..." My voice rose. Melissa caught my eye and tapped her index finger on her lips.

"Do you think for one nanosecond they'll let it go public at all?"

I blinked.

Luke went on. "Whoever is behind this is going to want to cover it up. Make sure nothing sees the light of day. And what do you think they'll do to the messenger who brought them the proof?"

I thought about the target on my back. It was growing larger. "I can't disappear forever."

"True. That's why I went to see Grizzly this morning."

"What for? What can he do?"

"Poke around, for starters. Find out who the key players are. Especially that asshole Stokes. Which is another reason why we're leaving."

I conceded. "You're right."

"Good. We'll drive up to Lake Geneva. Rachel too."

In spite of the situation, I smiled. "She'll be thrilled. She'll get to hang out at the Abbey spa every day. But what about Dad?"

"The security at his place is pretty good. He'll be okay."

This was true. With the bars on the doors and windows and a security guard 24/7, it can remind me of a prison more than an assisted living facility.

"Then we'll fly up to the cabin at Star Lake," Luke said.

The cabin at Star Lake was the place where Luke and I fell in love. Or should I say, the place where Luke allowed himself to love me. We make it a point to go up there every few months. He leaned over and cupped my chin. "Okay, sweetheart? You know I'm only trying to protect you."

I nodded. "But do you think the cabin is a good idea? There's no cell or Internet reception up there."

"Exactly."

Chapter Fifty-four

Thursday

Back home I called Rachel at work on my cell.

"Awesome!" she burbled. "I can go to the Abbey!"

"Sorry, but we won't be there long."

"Don't tell me we're going to that cabin in the middle of nowhere."

I decided to avoid a spat. I also didn't want to reveal the cabin's location on the phone. Although I was supposed to have pretty good encryption, you never knew. "I'll tell you when I see you. How soon can you get here?"

"I work until five."

"You have to get here earlier."

"Why? What's going on?"

"Rachel, I can't talk about it over the phone. Be here by three. At the latest."

"What do I tell my boss?"

Her boss, Betsy McNair, was a no-nonsense fiftyish woman. She loved Rachel; me less so. "Make up something. Tell her your mother is having a meltdown and needs you."

"That's what I told her the last time."

I rolled my eyes. "You'll think of something."

"How long will we be gone?"

"Bring enough for a week. Look, I gotta go. See you soon."

◇◇◇

It wasn't all bad, I thought as I threw together a suitcase. The day, one of Chicago's late winter gifts, was sharp and clear. Sunshine twinkled through the bare branches and glittered on metal like lighters at a rock concert. The drive up would be short, and we'd have nothing but five-star accommodations once we arrived. Luke lived in a mansion of which Thomas Jefferson would have approved, mostly because it was a replica of Monticello. How that happened is a long story that involves Luke's late father. There are only nine bedrooms, most with adjoining baths, and a dozen other rooms, not including the kitchen, but we make do.

While we were waiting for Rachel, Luke said, "My turn to talk. Grizzly and I were batting around something this morning."

"Okay."

He sat on the family room couch and patted the seat beside him. I sat down. "A few months ago a few Chinese nationals were indicted here in the US for stealing microelectronics designs from Silicon Valley."

"So?" I drew the word out, wondering where he was going.

"And a year before that the Justice Department indicted five other Chinese for hacking into American companies to steal technology."

I scratched my cheek. "Your point?"

"What we're facing with Hollander isn't exactly the same thing. If she really did sell the system to the Chinese, Hollander's is a case of insider theft, not hacking."

"I still don't get it. They're both crimes."

"When the government tries to go after hackers, whether they're Chinese, Russian, or whoever, they don't have a lot of success. Hacker attacks can be difficult to trace to specific individuals, and it's hard to arrest or even serve subpoenas to entities outside the US. It gets complicated."

I tilted my head. "Which means..."

"Which means if she's caught, Hollander could be holding the bag all by herself, criminally speaking."

"You mean the Chinese will just go on their merry way and build the anti-drone system anyway?"

"Right. They'll pin as much as they can on her, rather than risk political repercussions with us."

I pondered it. "Hollander is no dummy. She must have known that was one of the risks."

"We can't figure it out. Why would she go ahead, if she knew she would be the only fall guy? Or woman?"

"I have no idea, Luke."

"You had drinks with her. What did you think?"

I thought back to our meeting at the Happ Inn. "Actually, I kind of liked her. For a little while, at least. Then again, there's always someone who thinks the rules don't apply to them. Hollander fits the mold."

Luke shrugged. "Well, we'll have more time to think about it when we're at the cabin."

"By the way, next time you talk to Grizzly, can you ask him something?"

"Sure."

"Can you ask him about US drone strikes in Uyghur territory? How often they happen? You remember that article at the library."

"I'll ask him, but don't forget that drone strikes are one of the few areas where China and the US can cooperate. Even Russia can get into the act. Drop bombs on the Uyghurs rather than each other, and the superpowers can say they're fighting the war on terror together."

"That's what Grace said. It's interesting, though. There's no mention of the Uyghurs in any of the emails between Parks, Gao, and Hollander. All of it is couched in antiterrorist language: early warning systems, precise navigation that homes in on the target…things like that. Someone did mention the sophisticated weaponry being used by drug cartels. And there was even a snide comment about Amazon. But no Uyghurs."

"Does that surprise you?"

"I guess not."

Luke checked his watch. "Hey, where is your daughter? It's after three."

I noticed how Rachel became "your daughter" when things weren't going according to plan.

"I'll call her." I punched in her cell. It went to voice mail. "She's probably on her way."

Luke rose and started pacing. "We need to get going."

I let him pace for a few moments. Then: "Stop. You're making me nervous." I checked the time on my cell. "It's only ten after. What's so urgent?"

"We should have left yesterday."

"What do you know that I don't?"

"Let me put it this way. If Griz makes the calls I think he's going to, things might get hot."

"Lovely." I called Rachel back on my cell. Again I reached her voice mail.

Fear is contagious, and I was starting to get worried myself. To settle my nerves, I turned on the news. The weatherman had just told us it was going to be clear but seasonally cold when one of the anchors cut in.

"We have breaking news. We've just heard that a young woman has died in an automobile accident"—I sucked in a panicked breath: Rachel?—"on the Eisenhower Expressway." I sagged in relief. I-290, or the Eisenhower or Ike, as it's called, comes in from the west to downtown Chicago. Rachel would be taking the Edens, which is nowhere near the Ike.

The report cut to the scene of the accident shot by the news station's traffic helicopter. I gasped. A battered green Toyota had been totaled, and smoke was rising from the front of the car. An ambulance was on-site, and the news helicopter zoomed in for a close-up of a body in a plastic bag on a gurney. An Illinois state trooper, the cops who patrol the highways, was talking to a reporter.

The scene cut to a camera on the ground. The news reporter, a woman, talked into it. "The victim, who has been identified as Grace Qasimi, was pronounced dead at the scene. Although it's too soon to know exactly, authorities believe the steering failed, and she smashed into the guardrail head-on."

"Oh God!" A wave of nausea rose from my gut and settled in my throat. "Luke! Did you hear this?" I covered my mouth with my hand.

Luke hurried into the family room. "What's wrong? Is it Rachel?"

I could barely shake my head. "It's Grace Qasimi. Gregory Parks' girlfriend." I pointed to the television.

Luke stared at the TV and watched. Then, "Oh, Christ."

"What's going on, Luke? I can't believe it was an accident."

Luke pressed his lips together. "Neither can I."

"Then who?"

He came over and put a protective arm around me. "I don't know."

I remembered the man in the Baha'i Temple who'd been following us around. Was it him? If so, for whom was he working? The Chinese? Someone here? Apparently Grace had gone too far, but too far in what way? When? Whom had she offended? Whom had she threatened? I was terrified. I let myself collapse into Luke's arms, and we held each other.

Chapter Fifty-five

Thursday

Half an hour later tires screeched on the driveway. Rachel had arrived. I let out a relieved breath, only then realizing I'd been holding it. So did Luke, I noticed. I pulled myself together and met her downstairs in the garage.

I've always loved the way a garage smells. Whether it's the residue of gasoline fumes, or whether it seeps into the concrete walls and floor, it's unique. Almost addictive. Probably toxic as hell, too. After the news about Grace, though, I couldn't truly appreciate it.

"Sorry I'm late," Rachel said. "Betsy needed me to finish with a client, and then I had to go home—I don't even know what I packed."

"Luke will be pleased you're finally here."

She cocked her head. "What's going on, Mom?"

"It's complicated. It has to do with that video for Delcroft I didn't finish."

"Are we running away?" She grinned. "To the Hole in the Wall?"

"Actually, we are trying to get away from the bad guys."

"Holy crap. Really? How cool! I can't wait to tell—"

"Uh—you're not going to tell anybody. No one. Seriously. It could be a matter of life and death."

Rachel's smile faded. "Now you're scaring me."

I gave her a quick hug. "Sorry. No reason to be. Nothing bad is going to happen."

Luke clattered down the steps. "Good, Rach. Glad you're here." He seemed to have calmed down as well and turned to me. "I've been thinking. We should take two cars. It'll be safer."

"Safer?" Both Rachel and I exclaimed at the same time. Concern splashed across my daughter's face.

"Um, well, that was the wrong word." Luke backtracked. "Convenient. It'll be more convenient." He absently brushed his hand across his forehead. "I'll go in the pickup. You and Rachel follow in the Camry. We'll have dinner in Lake Geneva, then fly up to the cabin in the morning." He opened the garage door wider and proceeded to the pickup. "Don't forget to turn off your cells."

"Really?" Rachel said. "I can't listen to my tunes?"

"No. And it's nonnegotiable." His voice was sharp. "In fact, why don't you give your cell to me?"

Rachel sulked. "I can turn it off myself."

"Rachel, you can't just turn the phone to airplane mode and play music. It still gives off a signal," I said.

"I know."

Luke glanced at me as if to ask, "Can she do it?"

I was about to shrug, but Rachel surprised us both by handing her cell to Luke. I thought I knew my daughter. What did she have up her sleeve? Or, miracle of miracles, was she finally mature enough to appreciate the gravity of our situation? In any case, I smiled. "Problem solved."

"You too, Ellie."

"Got it. Only call if it's an emergency."

Luke shook his head. "It won't help. I'm turning mine off, too. But it's only an hour drive."

Chapter Fifty-six

Thursday

We headed out. It was nearly four, the sun starting to sink into the west. When we turned onto the Edens, Luke stayed in front of us. For a while I followed obediently: I sped up, slowed down, and changed lanes when he did. After about twenty minutes, though, I started to relax and let him drift a few car lengths ahead.

"I think we're good," I said. "No worries."

Rachel and I sang camp songs. Then we told each other jokes. Then we actually had an adult conversation. She and Q were definitely a couple; she seemed as surprised as I. Still, I could see how happy she was. Then something occurred to me.

"Did you tell him you were leaving?"

Rachel slouched down in the passenger seat. She wouldn't meet my eyes.

"You texted him, didn't you?"

"Mom, I had to. We had plans for tonight."

"I wish you hadn't."

"I didn't tell him we were going to the cabin. Which reminds me. Do I have to go with you?"

Suddenly she was a little girl again, unwilling to go to the doctor in case she'd be getting a shot. "I mean, I'm not involved in any of this. And it's boring. Can I stay in Lake Geneva? Please?"

"So you can go to the Abbey and have Q come up? Nice try."

She shot me a withering look, then stared out the window. The sun was still above the horizon; daylight was lasting longer. It seemed a promising omen.

I checked for Luke. He was a few car lengths ahead in the fast lane. I changed lanes and sped up. Soon I was going near eighty. My father says I have a heavy foot; in my defense, I think it's a waste of time and space not to fly down the highway as fast as reasonably possible.

By the time we were a few miles from the turnoff for Lake Geneva, the clouds that had been following us all day became tinged with pink and gold, and the sky turned that beautiful shade of dusky violet that ushers in twilight.

I thought about cooking dinner, then decided we should go to Jimmy Saclarides' family's restaurant. His mother and aunt ran the place and their reasonably priced Greek food came with crazy big portions. I started dreaming about spinach and feta spanakopita, and the fish spread that tastes like salty caviar whose name I can never remember. And lamb: roasted or skewered and marinated with lemon, rosemary, and who knows what else. My mouth was watering. I'd even pick up the tab.

I looked for Luke again but didn't see him. He must be already barreling down Route 50. I checked my rear view. About a mile back was a vehicle with flashing lights on its roof. The Illinois State Police. They were as bad as the cops in my village when it came to ticketing speeders. I'd been stopped more than once. I had to slow down.

I glanced over at Rachel. She was asleep. The candle she was burning at both ends was probably just a stump. I fixed my eyes on the rear view. The red and blue flashing lights were gaining. It didn't appear as if the cops were cruising for speeders but rather had a specific mission. I switched lanes to let them pass and made sure I wasn't going over sixty-five.

But the cruiser switched lanes too and positioned itself directly behind my Camry. The glare from the lights obscured the vehicle itself, but I could see the silhouette of a man at the wheel, and it looked like he was wearing the unique, wide-brimmed hat of a state trooper. A campaign hat, they call it.

It wasn't until the crackle from the microphone was followed by an amplified order that my stomach clenched.

"Camry with Illinois plates, pull over. Now."

Rachel came awake, stretched her arms, and looked out her side-view mirror.

"What's going on, Mom?"

"I was speeding, damn it."

She twisted around. I checked the rear view again. The cruiser was only about fifty feet behind us. The flashing lights still masked the vehicle and its occupants.

"Mom, that doesn't look like a police car."

"What are you saying, Rachel?"

"Don't turn around, but it kind of looks like a regular car except for the lights."

"But they have that microphone thing, and they just ordered me to pull over. They have to be official."

"I don't know," Rachel said. "Maybe we shouldn't."

"We have to."

"Don't you remember all those warnings on the news about fake cops and the fact that women shouldn't stop if they're alone on the road and it's dark? Even if there is a rotating light?"

"First off, it's not that dark. Yet. Second, we're not alone on the road. And third, when did you start watching the news?"

She shook her head.

Again, the amplified voice. "Pull over. State police."

I looked over at Rachel. "See?"

Rachel shrugged. She had a point. But so did I. Even if they weren't in a patrol car, they were still official; undercover cops maybe. And it wasn't dark; it was dusk. And Luke was—well, he wasn't in sight. I didn't have a choice. Trying to outrun the cops, the feds, or whoever they were was a bad idea. I slowed and eventually pulled onto the shoulder.

The vehicle behind us did too. What happened next was in such an accelerated and compressed blur of time, I felt as if we'd entered a space warp. The instant I came to a stop on the shoulder, the cruiser pulled around and wedged itself in front of the Camry, blocking my ability to slide back into traffic. Then a second car I hadn't noticed replaced the cruiser behind us. Three men including the driver jumped out of that car. Two men got out of the car in front. Too late I realized the "cruiser" wasn't a patrol car at all. It was just a four-door sedan. And none of the sedan's occupants wore the khaki uniform of a state trooper. Except for the campaign hat on the driver's head, they wore jeans, sweatshirts, and parkas. Rachel was right.

I jerked the wheel and gunned the engine in an attempt to get back on the highway, but they had me penned in. The passing traffic slowed, but no one stopped, probably figuring, as I would have, that this was none of their business. I considered rolling down my window and yelling for help anyway, but I didn't have time. I shouted to Rachel to find my cell and call the police.

While she was rummaging in my purse, one of the men started to pound on Rachel's window and motioned for us to roll it down. I shook my head. He pulled something out of his jacket. A pistol. He aimed it through the window at Rachel. I froze. Again he motioned for me to roll down the windows. This time I did.

A second man appeared on Rachel's side of the Camry, brandishing a second pistol. He went to the backseat window and fired a shot into the glass. It shattered, flinging shards and splinters of glass across the backseat.

"Cover your head!" I screamed to Rachel.

She did, but the man in the back was able to reach in the window and grabbed her hair.

"Unlock the doors," he ordered.

"No. I'm calling the police!"

"Mom...they're hurting me!" Rachel cried in a panic-stricken yelp.

Suddenly a third man appeared at my window, also holding a gun. He pointed it at me. I unlocked the doors. The one outside

Rachel's door opened it, the man in back released her hair, and both men pulled Rachel out of the car. She screamed.

So did I.

"Mama! Stop them!"

But the man on my side of the Camry climbed into the backseat, pressed me against the seat of the car, and grabbed me in a choke hold. I struggled to free myself but couldn't move. "Let go!" I tried to yell, but I couldn't breathe and the words were unintelligible even to me.

My outburst made him pin me against the seat more forcefully. While he had me hemmed in, the other two wrestled Rachel into the vehicle behind us. Only when they slammed the door did the man who'd been pinning me down release his grip. He came around to the front, opened my door, and snatched my keys out of the ignition. He raced back to the car in front, dove inside, and gunned his engine. I watched in horror as both cars screeched back into traffic and sped off with my little girl.

Chapter Fifty-seven

Thursday

I craned my neck trying to watch where they were headed, but it was getting pretty dark now, and the road was full of traffic. I couldn't tell which pair of taillights belonged to the car that held my daughter. Ten seconds, and I'd already lost her.

Panic washed over me, bringing with it a deep sense of despair, so deep I couldn't find bottom. Had this really just happened? I leaned my head against the steering wheel, seemingly paralyzed. Frigid air whistled through the car. I wanted to turn on the heat, but I couldn't; the bastards had taken my keys. Which also included my house key, the key to Rachel's apartment, and the key to Luke's place. I was stuck.

Luke. I had to call Luke. He'd know what to do. Thankfully, my bag was still crammed into the space between the front seats—they'd known exactly what they wanted when they overpowered us, and it wasn't money. I frantically fished out my cell, trying to avoid the bits of glass that were sprayed across the seats, and snapped it on. My location didn't matter now; they'd obviously known where I was since we left the house. How? Did Rachel leave her cell on by mistake? No. She'd handed it over to Luke. Was my cell somehow emitting signals? No. I'd just turned it on. I'd have to figure it out later; I couldn't concentrate. My hands shook as I punched in Luke's cell.

My call went to voice mail. I slumped in defeat. He'd turned his cell off. He'd said he was going to. He was obviously still on the road, still thinking we were behind him. How could my world be ripped apart so quickly?

"Luke," I said shakily, "call me right away. Rachel was kidnapped on 94. I—I don't know what to do!"

I disconnected, my gut a tight knot. The assholes had to be in Wisconsin by now. Was that where they were headed? Or would they turn around on a back road and race back to Illinois? My paralysis extended to my mental faculties. I didn't know what to do, whom to call.

The police. Of course. But which force? My village? No. It wasn't their jurisdiction. Jimmy Saclarides in Lake Geneva? Did I even have his number? I had to call someone. Doing nothing would let them get farther away. Then I realized in my half-crazy thought process that it didn't matter. Call 911.

A woman's voice answered. "What's your emergency?"

"My daughter has been kidnapped!" I shouted. "On Interstate 94. Please help me!"

The woman's voice was calm. Even soothing. "What's your location, sweetheart?"

"I just told you!" I screamed. How stupid was she?

"Where on 94 are you, honey?" Still calm. Rational.

"I don't know," I sobbed. I gazed around. Where the hell was I? Wait. I did know. "A couple of miles before the state line and the turnoff to Lake Geneva. South of Route 50. In Illinois."

"Good girl. Wait there. Help is on the way."

Three minutes passed. I know because I called Luke every few seconds, hung up, checked the time. I wondered whether to get out of the car, but with the onset of night, the temperature dropped, and even with the windows down, it was still warmer inside than out. I recalled there might be a blanket in the trunk, but I didn't have a key to open it. Then I remembered the lever on the side of my seat that opened the trunk automatically. Clearly, my brain was sluggish. I pulled the lever, got out, and found the blanket. I draped it around my shoulders and climbed back into the car. Traffic was still slow, but again, no one stopped. Two more interminable minutes passed. The warp speed of the kidnapping had evaporated; now time moved in ultra-slow motion.

Night had fallen. I was alone on the highway, and my Rachel, my heart, was gone. If I didn't have Rachel, I had nothing. My eyes grew wet. Tears rolled down my cheeks, building to a steady stream. Along with them came wracking sobs. I buried my face in my hands. I didn't even try to stop.

Chapter Fifty-eight

Thursday

The first state trooper to show up had rosy cheeks and a sparse blond mustache and looked about sixteen. His hat was tipped back like some latter-day Lone Ranger. A heavy jacket covered most of his uniform. He'd pulled up behind me, Mars light flashing. He got out and walked over to my side of the car.

"Good evening, ma'am. May I see your license and registration?"

I lost my cool. "Are you kidding? My daughter has been kidnapped! Look—there's her purse." I twisted around. "And there's her suitcase in the back! This isn't a damn traffic stop!"

He cut me off. "Ma'am, please calm down. I need your license and registration."

"Can't you see we're wasting time? They went north, but for all I know they could have turned around. Please...listen to me!" I flailed my hands wildly. An urgent energy was building inside me, an energy that had nowhere to go.

His voice grew tight. "Ma'am. I understand your distress. But before we move on, I need to confirm you are who you say you are."

I heard Luke's voice in my head telling me to calm down and comply. That there was no sense getting off to a bad start with the authorities, even though Baby Face barely counted as one to me. I rummaged in my glove compartment, pulled out my registration, and handed it over along with my license. "Please hurry. It's my daughter."

He nodded and went back to his cruiser.

I started to shiver. Traffic had thinned. Oncoming headlights winked through the dark, but they looked like they were mocking me. At least there was no snow. Where was Luke? Why hadn't he called? More important, where was Rachel?

I forced myself to focus. It didn't take a genius to figure out who was behind this. Stokes had practically announced his intentions when we met at Solyst's. He'd made it clear he wanted the goddammed flash drive, and he'd get it any way he could. Kidnapping my child, the most despicable act any mother could ever imagine, was just another operational tactic for him.

Naturally, there was no way for me to get in touch with him. No phone number, no email. I'd have to wait for him to make contact. In his own good time. Christ. Slowly my panic and despair turned to anger. He'd orchestrated every move, and he'd succeeded. He must have slapped a GPS tracker on the Camry at some point and had been following me ever since. Probably at Solyst's. I recalled how I lost sight of him for a short time after he got out of his car but before he came into the bar.

I kept fisting and releasing my hands. No way could I compete with a slick operator like Stokes. I needed someone who could stand up to the asshole. Someone who could give as well as he got. Who wouldn't let him walk all over us more than he already had. And someone who could find Rachel and bring her back to me. Alive and safe.

I stared at the oncoming cars. That someone wasn't going to be Luke. When he heard about this, he'd go ballistic, and rage would cloud his judgment. It might be Jimmy Saclarides—he *was* Lake Geneva's chief of police—but he might not be the best person to deal with an arrogant jerk like Stokes. I needed someone—I jerked my head up. I knew the perfect candidate. Someone almost as arrogant and calculating as Stokes. I scrolled through the contacts on my phone, found who I was looking for, and punched in the number.

"Special Agent Nick LeJeune's line…"

"Is he there?"

"He's in the field. Who's calling?"

"Ellie Foreman. Tell him to call me as soon as he can. It's an emergency."

Chapter Fifty-nine

Thursday

By the time Baby Face, whose name, I learned, was Chadwick, came back to the car, two more cruisers had pulled up on the shoulder, and a gapers delay was building on the highway.

I got out of the car and stamped my feet. Chadwick carried a thermos of coffee, which he offered me. I took it as a peace offering and gratefully accepted. An officer from the second cruiser, older and clearly more senior than Baby Face, introduced himself as Lieutenant Wickham and asked me to go over exactly what had happened. In the middle of our interview, my cell beeped. I checked caller ID. Finally. Luke.

"I'm sorry. It's my boyfriend. He doesn't know."

"Make it brief," Wickham replied.

I nodded.

"What the hell is going on, Ellie?"

Hearing his voice switched on my emotional spigot, and I wanted to cry. But I couldn't. I wouldn't. Not until— No. I wouldn't let myself think about that.

"Rachel's been kidnapped." My voice sounded shaky.

There was a long pause. "How?" Controlled fury lined his voice.

As I told him the story, Wickham listened too and made the occasional note. Was he trying to determine whether I'd left anything out?

"I'll be there in twenty minutes."

"Luke, they took my little girl," I wailed.

"Hold on, honey. I'll be there soon."

I disconnected. Wickham said, "Okay, first we're going to issue a possible abduction alert. Can you describe your daughter and what she was wearing?"

Rachel had still been dressed for work when we left the house. "Jeans, one of those paisley retro vests, a blazer, black boots." I ran a hand through my hair and paced. "She's about five-six. Curly blond hair. Gray-blue eyes. She's twenty-five. Slim..." I stopped abruptly. What if I never saw those curls again? Those beautiful eyes? Terror raced up my spine, threatening to overwhelm me. I covered my head with my arms and bent over. I wanted to curl into a fetal position on the shoulder of the highway.

Wickham must have recognized the signs of shock, because he gently put an arm around my shoulders and led me to one of the cruisers.

"Why don't you sit in here and get warm?"

I nodded unsteadily.

He picked up his radio and started to issue instructions for the alert. I sat in the backseat trembling and dazed.

My cell buzzed again. I checked the incoming number. LeJeune.

"What happened, Ellie?"

"Rachel was kidnapped."

"Holy shit, *cher*. Where are you?"

"Just south of the Wisconsin state line, I think."

"Where do you think they went?"

"I don't know." Somehow, through my panic-induced haze, I realized what he was really asking.

"They could be headed to Wisconsin. Across state lines."

"I'll be there as soon as I can."

An hour later, it must have looked to passing drivers like we were having a tailgate party on I-94. In addition to my car, three state trooper cruisers, Luke's pickup, LeJeune's Spyder, and Jimmy Saclarides' Lake Geneva police car were all parked on the shoulder. Luke had obviously called Jimmy. I got out of the cruiser and joined them.

I knew enough about law enforcement to know there could be a tussle over jurisdiction of the case. I also knew that if the kidnapping crossed state lines, it was a good bet the FBI would step in. To be honest, I was relieved to have LeJeune on my side. He might be full of himself, but I'd rather have a seasoned FBI agent than Baby Face Chadwick.

First they designated my car a crime scene. LeJeune and Jimmy conferred with the troopers. Jimmy said he could call in evidence techs from the Walworth County Sheriff's Department, but Wickham cut in.

"Chief, that's mighty nice of you, but the state police have an excellent crime lab. They're already en route."

LeJeune nodded. "Good move, Lieutenant."

"Of course," Jimmy said. "Much better." He said he'd have my car towed to Luke's when they were finished.

I sucked in a breath. "Oh my God, I forgot to tell you something critical!"

The lawmen and Luke looked over.

"The driver was impersonating a police officer. He was wearing one of your campaign hats. And they had lights and a siren on the car."

Wickham narrowed his eyes.

"Yes, but the car wasn't a patrol cruiser. It was just—just a car."

Wickham reviewed his notes on his iPad. "You said it was a dark four-door sedan."

"That's right. I forgot about the siren and lights."

"I'm glad you remembered." He got on his cell and punched in a number. He walked a few steps away from us, and I heard him discussing what I'd said.

I started to shiver again. Luke put his arm around me. "It's going to be okay," he said. "We'll find her."

I gave him a perfunctory nod.

Wickham came back just as we heard the chop of helicopter blades above.

"Crap," LeJeune said. "Fucking media vultures." He turned to Wickham. "Look, I'm just here in an unofficial capacity right now. Miss Foreman's a personal friend. But I'd like to run this thing up the chain of command and have us deal with it. What do you think?"

Wickham took a look at me, Jimmy, and Luke, then back at LeJeune. "I don't have a problem with that."

I sagged in relief. I almost threw my arms around him.

LeJeune's response, naturally, was more subdued. "Great. We'll work with your crime lab people, of course."

Wickham nodded.

"One favor." LeJeune pointed upward. "Can we keep this cluster fuck quiet? I mean, I know you have the alert out, but could you tell the media *this* is just an accident and you're investigating?"

The hint of a smile flashed across Wickham's face. "No worries there."

At least something was going right.

LeJeune shook Wickham's hand. "Thanks, man. In the meantime, *cher*, let's you and Luke and I go to that truck stop up yonder and get you some food."

Chapter Sixty

Thursday

Twenty minutes later Luke, LeJeune, and I walked into a truck plaza not far from the "accident." The neon lights splashed across the place were too bright, and the country music blaring from overhead speakers grated. I concentrated on breathing. In. Out. In.

LeJeune led us into the restaurant area, which was a kind way to describe the dozen wobbly tables, plastic chairs, and sticky booths. There was only one other couple at a table, he with a grizzled beard and big gut, she in turquoise sweats and big hair that hadn't been in fashion since Farrah Fawcett. But the place was warm, and we—at least I—needed a respite from the horror.

It was a cafeteria-style eatery, and without asking, LeJeune got up and returned with sandwiches, chips, and coffee. "Don't tell me you don't get anything for your taxes. This is on the feds, my friends."

"Thanks." I still had the blanket draped over me; I pulled it closer.

"So before we start, I need you both to know something," LeJeune said.

Luke, who had been holding my hand since we left the highway, let it go and cocked his head toward LeJeune. I unwrapped the cellophane around my sandwich.

"You remember I was investigating the IED that destroyed your hacker friend's office, right?"

I nodded. "Zach Dolan."

"I was pulled off the case."

I looked up. "Why?"

"Good question, *cher*. Someone ran it up the flagpole and it came back tagged with some bullshit about national security. It was handed over to the military."

"DIA?" Luke asked. He and I exchanged glances.

LeJeune watched us. Then: "Apparently, I'm missing something here. Care to fill me in?"

I took a bite of my sandwich. It tasted like paper and cellophane. I forced myself to chew, then washed it down with coffee. I could use the caffeine. I had no plans to sleep until Rachel was back.

"A lot has happened since Dolan's office was destroyed." I explained everything from Parks to Stokes to Hollander to my conversation with Grace Qasimi and her subsequent "accident." Luke added more information about his relationship with Grizzly.

"There's one more thing," I added when Luke finished. "I lied to you about not making another copy of the flash drive. I've had it with me since Parks died."

"You think I didn't know that?" He squinted. "What the fuck did you start, Ellie?"

"That's not fair, Nick. It started when I got fired from a job. I was just trying to find out why, so I made a phone call. Anyone would have done the same thing."

Neither Luke nor LeJeune replied. In fact, they traded looks that, in other circumstances, might have been considered smiles.

"Am I wrong?"

"Most people," Luke said, "who get fired from a job go home and nurse their wounds with a fifth of vodka. Or bottle of wine." But he put his arm around me when he said it.

"Things just kind of escalated," I said.

"I get it." LeJeune bit into his sandwich. "Well, this sucks."

I wasn't sure if he meant the sandwich or the situation. Or both.

"What do we do now?" I asked. "Can you put out an APB on the SUV?"

"Already done, but if they're as clever as they should be, we won't find it."

"What else?"

He shook his head. "There's not much to do except wait."

"For him to contact me."

LeJeune nodded.

"I just can't sit around and wait for some asshole to call."

"You have to, Ellie," Luke said. He looked over at LeJeune. "Does it matter whether she's at home or with me in Lake Geneva?"

"Probably not. Everyone uses a cell these days anyway." He took another bite of his sandwich—I couldn't tell if it was beef or ham—and chewed thoughtfully. Then: "Given what you've just told me about all these spy games, I'm not sure you have all that much to worry about."

I exploded. "What are you talking about? Some creep, probably Stokes, kidnapped my little girl! You're making it sound like some kind of prank. Maybe if you had kids of your own, you'd understand. I really—"

LeJeune cut in. "Calm down, *cher*. And listen to me. Yes, he crossed the line when he took Rachel. No argument there. But I would bet my badge that this is all for show. He wants to let you know he has the upper hand and can make things happen."

Luke nodded. "He wants to bust your balls."

"Great. So now we're playing the who's-more-macho game." I glared at them both. "Like I said, it's not your daughter."

"Which is why you're going to hand over the drive," LeJeune said.

My gut reaction was to argue. "I don't see why I should I let him get away with it."

"Because if you don't, Rachel really *could* get hurt," LeJeune said. "He's got you over a barrel."

"Which he's probably enjoying," I said.

"Ellie," Luke added, "you were talking about giving it back to Delcroft anyway."

"Yeah, but it would have been on my terms."

No one said anything.

I slumped against the back of the booth, unexpectedly exhausted. I looked from LeJeune to Luke. "You're both right, of course. He can have the damn drive. I just want my baby back."

"So," LeJeune said. "No more waging the battle of justice. Tilting at windmills, bearing the torch of democracy?"

I shook my head. Tears welled in my eyes.

He tilted his head. "You know something? I think I like you better when you're feisty."

My tears dried up, and I shot him a narrow-eyed glance.

Luke spoke up. "You know, there's another issue we haven't talked about."

"What's that?" I asked.

"What if it isn't Stokes who kidnapped Rachel? What if it was the Chinese government?"

"Possible." LeJeune pushed his sandwich away and opened his bag of chips. "But unlikely."

"Why?"

"About a year ago the US indicted six Chinese citizens here in the country for stealing technology."

"Luke and I were just talking about that."

"But the litigation is moving at a snail's pace. Very few cases have come to court. And no one expects them to."

"Which means the Chinese have carte blanche to do whatever they want? Maybe Stokes is taking orders from the Chinese. Along with Hollander." I slid closer to Luke. "What if Rachel ends up in Beijing?" I stopped. "You know, LeJeune, your bedside manner needs work."

LeJeune flipped up his hands. "Look, I wouldn't be doing my job if I didn't lay out all the possibilities. Sure, it could be the Chinese, but the way it went down feels more personal. Less political. And you have to ask what the Chinese would get out of kidnapping your daughter."

"Revenge for the indictments we just talked about."

Luke shook his head. "They would have done it differently, Ellie. Think about it. All China wants is DADES. They don't give a damn what happens to the people who they bought it from. Including their own citizens."

"Except they paid a boatload of money for it," I said.

"Right," Luke said. "And from the contents of the flash drive, it appears they already got what they paid for."

LeJeune picked up a spoon and tapped it on the table. "It's a long shot. We can't force them into our legal system. Their passports are their get-out-of-jail-free card."

I leaned back. "You know something? With everything you're both saying, I'm having trouble separating the good guys from the bad."

"Welcome to my world," LeJeune said. "There are a lot of players in this game, and someone is going to be outplayed. I'm here because I don't want it to be you. Or Rachel. Don't forget—everything points to Hollander as the guilty party. American citizen. Ex-military. Now a traitor. When this gets out, America will go nuts. Like they did over Snowden. But this will be worse, because it's a fait accompli. It's done. They're going to crucify her." He paused. "But I have a team out looking for Stokes."

"You're not going to find him," Luke said. "He's already holed up somewhere with Rachel."

"I know that." He threw the bag of chips down in disgust. "But I can still pay a visit to his employers."

"You're going to Delcroft?" I asked.

"Damn right I am." He glanced out the window. "Tomorrow morning."

"Do you really think they'll tell you anything useful?" Luke said.

"We'll find out. And even if we don't, they're going to have to deal with the fact that their so-called security chief is a felon."

"If he's the one who kidnapped Rachel," I said.

"Read the tea leaves, *cher*," LeJeune said.

I set my coffee down. The china cup clinked against Formica. "You can read whatever fucking tea leaves you want. As long as you get my daughter back alive."

Chapter Sixty-one

Thursday

We arrived at Luke's just before midnight. LeJeune followed us to the house and coached me on how to handle Stokes' call. Afterward, we settled in Luke's kitchen. The room had a gas fireplace at one end, and Luke turned it on. An ugly couch in tartan plaid sat in front; I always kidded Luke about it—only WASPs with absolutely no taste would have it in their home, much less their kitchen. He would reply that I must have known his parents.

Tonight, though, there was no ribbing. I was drained, but a feverish urgency wouldn't let me relax, much less sleep. Luke and LeJeune switched from coffee to beer and camped out on the couch, but my full-blown case of *shpulkes* kept me pacing back and forth.

"You're sure he'll call?"

"Of course he will, *cher*. He's just waiting for you to reach that panic stage where you'll do or say anything to get Rachel back."

"In that case, he should have called hours ago."

"Got a present for you," Nick said. He pulled out something about the size of a quarter from his jacket pocket and tossed it on the coffee table.

Luke leaned over. "The tracker."

LeJeune nodded. "He's known where you've been for a while."

"That includes the Baha'i Temple and the library, doesn't it?"

He frowned. "Why?"

I told him about the man who'd shown up while Grace Qasimi and I were talking. And the video clips about the Uyghurs that disappeared from the Internet.

LeJeune pulled out his cell and made a few notes. "I don't know about those videos, but do you know how to reach this Qasimi woman?"

"You can't," I said.

"Why?"

"She was killed on the Eisenhower Expressway a couple of hours ago."

LeJeune's eyebrows went sky-high.

"I don't think it was an accident."

"Because…"

"Because of what I just told you. She was Gregory Parks' fiancée. She was the one who told me about the Uyghurs. And that Gregory was a double."

LeJeune chewed his lip. "What about friends? Relatives? You know anyone who knew her?"

"She obviously knows someone up at the Dragon Inn North. She got them to pass me a message."

"Good. I'll start there."

Panic swirled in my belly. "Wait. You're not leaving, are you?"

He smiled. "Luke can handle you." He shot him a sidelong glance. "Probably a lot better than I can."

My eyes went wide at LeJeune's—well—I would have to call it modesty. That was the first time I'd ever seen it. Had I not been so miserable, I might have had a comeback. Instead I let it go.

"There's one more thing, guys," I said. "What do we do about Dad? I haven't told him yet. But if I don't, he'll never forgive me."

Both men were quiet for a moment. Then Luke said, "I wouldn't say anything yet. If you don't hear anything by tomorrow night, then we can reassess."

"I agree," LeJeune echoed. "The fewer people who know what's going on, the better. More controllable."

I stopped pacing. "Controllable? How do you control a kidnapping? You just finished telling me he holds all the cards."

"True."

"So we have no options."

"Maybe, maybe not. He needs the flash drive, right?"

I nodded.

"In fact, he has to get it. Or so he thinks."

I nodded again.

"That may mean we can dictate how and when."

"And put Rachel in more jeopardy? No way." I went to my bag and started digging inside for the flash drive.

LeJeune let out a strained breath. I could tell I was trying his patience. It had been a long night. "Not necessarily."

I kept fishing for the drive in my bag. LeJeune watched me. He looked like he was going to explain when I threw my bag down on the couch. "Oh crap!"

"What?"

"The flash drive. It's not here. In the rush to get away, I think I left it back home. And Stokes knows from the tracker that I'm not there. What if he breaks in to get it? Then he doesn't need Rachel at all. He could do anything he wanted with her," I wailed. "Christ! What are we going to do?"

LeJeune got to his feet. "Don't worry about that, Ellie."

"What do you mean, don't worry? Of course I'm—"

"I have six agents outside your house right now. No one is going to break in unless it's us."

"Really?" For the first time all evening, I allowed myself a deep breath. "Thank God. Thank *you*."

He nodded and zipped up his jacket. "But I'm going to get it. You want to give me your key?" He paused. "Unless you're okay with a B and E, Bureau-style."

I almost smiled. Almost. "Yup."

"What do you mean 'yup?'"

"You will have to do a B&E. The assholes took off with my keys."

LeJeune sighed. "Of course they did." He squeezed his eyes shut then opened them again. "Don't worry. We'll be careful."

I raised my eyebrows.

"The best thing you can do is try and get some rest," he went on. "He'll call. But it won't be tonight. It may not even be tomorrow. But he will."

Luke came over and put his arms around me. "Listen to him, Ellie. He knows what he's doing."

I swallowed.

"Where is it?" LeJeune asked. "The drive."

"Probably in my desk drawer. Upstairs in my office."

"Okay, *cher*. I'll be back tomorrow."

Chapter Sixty-two

I'd rehearsed what to say to Stokes so many times that the call, when it came the next night, was almost an afterthought.

My memory of the twenty-four hours prior was hazy. There were alternating periods of grief, terror, and guilt. I recalled a flood of tears, hours on the bed in a fetal position, Luke's arms around me. I remembered the sweet smell of Rachel's baby skin after she'd had a bath. The way she went all out for soccer when she was fifteen. How she nearly ran me over when her father taught her to drive. I might never see, hear, or touch my little girl again, and it was my fault. If only I hadn't become so obsessed with that damn flash drive. When would I learn? Thoughts like those would restart the tears, and the cycle would begin anew.

There were a couple of calls from LeJeune, one telling me he'd picked up the drive, another saying he had interviewed Gary Phillips at Delcroft but didn't learn anything significant.

"I'll say one thing for those corporate guys," LeJeune said. "They toss the bullshit around better than most anyone else. Except lawyers."

Jimmy Saclarides dropped off my Camry in the driveway. The crime lab techs had been all over it but hadn't retrieved much beyond shards of broken glass and the detritus of bank receipts, grocery lists, and Starbucks cups. He was ready to leave, but Luke asked him to stick around.

I felt paralyzed by a profound lassitude; it was hard to even muster the energy to go to the bathroom. At about five, Luke walked me into the shower, soaped me up, and washed my hair. Then he led me down to the kitchen, heated up some soup, and forced me to take a few spoonfuls.

My cell hadn't been more than a few inches away all day, but I tried not to stare at it. If I did, he wouldn't call. If I ignored it, he wouldn't call either.

It reminded me of a joke Rachel and I shared about parking karma. I have it; she wants it. I seem to be able to park in the best spots on Chicago city streets for free, or at least a minimal amount of money. She called me one night after circling her Wrigleyville apartment for twenty minutes trying to find a spot. While we were chatting, I told her I'd put it out in the universe. "Give Rachel some parking karma," I intoned in a mantra-like manner.

Thirty seconds later, she squealed. "OMG. A spot just opened up. Right in front of my apartment. You're amazing, Mom!"

We'd laughed so hard I almost spit out my wine.

Now I wanted to cry. I needed cell phone karma.

LeJeune showed up while Luke was making ginger tea. He took one look at me, saw how distraught I was, and directed most of his conversation to Luke and Jimmy.

"I want to brief you on what we found out about our pal. Warren Stokes is from Oklahoma. He enlisted as soon as he was eighteen. Right around the First Gulf War."

Luke's eyebrows arched.

LeJeune rubbed his nose. "He was attached to the Eighteenth Infantry Regiment. Saw a little action, but most of it was mopping up. When he came back he applied to the Agency. They told him he needed a college degree, so he took night classes at Prince George's Community College outside DC. He spent days as a security guard. At one point he applied for the DC police department but didn't make the cut."

"Really."

LeJeune nodded. "But he did do one smart thing. He learned Arabic."

Luke's eyebrows arched even higher.

"After 9/11, he convinced the Agency he was almost fluent."

"Was he?" I cut in.

"Who knows? But they took him and sent him to Afghanistan. He was back and forth for a couple of tours. Best I can tell, about five years."

"That's a long time."

LeJeune nodded. "Then, all of a sudden he's out. Instead of riding off into the sunset, he sets up Stokes Security. Hires a marketing company, and within a year he's got half a dozen clients. A year later six more. He adds a bunch of ex-spooks, pretty much all military, Agency, Bureau, Secret Service. Most of them with a talent for hacking. A few months ago he gets the Delcroft account."

"He's not stupid," Luke said.

"Agreed," LeJeune said. "If his guys really can hack into people's computers, there's no telling how much dirt he can pull up."

I sipped the tea. It felt soothing. "Are you saying he blackmailed companies to get clients?"

"Like I said, who knows?"

"Why did he leave the Agency?" Luke asked

"It's not clear. I'll let you know when I find out. Meanwhile let's focus on the exchange."

Chapter Sixty-three

Friday

And that's when my cell buzzed. All four of us stared at it. I checked the caller ID panel. Caller unknown. I held it up so LeJeune and Luke could see. They both nodded. I took a deep breath, pushed the green light, and put it on speakerphone, as Nick had instructed.

"Hello?"

No hesitation on the other end. "You know who this is, I assume."

"Yes, Mr. Stokes," I said for their benefit.

"And you know what I want."

"Yes."

"Well?"

"I need to talk to Rachel. Make sure she's okay."

LeJeune had said he would probably say no but to tell him all bets were off until I heard her voice. To my surprise, though, he didn't object. "Of course."

There was a swish of air. A moment later, I heard, "Mom?"

Her voice on the other end of the phone was like my birthday, Mother's Day, and Christmas, all wrapped up in one. "Rachel. Oh my God. I love you. I am so sorry. Are you okay?"

"Well, actually I am. I was scared shitless at the beginning, but it's okay now."

I started to giggle. I knew it was a nervous reaction to the stress and fear. But I couldn't help thinking how mature she sounded.

"What's so funny?" Rachel asked.

"Nothing, honey." Still, she wasn't with me, and in the space of a few seconds, my giggles turned to sobs. Luke squeezed my free hand.

Rachel picked up on my tears. "Don't cry, Mom. Really, I'm fine. They bought me McDonald's for dinner last night. And KFC tonight. And one of the guys is a pretty good— Look, I can't stay on the phone. He's motioning me to get off."

Was this my daughter? She sounded so level-headed and calm I would have thought she was at camp, not the captive of some ambitious, overreaching covert operative. Was I overreacting? Was all the hysteria and anxiety misplaced? "Baby, we're going to—"

But a sudden swish on the phone told me I was no longer talking to Rachel. My fear ratcheted up.

"Satisfied?" Stokes said.

"I want to talk longer."

"Not now. By the way, you can call off the feds. I know they're listening."

All four of us exchanged glances. LeJeune leaned back with an expression that said he might have underestimated Stokes.

"And you can tell the rest of the gang we're going to do you a big favor."

"What's that?" I said.

"I know you're in Lake Geneva. And you now have the drive."

"How do you—"

He ignored the question.

"There's an airstrip behind the Lodge, the fancy resort up there."

"I know it." I glanced over at Luke and Jimmy. The three of us had history there.

"Be there at two am. You give us the drive; we'll give you your daughter."

"How do I know you won't pull a stunt at the last minute?"
"You don't." He paused. "No weapons. No floodlights or cameras. No comms. Maglites and binoculars are okay. Most important, no one comes before two am. If my team sees anyone they don't recognize, anyone ferreting around, prepping, or planting land mines or flares, the deal is off, and you'll never see your daughter again." Another pause. "Oh, and *you* will hand over the drive. Not your FBI pal or your boyfriend. Got it?"

I was about to reply, but he disconnected.

Chapter Sixty-four

Friday

"Something's off." LeJeune got up and started to pace.

I followed him with my eyes. "What?"

"It's too easy."

"Maybe to you. I thought he made it pretty clear. No weapons, comms, flares—"

He cut me off. "That's par for the course." He stopped pacing but continued to look tense and coiled, ready to spring into action. "Why would he stipulate *you* have to hand the drive over? I don't like it." He turned to Jimmy and Luke. "Tell me about the airstrip."

Jimmy spoke up. "It's about a mile-long strip at the back of the property. It's deteriorated over the years. Broken concrete. Weeds. It was built to fly in performers and stars who appeared at the Playboy club."

"And the big rollers," Luke added.

"What's off to the sides? Who monitors it?"

"It's a private strip. Only people like Luke use it."

"You have your own plane?" LeJeune asked.

"I do," Luke answered. "But it's not restricted. You need to fly in or out, it's not a problem. Sometimes the city of Lake Geneva supports the strip with some funding. Sometimes they don't."

"There are woods on one side," Jimmy took over. "The resort property is on the other. There's a small hangar on one end, surrounded by an equipment shed and rows of seedlings and flowers that make up the resort's nursery."

"Can my men take positions in the woods?"

"Probably. But I don't know how you're going to get them there ahead of time."

"Is there any other way to get to the airstrip?"

"You mean besides going through the resort?"

LeJeune nodded.

"There's an abandoned dirt road that runs parallel to the strip and connects with County Route 45," Jimmy said. "But it's a quarter mile to the airstrip on unpaved land. They better hope they have off-road tires."

"What about eyes in the sky?"

"It won't be a great view," Jimmy said. "Too much woodland."

"Still, we'll get a sat on it." LeJeune pulled out his cell, then stopped. "Of course, he will too, now that I'm thinking about it."

"Stokes?" Luke asked.

"He was Agency. He'd know the right people to call. Monitoring sats is one of the most boring jobs in the world. For a pocket full of money, those monitors will do anything. This'll seem like the Kentucky Derby to them."

"You would know," I said. LeJeune was from Louisiana. Close enough.

He whipped around. "Feeling better, eh, *cher?*"

I allowed myself to smile.

"Good. Because you're going to need balls of steel in a while."

My smile faded.

He looked at his watch. "We've got two hours. My team will be here in fifteen. I'll reconnoiter with them and come up with a plan."

Fifteen minutes later, a swarm of men in a van and two unmarked cars arrived. I was forced out of my sluggishness to make huge pots of coffee. They'd brought three dozen doughnuts, which surprised me. I thought cops had the market sewn up. After getting coffee and taking their treats, they went back outside to talk with LeJeune. Luke and Jimmy went with them.

I stole one of the doughnuts and peeked outside while I ate it. A group of eight men, all wearing their navy FBI jackets with yellow letters, stood in a semicircle around LeJeune. I couldn't hear what they were saying, but I saw a few nods. Others shook their heads. One man started scraping his foot on the gravel driveway. It was a cold night, but not brittle, a sure sign winter was loosening its grip. And thankfully there was no snow.

After ten minutes the men dispersed and took off in the van. Jimmy went with them. Luke and LeJeune came back into the kitchen.

"That's one good thing…," Luke was saying.

"What's good?" I asked.

"They traced Stokes' cell."

"Really?" I brightened.

"Yeah," LeJeune said. "But if he's worth his salt, he anticipated we'd get it. He's probably using a burner."

I rubbed my arms, feeling chilly in spite of the fire. "Well, it's something. Where did your men go?"

"To stake out the woods beside the airstrip."

"What happens if Stokes finds them?"

LeJeune waved a dismissive hand. "What he said was bullshit. He knows we'll be there. He's probably got *his* men positioned already."

A pulse of anxiety streaked up my spine. "I don't get it. If you send your men out and he sends his, and you both know it, what's the point? What's to prevent all-out Armageddon?"

"That's why we game it out ahead of time. Stokes knows that. He's figuring out his options now. Don't worry about it."

I wanted to slap him. The old LeJeune was back. Telling me not to worry my pretty little head about anything.

"Well, I am worried. You guys are playing games with the life of my daughter!" I turned to Luke. "What do you think, Luke?"

"I think you should listen to the FBI."

"You too?" I glared at him. "Please. Someone tell me something this pretty little head can understand that won't ruin my pretty little manicure when I belt you both in the face."

Luke raised his hands in a back-off gesture, but LeJeune grinned.

"She's baaack," he cracked. "Seriously, though, sit down and I'll walk you through the plan."

"What plan? I walk down the airstrip from one direction. Rachel and Stokes come from the other. I give him the drive. He gives me Rachel."

"Not so simple. First of all, it won't be him. It will be one of his proxies. He doesn't want anyone to get a camera shot of his face. Which, of course, we would do. But that's not the main thing. The asshole has got some play up his sleeve."

"What kind of play?"

"I don't know. But there is one. Got to be. His conversation with you was too vague. He didn't say anything we didn't expect. We have to make some assumptions."

"Like what?"

He didn't answer, then shook his head. "We're at a disadvantage."

I raised my hand. "Including me."

He smiled. "That's why you have us. We'll have your back."

"So you are bringing guns."

LeJeune rolled his eyes. "Of course we are. So will he."

Again, I asked Luke, "Are you okay with that?"

"Ellie, like I said, he's the professional. Listen to him."

"So what do I do?"

"You walk down the airstrip, give the guy who's with Rachel the drive, lead Rachel back. But expect the unexpected. Be prepared."

"Hey, that's one hell of a plan, LeJeune."

Chapter Sixty-five

Saturday Morning

We took off around one thirty in Luke's pickup. Ten minutes later we reached the Lodge. Driving past the entrance brought back memories of the summer I produced a video for them, the summer I met Luke. Now we meandered through twisty roads, empty and bare at this hour, and pulled up to the hangar at the end of the airstrip. LeJeune's men had already arrived, their bright yellow letters visible even in the blackest part of the night. I counted more than a dozen of us, including three officers from the Lake Geneva police. All to rescue one young woman. Most of the officers had shoulder mics and cell phones clipped to their waists. Most carried Maglites. If they were carrying guns, which I assumed they were, they kept their weapons holstered and well out of sight.

One of the FBI men worked off a clipboard, estimating the distance between the hangar and the opposite end. I wasn't sure why. Jimmy had already told them it was about a mile. While they were working, I wandered over to the hangar. I'd been on the airstrip a few times but never at night. It was in pretty bad condition, as I recalled, studded with chunks of cracked asphalt and rocks. Then again, no airplanes were ever scheduled to take off or land. Except Luke's. And the executives from the resort.

I followed LeJeune over to the guy with the clipboard. "We have no clear lines of sight because of the woods," he told Nick. "But at least there are no buildings, except for the hangar and equipment room, and they've been searched and cleared."

"How will Rachel get here?" I asked.

"She'll likely be in a van or SUV." The FBI guy pointed to the far end of the airstrip. "They'll come in from that end."

"Do you think they'll try anything? A double-cross or something?" I asked him.

He looked over at LeJeune, who replied, "Well, that's the sixty-four-thousand-dollar question, isn't it, *cher?*"

I rubbed my forehead, trying to suppress my anxiety.

LeJeune walked over to a small knot of officers. He beckoned me to follow him. "Come over here, Ellie. We need to wire you up."

"You didn't say anything about a wire."

"It's for your protection. I want to hear everything that's said, and I'll be whispering in your ear what to say back."

"What if Stokes spots it?"

LeJeune shrugged. "It doesn't matter. What's the worst that could happen?"

"He has his goons rip it off and kill Rachel."

"I think the possibility is pretty slim. He doesn't care about anything except that drive."

I kept my mouth shut. One of his men pinned a mic under my jacket and worked a tiny earpiece into my ear.

"Now put your hat on."

I did.

"Good." LeJeune made a call on his cell. "We're pretty exposed. Nothing we can do about that." Was he talking to his boss?

"So we either get double-crossed or we don't…Yeah. Got it." He disconnected, turned to his men. "Those of you with radios, let's make sure we're on the same frequency. Channel four." Then he called out to Luke.

"You got your b-nocs?"

Luke held up his binoculars. "Infrared."

LeJeune nodded. "You'll be our eyes."

"You got it," Luke said.

Two vans lurched into sight at the opposite end of the strip.

"Okay, men," LeJeune called out. "Show's starting."

Luke brought the binoculars to his face and peered through them. "Two men exiting the first van. One is the driver." I heard a faint thud as a door slid shut. "One man exiting the other van. Passenger side." Another thump. "Looks like there are three inside the second van."

All at once, the headlights of the first van blinked twice.

Jimmy blinked the headlights of his cruiser in response.

"How many?" LeJeune asked.

"Counting Rachel, six visibles," Luke said.

"Let's hope there's not another vehicle idling in the woods."

No one answered.

LeJeune looked at me. "You got the drive?"

I nodded shakily and slipped it out of my jacket pocket.

"You know what to do."

A couple of the FBI guys snapped on their Maglites, aiming them at me like spotlights. I started forward.

"Slower, Ellie. I know you want Rachel. But no sudden moves. You got it?"

I tensed. I was only a few yards from the hangar, but a wave of isolation washed over me as if I was the only living person in the world. I had LeJeune in my ears and Luke on my back. Still, I prepared to do battle like a gladiator fighting solo in the forum.

From the corner of my eye I spotted the woods. FBI snipers were somewhere in the dense brush. Then again, LeJeune had said Stokes' men would be there too. I wouldn't count on help from that direction.

A minute later, the second van's doors opened again. A figure got out from the front passenger seat.

"Is that Stokes?" LeJeune asked.

"I can't tell," I said. I'd met him only once. It was a stocky figure, though; it could have been him.

"Able, you got your camera out? Try and get as many shots as you can."

"Roger that," a voice said in my ear. "But they're not gonna be very good."

"Don't worry about that. Just get them."

The back door of the van slid open and another figure got out. Rachel.

"Okay. Daughter is out," Luke said. "The men in the other van are out too."

"By the way, *cher*, the home office says we have eyes on us." He spoke into his cell. "Are you seeing anything out of the ordinary?" There was a pause. Then: "Good. Start walking again, Ellie."

I took a few more steps forward.

The man who may or may not have been Stokes went around to the back of the van, opened the door, and removed something bulky. I narrowed my eyes, trying to see what it was, but I was too far away.

LeJeune caught it too. He talked to the satellite monitor. "What's going on, Skylight?" A pause. "Well, get your fucking eyes closer. Luke? You see anything?"

"Not yet."

The man took whatever he was holding and carried it back to where Rachel stood.

"What's going on, guys?" I asked.

"Looks like he's putting something on her," Luke said. Then after a pause, he cried out. "No. It can't be."

"What? What is it?" A fresh wave of tremors shot through my hands.

Luke started to say something but suddenly went quiet. I whipped around. LeJeune was making the zip-it motion with his fingers. I shaded my eyes from the glare of the Maglites. "What the fuck is going on?"

"Turn around," LeJeune said in my ear. I did. "Now, Ellie, I don't want you to react. You understand? Pretend I didn't say a word."

"Why not?" My voice was high and scratchy and tentative.

"He's putting a suicide vest on her."

Chapter Sixty-six

Saturday

I screamed in terror. "No! Get it off! Take it off! Someone!" I started to shake uncontrollably. "Not my baby. Not this."

"Steady, Ellie. Keep it together," LeJeune's voice said in my ears. But all I wanted to do to was throw myself in Luke's arms. This wasn't part of the plan. He'd make it go away, wouldn't he?

I yelled into the mic. "How can I? He's going to blow her off the planet. LeJeune, do something. Shoot the motherfucker. Right now!"

"Calling his cell."

I whipped around. After a few minutes, he shook his head and pocketed his cell. "Like I thought...He's using a burner."

"Fuck. What are we going to do?" I cried. I wrapped my arms around my chest. It was the only way to keep myself from sinking to the ground. I squeezed my eyes shut. This was the stuff of crazy Islamic jihadists or ISIS. The sort of desperate action you'd expect from brainwashed individuals with nothing left to lose. This didn't happen in America's heartland. This had to be a surreal nightmare that would disappear when I opened my eyes.

Except it wasn't. And it didn't.

I squinted, trying to see how Rachel was handling it. She was too far away and it was too dark to make out much, but her body language said it all. Rigid. Uncompromising. Arms and legs moving stiffly, like a marionette. She had to be terrified.

"Listen to me, Ellie," LeJeune said. "Remember I told you to expect the unexpected? This is it."

I glanced toward the woods, half-expecting to see the FBI snipers taking aim.

LeJeune read my thoughts. "We can't take them down. What if they hit Rachel instead? Plus, it would start a firefight, and no one, including you or your daughter, would walk away."

My voice cracked. "What are we going to do?" I was sobbing.

"You're going to have to deal with it." Nick's voice was laced with tension.

"I'm going to ask them to put it on me instead." And with that I started walking forward briskly, waving my arms.

LeJeune talked into my ear, and his orders made me realize our two-way communications were being overheard by the rest of his team. "Take your marks, Officers, but don't shoot. Got that?"

I heard a chorus of "Got its" and "Ten-fours" in response.

"You can do this, *cher*. We got your back."

I forced myself to take a deep breath. And then another. I tried to shove my fear to the back of my brain. My mission was to get Rachel. Give him the goddammed drive. I started forward again. As I did, the man who could be Stokes got back in the lead van.

"He's back in the van," Luke said.

"Directing traffic," LeJeune said.

"I'm going to kill that asshole," Luke said.

"Calm down, Luke," LeJeune said. "Ellie, you okay?"

I wasn't, but I nodded. One of Stokes' men and Rachel were waiting at the opposite end of the airstrip.

LeJeune shouted, "Bring her halfway."

An arctic breeze suddenly flared, and I wanted to wrap my wool muffler around my neck. But I figured any unexpected movement on my part might backfire and start a firefight. I shoved my hands into my pockets.

The man led Rachel toward the middle of the airstrip. As she got closer, I could see a glazed, frozen look on her face. She resembled a manikin in a department store, her casual manner on the phone the night before long gone. As we came within one hundred yards of each other, the goon drew something out of his side. A pistol.

"Do you see that, Nick?" I breathed.

LeJeune shouted out again. "I thought there would be no weapons."

"Boss changed his mind," the goon said.

"Take the vest off the girl."

I swear I saw a smile appear on the man's face as he shook his head. "Boss says take it or leave it."

LeJeune whispered in my ear. "Balls of steel, *cher*. We're almost there."

"Yeah, and then he'll pull the cord, and she'll be blown to bits," I whispered back.

"Have faith. By the way, Luke says he loves you."

I halted. That Luke would tell LeJeune to say that, and that LeJeune actually *told* me, made a difference. I suddenly felt more centered. Less alone. More than a dozen people, including the man I loved most in the world, were looking out for us. Maybe it would work. Still, I vowed to never again watch any movies or shows about terrorism.

I approached the man and Rachel steadily but with caution. Rachel was dead quiet but kept walking stiffly, as if she knew any wrong move would end in disaster. Then she stopped.

My heart banged in my chest. What now?

She leaned toward the man and asked something. I couldn't hear what it was.

He nodded and pointed forward. She started walking again. My mouth went as dry as a desert. I wanted to scream, "Stop. Just stop." I opened my mouth. Nothing came out.

It seemed like forever, but eventually we were only about fifty feet apart.

The man stopped. So did Rachel. I did too. The man looked familiar. I realized he was one of the men who'd been camped out at my neighbors', the Schomers'. In the pickup. It seemed so long ago. As if it was another life.

Now the goon raised his pistol and aimed it at my chest. Time stopped. I gagged. "Any wrong move, I shoot. And that's the signal for the boss to activate the vest."

I managed a weak nod.

"Give me the drive."

"Let Rachel go first."

"It doesn't work like that. You first, Ms. Foreman." I could have sworn he was smirking under his breath.

"Why?" I couldn't help it.

There was silence for a moment, and I knew that, like LeJeune's voice in my ear, Stokes was talking to his man. "We planned the meet-up here. Let you talk to your daughter on the phone. Both good-faith gestures. Your turn."

I looked back at Luke and LeJeune, wondering if I should make the move. Then I realized the goon was right beside Rachel. He didn't want the vest to blow up any more than I did.

I stepped forward slowly. "It's in my pocket. I need to put my hand in and get it out."

He nodded. Oh, how I wished I had my father's Colt in there instead of the drive. I would shoot the bastard, no questions asked. Instead, I slipped my hand in and brought out the two-inch piece of plastic that was now the only thing standing between my daughter's life and her death. I wanted to fling it at him, grab Rachel's hand, and fly back to the hangar. But I couldn't. I stepped forward. He held out his hand; I gave him the drive.

That was it.

I didn't expect a thank-you, or any gratitude, but I didn't expect what he did next. He holstered his weapon, whirled around, and sprinted back to the van at the edge of the airstrip, leaving Rachel and me in the middle of the strip.

"Oh, baby!" I went toward her with outstretched arms.

"Don't, Mom. Don't move a muscle. Do you hear me? Stokes is going to push the remote."

I froze and stood stock-still. He wouldn't. He couldn't.

Rachel stared at me, her eyes wide with panic.

I heard running steps behind me. "Don't move, Ellie." LeJeune.

"Rachel, you too." It was Luke. "Don't turn around. We have to get that thing off."

"Hurry!" I shouted. "His guy is almost back at the van!" His other men were piling into the two vans. One of the engines started up.

Luke went to Rachel and shone a flashlight at the vest. Then he looked up at Rachel. "Where's the clasp? How did he fasten it on you?"

"There's a hook at the top and bottom. On the inside."

"Good girl," Luke said. "Now just stand still. I'll do the rest. It'll all be over soon." He handed the light to LeJeune, who aimed it at the vest.

I followed Stokes' men with my eyes. "Oh, shit. The last man is climbing in the van. You've got to get it off. He'll explode it any second!"

The wind was picking up. I shivered. I needed my little girl. She needed me. We were only a few feet apart, but it could have been miles.

Luke managed to unhook the clasp at the top of the vest. "Almost there. Hang on, everyone." He went to work on the bottom. As he was looking for the hook, the second van roared to life.

"Luke, hurry! Please! It's now or never!"

Luke found the clasp, unhooked it, and carefully took the vest off Rachel. She ran into my arms.

"Get rid of it!" LeJeune yelled.

Luke wound up as if he was going to serve a volleyball, took three running steps and heaved it toward the side of the airstrip away from the woods.

"Okay, everyone. Run!"

The four of us sprinted like professional runners. We were almost back to the hangar when the vest exploded. The force of the blast threw us to the ground. I crawled over to Rachel, covered her body with my own, and watched a giant orange fireball rise into the night sky.

Chapter Sixty-seven

Saturday Night and Sunday

The next morning I decided to drive to the drugstore in Lake Geneva to buy a night-lite. Luke, Rachel, and I had arrived back at Luke's at about four in the morning. Rachel hadn't said a word since she'd been released, and the look of terror on her face told me everything. She refused to let me get farther than a few feet away from her, so we both crawled into a bed in one of Luke's guest rooms. She wouldn't let me turn out the light and wriggled as close to me as she could. I held her for what seemed like hours until I finally heard the deep, even breathing of sleep.

Between the overhead light and the stress of the past two days, there was no way I could sleep. Trying not to disturb Rachel, I climbed out of bed around seven and went downstairs. Luke had brewed a pot of coffee and was drinking it at the kitchen table. Dark circles gouged the pockets under his eyes, and he had the roughness and stubble of someone who hadn't slept or showered. A pad of yellow legal paper lay in front of him, and he was making notes that, from across the room, I couldn't decipher.

I went to him, put my hands on his shoulders, and kissed the top of his head. "Thank you," I whispered. "For everything."

He didn't turn around but reached up and squeezed one of my hands. I buried my head in his neck and nuzzled his cheek.

"It's not over, you know," he said. His voice was raw.

"You didn't sleep, either."

He shook his head.

"What are you doing?"

"Making notes."

"Why? For interviews with the FBI and the cops?"

"Among other things."

I straightened up, went over to the coffeepot, and poured myself a cup. "What other things?"

"He's not going to get away with it."

I faced Luke. "He already did."

"That's not what I mean, Ellie." I inclined my head. His tone was one I hadn't heard in years: heavy and solemn and freighted with smoldering anger. It reminded me of the first time we'd met. When he'd been accused of murder.

"What are you going to do?"

"How's Rachel?" he asked, dodging my question.

"She refuses to let me to leave her side. But she's finally asleep. With the lights on."

"So why are you leaving her?"

A trace of irritation came over me. I wasn't leaving her. Then again, we were both exhausted, physically and emotionally. We were apt to say things we didn't really mean. At least I was. I forced my irritation down. "I'm going to the drugstore to pick up a night-lite. Do you need anything?"

"Why don't I go instead?" He stood up. "I'll get some groceries too. What should I get?"

"Whatever you want." I crossed the room again and put my arms around him, relieved that I didn't need to leave my little girl.

He hugged me back. "You know, there are going to be a pack of people here this afternoon. Do you think Rachel's up to it?"

"If she's not, they'll just have to wait until she is. They can talk to us instead. She's in bad shape, Luke."

"I'll tell Jimmy. He's already called."

I stepped out of his embrace. "I've been wondering about something. Do you think the vest exploded because you threw it off the airstrip? Or did Stokes activate it when they were speeding away?"

"I don't know. I guess we'll have to wait for the forensics analysis."

"Will it make any difference? I mean, no one is going to blame you for doing that, are they?"

"Just let them try."

I rubbed the back of my neck. In a way, I was reluctant to revisit what had happened the previous night. Not because it would bring back the terror of the events. I was afraid of my own rage. It had been building ever since we got Rachel back. A clear, pure rage. I wanted to tear Stokes from limb to limb. I knew I could do it. He had put my daughter through hell. Threatened the most vulnerable person in my life. And scared the shit out of a lot of other people. If revenge could ever be justified, this was the time. In fact, the strength of my feelings scared me.

Luke shrugged into his jacket. "Okay. I'll be back in a while. If anyone calls, just let it go to voice mail."

"I'm going to lie down with Rachel. Don't forget the night-lite."

Chapter Sixty-eight

Monday

Gary Phillips was not looking forward to his meeting with Stokes. The security chief had asked to meet him in an out-of-the-way alley in the South Loop, near Manny's Delicatessen, at seven in the morning. Phillips had been reluctant to agree, and now that he'd taken a cab over, he worried a hand through his salt-and-pepper hair. It was a habit he'd picked up in college, and he'd thought he'd licked it. But it came back, especially during stressful times. And a visit from the FBI alleging that Delcroft's security chief had kidnapped a young woman, on top of the other crimes he'd committed, had been plenty stressful. No wonder Stokes was lying low.

Phillips' only rationalization for coming was that he needed to know exactly what Stokes had done in order to manage damage control. He stamped his feet. It was a sunny day, with a metallic blue sky, but it was cold. He pulled out his leather gloves, put them on, then turned up the collar of his North Face parka.

He checked his watch; Stokes was always prompt no matter where they were meeting. He gazed around. Like some Chicago alleys, this one was cracked concrete with a pothole in the center. The back doors of a dozen small offices and stores, separated by chain-link fences edging the property lines, opened onto one side. A few small buildings, warehouses probably, occupied the other side. A set of green Dumpsters sat at each end, both releasing rancid odors. The husk of an old Chevy on blocks lay in one yard.

A cab pulled up to the south end of the alley and the back door opened. A burly figure emerged. Stokes. The man made his way over leisurely, as if they had all the time in the world. When they were close together, he said, "I got Parks' flash drive."

Phillips let out a breath. They were back to that. Murder in the first degree. Now kidnapping. And attempted murder. At least he'd called his lawyer.

"I had a visitor over the weekend. At my house in Winnetka."

"From the FBI, I'll bet."

"Exactly. They're looking for you. What the fuck did you think you were doing kidnapping the Foreman girl?"

"It was—necessary."

"And the suicide vest? Are you completely insane? Do you know how much shit the company will have to shovel to contain this?"

"I realize you think it was over-the-top, but I considered it a matter of national security. We had to know exactly what Hollander was doing with Gao. Now we do."

"Yeah, well, now that we know, I can let *you* know that you're fired."

Stokes tilted his head. "Riordan's the only one who can fire me."

"He did. This comes from him," Phillips said.

"He'll change his mind when he sees what I have in my possession."

"What's that?"

"I got the intel we needed. Hollander is definitely a traitor. The emails prove it."

Phillips shifted his feet. "You decrypted them?"

"They already were." Stokes brushed a finger between his nose and upper lip. "We hit the jackpot. We had Hollander's emails to Parks, but now we have the correspondence from Parks to Gao. There are emails about payments, who gets what and when.

Attachments of blueprints, too. And the three of them met in the Bahamas a few months ago to discuss the deal." Stokes puffed out his chest. "It gets even better."

"I want a hard copy of all those messages ASAP," Phillips said.

"I don't know." Stokes folded his arms. "They're on a need-to-know basis."

"You'll have them on my desk by the end of the day." He looked at his watch. "Riordan's orders," he added.

Stokes gazed at him as if he was unsure what to say. Phillips couldn't resist a smirk.

"He's turned the whole matter over to me. Doesn't want to get his hands dirty." When there was no response from Stokes, Phillips added, "As to relieving you of your duties, feel free to call him if you don't believe me." He shoved his hands in his pockets. "Anything else?"

"What do you mean?"

"Anything else you want to tell me? Where you're going. Where we can find you."

"You won't find me. I'll contact you. And you should know something. Even if I give you the emails, I'll be keeping a set for myself. Just in case."

Phillips knew Stokes was trying to intimidate him. But he was having none of it. "Remember at our last meeting you said you had two words for me?"

"Yeah. Aldrich Ames."

"Right. Well, I have two for you." He paused. "Plausible deniability. You've gone rogue."

Stokes didn't answer for a moment. Then: "If you tell the FBI where you think I am, I'll go to the media with all of it. From the beginning."

"Uh-huh." Phillips wasn't cowed. He knew Stokes wouldn't do a goddammed thing that brought more attention on him. But just to be sure, Phillips would make a call when he got back to his office. To his contact at DOD. First he'd chew him out for not having better intel on Stokes from the beginning. Then he'd tell him what he wanted done.

"Well, this has been a good meeting. Now, if you'll forgive me, I have a busy day. Have the package on my desk by five. Oh. Be sure to contact HR before the end of the day. They'll be happy to recommend outplacement opportunities for you."

Stokes glared at Phillips, which gave Phillips a tiny thrill. He hid his smile as he strolled down the alley back to the street, leaving Stokes where he belonged—by the Dumpsters.

Chapter Sixty-nine

Monday Night

Phillips was still working in his office after dark when his office phone buzzed. "Phillips."

"Mr. Phillips, sir, this is Henry Harding in Engineering."

To Phillips' surprise, Stokes had messengered the hard copies of the emails to Phillips just before five. Phillips promptly had the set copied and sent for Harding, the acting chief of engineering in Hollander's absence.

"This is a highly confidential project, Harding. No one is to know anything about this. Understand?"

Harding, a fortyish man with glasses, off-the-shelf suits from Men's Wearhouse, and ties that were twenty years out of date, nodded. "Yes, sir."

"I want you to compare these papers to the originals. You know, the schematics and blueprints. Make sure they're identical." Phillips still couldn't believe Hollander had committed treason. It just made no sense.

Harding swallowed. Phillips knew the man had questions, but he seemed to understand the delicacy of the matter. He kept his mouth shut.

Now he was on the phone. "What can I do for you, Henry?"

"I think you better come down. There's something you're going to want to see."

Phillips took the elevator two floors down and found his way to the Engineering Department. Harding was waiting for him, so he didn't need to swipe his key card. Harding led him into a conference room where an old transparency projector sat on the middle of the table. Phillips remembered transparency machines from his early days in marketing. He was surprised they were still in use. Well, maybe not. It was a well-known fact that engineers used the most advanced technology in some areas, but still wore pocket protectors and used obsolete technology in others.

Harding had rolled up his sleeves, and he was pale, as if he hadn't seen daylight in weeks. Then again, he probably hadn't. Like most of the other Delcroft engineers, Harding was a workaholic. He looked wrung out, and his posture was stooped. But behind the weary appearance was a keen mind with sharp analytical skills. Harding leaned over the projector and snapped it on. An image of two documents side by side lit the screen.

"Take a look at these. They're both diagrams of the navigation system for DADES."

Phillips frowned at the images. "What am I looking for?"

"Do you see any difference between them?"

Phillips wasn't an engineer. He'd barely passed basic physics at Yale. He shook his head. "They look identical to me."

"Look on the right side of each diagram." Harding turned on a laser pointer. "See the connections and wiring?"

Now that Harding pointed them out, Phillips looked more carefully. "They're different. One has wires going to one box, the other to that rotating thing, whatever it is."

"Exactly. Now look at these." Harding slapped two new images on the machine and used the pointer to circle the area on which Phillips should concentrate.

"They're different too. Subtle but different."

Harding nodded.

"Are you saying what I think you're saying?"

Harding smiled. "Yes. The one on the left is the real deal. Straight from the vault. The one on the right is what Hollander sent to Gao through Parks. Somehow, it's been adulterated. Changed. It won't work worth a damn."

Phillips' jaw dropped, his mouth agape. Then he started to laugh so long and hard that Harding looked bewildered. The engineer probably thought Phillips had lost his mind. But Phillips couldn't bring himself to stop.

Chapter Seventy

Wednesday

Rachel and I spent the next few days at Luke's. Rachel was showing what I found out later were classic signs of PTSD. She slept only in spurts and woke up screaming with nightmares. When she was awake, she was moody. She would stare into space, distant and remote; a moment later, she grew consumed with terror.

That happened after she woke up. She hardly said a word during breakfast, but she did wolf down her eggs and toast. I was glad her appetite seemed to be okay.

When she was done, I said, "You feel like taking a shower?"

She gave me a vague nod and trudged back up the stairs. I was loading dishes into the dishwasher when I heard her scream.

"Mama, where are you? I need you!" She often calls me "Mama," not "Mom" or "Mother," when she feels helpless.

I raced upstairs and found her crouched on the bathroom floor, naked. She was trembling all over, as if she was outside in the cold. I covered her with a towel and led her back into the bedroom.

I stayed with her all day, holding and cuddling her and reminding her it was all over and she was safe. I figured we'd talk about the rest of it when she was ready. I also suspected she might need professional help. What twenty-five-year-old woman wouldn't be freaked out after straddling the fragile line between life and death? Strapped into a suicide vest, knowing one false move by her or someone else could obliterate her and the people around her? I was her mother, but even I could only guess at the abject horror that claimed her.

The police and the FBI were in and out of Lake Geneva. Mostly LeJeune and Jimmy Saclarides, both of whom, thankfully, Rachel already knew. Others came with them, but no one pressed Rachel. Instead, they conducted a series of interviews with Luke and me. I wasn't sure if the men who came with LeJeune were with the Bureau; they might have been from another federal agency, maybe Homeland Security, maybe CIA. I made a mental note to ask Nick afterward. Even LeJeune and Jimmy had been debriefed, they said, and were preparing detailed reports.

The media, of course, heard rumors about the explosion as well as of federal agents overrunning the Lodge. Jimmy took the lead and explained in a press conference that a gas tank near the airstrip had ruptured. No one was killed or hurt, and property damage was minimal. That held the media's interest for about a nanosecond, and they went away. I was impressed.

By the third night Rachel seemed to have gained some equanimity. She wasn't herself, but she did acquiesce when I suggested takeout from Saclarides for dinner. I was rewarded with a smile when I mentioned taramasalata, the pink fish roe appetizer she loved. I phoned it in and had a pleasant conversation with Jimmy's aunt, who asked how she was doing. When I got off, I told Rachel lots of people cared about her.

She seemed pleased, then, for no apparent reason, suddenly burst into tears. I put my arms around her and led her to the kitchen, where I poured her a glass of wine. It might not have been the recommended tonic, but it did seem to quiet her. I poured one for myself, too, and as we were sitting down, I asked, "Do you want to see Q?"

Her eyes went wide, and the expression in them made me think she might panic again. Then she calmed down. "No. I can't."

"Why not?"

"I—I don't know. I—I don't want him to be associated with this—this thing."

I thought I knew what she was saying. I smiled. "Okay. He's been calling. He just wants you to know he's concerned. His exact words were"—I cleared my throat—"I miss her."

She sipped her wine and gave me a sly smile.

That was when I knew she would be okay.

Chapter Seventy-one

Wednesday

An hour later Luke went to pick up the food. Rachel and I dozed on couches in his family room. I was just drifting off when the house phone rang. I figured I'd better answer it. I went into the kitchen and picked up the extension.

"Ellie? Grizzly here."

"Hey, Griz. What's going on?"

"I have some information for Luke."

"I can pass it on if you'd like."

He paused. Then: "Sure. I guess it would be okay. Tell him I found out more about Stokes."

I stiffened. "What about him?"

"How much do you know about his background?"

"Just that he was in the CIA."

"That's right. Well, he left under somewhat mysterious circumstances."

"Yeah?"

"I made some calls and discovered he was kicked out."

I straightened up. "For what?"

"Apparently, he was in Afghanistan and got hold of some intel about the Taliban that he passed on to the military."

"And?"

"It was lousy intel. Half a dozen American soldiers went into a village and were slaughtered. The general in charge called the Agency and told them the army would never work with the guy again."

"Really."

"Yeah, but because he was with the Agency so long, they agreed to keep it under wraps."

"Why am I not surprised?"

"After what he did to you and your daughter, neither am I."

"You think Delcroft knows about this?"

"I wouldn't count on it. My sources are on deep background."

"You rock, Griz."

"I know."

I walked the phone into the family room. Rachel was asleep. At least her eyes were closed. I went back into the kitchen. "What prompted you to find this out, Griz?"

"I told you. I nosed around."

"Sorry. Wrong question. Why were you looking for it?"

There was a slight hesitation. "I thought you knew. Luke asked me to."

When Luke got back, I told him about Grizzly's call and what he'd said. Luke walked into the kitchen and started unpacking the cartons of food. I followed him in.

"What are you doing, Luke?"

He threw me a glance over his shoulder. "Getting dinner ready. How's Rachel?"

I planted my hands on my hips. "Don't try to change the subject. You know what I mean. Why are you looking into Stokes' background?"

"Isn't it obvious?"

"Pretend it's not."

"I want to dig up as much dirt on the asshole as possible. And then make it public. Along with what he did to you and Rachel."

"What if I don't want that?"

"Why wouldn't you?"

"Um…there's something called privacy. I know there's not a lot of it left anymore, but I'd like to hold on to the tiny fragments we still have. And I don't want Rachel's situation out there. She's still fragile. What if some idiot wants to finish what Stokes started?"

Luke turned around. "I don't think that's going to happen. And your names aren't going to be public."

"How do you figure that?"

"You'll see."

I took a deep breath. I loved Luke. I trusted him with my life. But this side of him, this angry, vengeful mind-set, wasn't like him. Still, I owed it to him to respect his motives. I knew they sprang from his desire to protect us. To make sure whatever threat was out there would be neutralized. I sighed and got out plates. "Whatever you're up to…please…be careful."

Chapter Seventy-two

Friday

Two mornings later LeJeune showed up after breakfast. Luke was outside pruning a couple of bushes. Then he was going to prune one of the trees. He liked playing lumberjack.

"Hey, Nick. Did I ever thank you for everything you did the other night?"

"No need. It's what I do. Got a couple of answers for you." He looked around. "Luke here?"

"I'll get him."

"Where's Rachel?"

"Still asleep."

"Good. She doesn't need to hear this."

I went to the back door to tell Luke that LeJeune was here. He came in a minute later and shook hands. I was pleased. Whatever tension had flared between them had evaporated since the kidnapping. I sensed they'd developed a mutual respect. It might even ripen into friendship.

We all sat in the family room. "So we analyzed the bits of explosive material at the airstrip."

"Tell me it was military-grade C-4," Luke said.

LeJeune tipped up the ball cap he always wore. "That's exactly what it was, my friend. The kind of material Stokes could easily get his hands on."

Luke stood and folded his arms. He started to pace the room.

LeJeune went on. "Preliminary forensic analysis indicates the timer was set to go off."

"Which means Stokes was going to kill Rachel," Luke said.

I felt myself gag. My hand flew to my mouth. I ran to the bathroom and threw up. It took me ten minutes to compose myself. As I came back in the room, I was calm. "What are your plans for capturing the motherfucker? He's got to be put away forever."

"That won't be necessary, *cher*." LeJeune looked from Luke to me.

"Why not?" Luke's voice was loud, accusatory.

"Because Stokes is dead."

A chill washed over me. "What?"

Luke stopped in his tracks. "When? How?"

"A car bomb in his van. Planted sometime yesterday. When he and two of his guys started the van last night, it all went boom."

"Who did it?" I asked, my voice preternaturally calm.

"We don't know." LeJeune looked over at Luke.

So did I. Was I imagining it, or did Luke not look as surprised as he should have? He stood rooted to the floor, arms still folded. Then he started to gently rock back and forth.

LeJeune smiled. "Well, *cher*, that is a separate investigation, which, I'm happy to say, is not my assignment. But I will do my best to keep you informed."

Luke continued to rock. And wouldn't meet my eyes.

"What's going on?" I asked.

He said nothing. Then he stopped rocking, straightened up, and shrugged. "Your guess is as good as mine."

I wanted to believe him. I looked down and stared at the area rug in the family room. It was a beige Indian design, with threads of red and brown. Very earthy. Plush. Masculine.

"I suppose it could have been Delcroft," I said.

"Why do you think that?" LeJeune asked.

"This all began with Hollander selling DADES to the Chinese. Maybe Delcroft decided to expose it themselves, rather than let Stokes feed it to the press and take the glory—"

Luke cut in. "Come on, Ellie. Do you really think Delcroft would sanction a murder?"

"They might have," I said. "Remember Gregory Parks? I never thought he committed suicide. I've always wondered if someone gave him a shove."

"Someone named Stokes?"

I nodded.

LeJeune shook his head. "It's possible. But the Bureau doesn't think Delcroft had anything to do with it. Too risky. Even though they're gonna pay a price for hiring Stokes in the first place. The means don't justify the end."

"Then who?" I asked. "The Chinese? Admittedly, they probably understood everyone would be better off without Stokes poking around. And pissing everyone off in the process. But to actually sanction a murder on US soil? I don't know."

We were all quiet for a moment. Then LeJeune looked over at Luke. "What do you think, Luke?"

He hesitated. Then: "I couldn't tell you."

Another pregnant pause.

I ended it. "So does Delcroft know about Stokes' 'off-the-books' activities?"

LeJeune said, "They do now. I had the pleasure of meeting with someone named Phillips."

"Gary Phillips. Deputy COO. Pretty high up the food chain."

"I told him everything." LeJeune was still watching Luke.

I decided not to pursue it. "Hey, you guys. There's something I don't get. If Stokes was kicked out of the CIA, why did Delcroft hire him?"

"Phillips claims they didn't know about his background," LeJeune said.

"Do you believe him?"

LeJeune shrugged.

"Delcroft and the military are obviously in bed with each other," I went on. "And even though Grizzly claims his ouster from the CIA was covered up, Delcroft has access to information we don't."

"I guess it depends on how much you believe Phillips," LeJeune replied. "By the way, who's Grizzly again?"

"A friend of Luke's in the navy. A commander up at Great Lakes."

"Oh, that's right." LeJeune continued to gaze at Luke.

"Or…" I got up from the couch and started to pace. "Maybe Hollander was behind it. Maybe Stokes was blackmailing her… or at least threatening to blow her 'arrangement' wide open. That could be a powerful motive."

"Maybe…," LeJeune said.

Both of us looked at Luke. He said nothing.

Chapter Seventy-three

Friday

LeJeune left a few minutes later, promising to keep in touch.

Luke made his way toward the door that led to the backyard.

"Hold on there, partner...," I said.

He stopped.

"What did you and Grizzly do?"

He turned around. "What are you talking about?"

"Luke..."

"How do you know I did anything?"

I bristled. "Stop with the games. I may be preoccupied with Rachel, but I'm not totally unaware."

He kept his mouth shut.

"If you had something to do with Stokes' death, you're just as bad as him."

Luke made a stand. "Ellie, you do realize this is all speculation on your part. You have no evidence."

"Except Grizzly's call."

He shoved his hands in his pockets. He wouldn't meet my eyes. "If I did anything at all, which I'm not saying I did, it was only to protect you and Rachel."

"Give me a good reason why I should believe you."

"Because I love you. And because Stokes was going rogue. He was way over the top."

"Look. I'm not sorry he's dead, okay? I'm glad he won't be able to hurt my baby again. But if you had something to do with it"—I felt my anger build—"that's a different issue. So. Did you?"

"I'm not going to answer that question. But you're right about one thing. This is a different issue. I know you're independent. I know you have your crusades. But sometimes you get in over your head and you need help. You either allow me to take care of you and do the right thing or you don't."

"Was killing a bad guy the only way to rescue me?"

"Don't be naïve. Sometimes it is and you know it. If your life is on the line and I have the resources or the contacts or the skills, well..." He didn't finish. He didn't have to.

Luke and I had reached a pivotal point in our relationship. There was no question I suspected him—at the very least—of passing information to Grizzly, who probably passed it to others, who made the decision to take Stokes out. But an assassination? Wouldn't it have been more effective to lock him up? Send him to a stateside Guantanamo, or a black-ops rendition site, and make him live out his days regretting his misdeeds? Although I hated the man for what he did to my daughter and me, forcing him to spend every day of his remaining days pondering and, perhaps, even atoning for his sins seemed to be a more powerful punishment than executing him.

Then again, I had never served in the military or an intelligence agency. Luke, Grizzly, and LeJeune had. They might know something about the man's conduct I didn't. They had been and still were a part of the perpetual state of war in which our country seems to exist; maybe it changes one's values and the way "soldiers" deal with rebellion, authority, and crime. Maybe war makes it easier to mete out retribution and punishment.

At the heart of it, though, was the personal relationship between Luke and me. As loath as I was to admit it, I do have a tendency to get in over my head. I do need to be rescued at times. Barry hadn't been able to. Neither had David. But Luke was begging for the job.

He stood before me now, marshaling his thoughts. Finally he said, "I don't know who killed Stokes. But I know why. He infected every person and organization he interacted with. It turns out a number of people wanted him dead."

It was my turn to say nothing. If I continued to pick at the scab of Stokes' death, I was pretty sure I'd discover Luke had played a role. So was I ready to condone a partner who actively pursued the assassination of another, as odious as that person was? Was I able to concede that maybe—just maybe—I needed someone in my corner to depend on? It was a huge risk to trust someone implicitly. Unconditionally. What if he took advantage of that trust and hurt me? What if it didn't work out? This living "in the gray" wasn't easy.

I had to make a decision. I mulled it over. "Just tell me one thing. Is it over?"

His brow smoothed out, and his body relaxed. His eyes filled with the soft, bottomless warmth I usually see. "Yes. The part that involves you and Rachel is over. Nobody will be coming after you anymore. I guarantee it."

"What about being hacked? Will NSA or whoever the hacker of the month is stop listening in on my life now?"

"I can't promise that. But I suspect once they find out how mundane and normal your life is, they'll lose interest."

I nodded. "Because of what you did."

He kept his mouth shut but shifted his weight. I was glad he didn't try to embrace me. It was going to take time for me to put his behavior in perspective. Right now all I could think was that the "soldier" I loved was not the person I thought he was. Nor was the country we lived in the country I thought it was. Both thoughts left me with an uneasy feeling.

Chapter Seventy-four

Sunday and Monday

On Sunday we drove back to my house. Rachel would stay with me for a while, until she was strong enough to resume her life. I called Barry, who came over right away. She flew into his arms. It made me realize that although he and I couldn't make it work, he cared about Rachel as much as I did. That was a good omen. I smiled. Barry caught my eye during their embrace and smiled back.

Both Rachel and I had a good night's sleep, but when I woke up, the skies were threatening. An hour later it rained, a cold, dreary rain that makes me want to huddle under the covers. I was about to do just that when a chauffeured limousine pulled up to the curb. A uniformed driver got out, opened an umbrella, and trotted around to the back of the limo. A gray-haired man wearing an impeccably tailored suit emerged. The limo driver handed him the umbrella, and the man proceeded to my front door. I felt the flash of recognition.

Gary Phillips. Deputy COO of Delcroft.

I went to the door and opened it just as he reached the porch but before he pushed the doorbell. If he was surprised, he didn't show it. "Good morning, Ellie. Do you have a few minutes?"

I showed him into the family room and brought him a cup of coffee. He sat in my father's chair, took a sip, then placed it on the side table. I sat on the couch.

"You heard the news about Stokes, I assume?"

I nodded.

"On behalf of Delcroft Aviation, I want to offer you a formal apology for the—the terror and anguish you and your daughter suffered. And make no mistake, it was a terrorist action. Stokes deserved what happened to him."

Was this a tacit exoneration of what Luke had done? Was he telling me that Luke indeed was an active player in Stokes' assassination?

"And we want to compensate you for your suffering. I know money can never—"

"I don't want your money," I cut in.

His eyebrows shot up.

"But I do want some answers."

He reached for his coffee. "You're entitled. Ask away."

"Why did you hire Stokes in the first place? What happened to your due diligence?"

"We thought we did it right. It turned out the report we got was a fabrication. It was full of—well, simply put, lies."

"You didn't know he'd been kicked out of the Agency?"

"We did not. Stokes clearly had allies in high places protecting him." He cleared his throat. "That, by the way, is being looked into right now."

"Gregory Parks. He didn't commit suicide, did he?"

Phillips tightened his lips and said nothing for about thirty seconds. Then: "No. He didn't."

"Stokes pushed him."

Phillips nodded. "Yes."

"When did you know that?"

His answer was slow to come. "Long enough for me to be charged with a felony if someone wants to."

I jerked my head up, surprised by his candor.

"What about Charlotte Hollander? What are you going to do? She sold DADES to the Chinese."

"Well, actually, that's the other reason I'm here."

I inclined my head.

"The schematics, the blueprints, for DADES that were sent via Charlotte's emails to General Gao had been adulterated."

"Adulterated? How?"

"They were changed. Simply but effectively. If and when the Chinese copy and manufacture them, bottom line, they'll end up with nothing. DADES won't work."

I went rigid. "You've got to be kidding."

He shook his head. "By the way, this is top secret. No one outside the company knows this. Just the chairman and me. And one of the engineers."

I tried to wrap my head around the news. "Who changed them? How did they find out? What are you going to do?"

Smiling, he held up a hand. "I'll answer all your questions. But one at a time. We compared the attachments—you know, the schematics and blueprints—on the drive from Parks, the one you handed over to Stokes, with the originals in our vault. The differences were clear."

"And?"

"As I said, it was a subtle but effective strategy. A conduit led to the wrong box. A wire here and there was misplaced. Altogether, it was enough to render the product worthless."

"Who did this?"

"It had to be Charlotte."

"Not Parks?" I said.

"No, it was Charlotte."

"How do you know?"

"Because the changes started on her computer. What she sent Parks was not what she designed. And that's what Parks sent to Gao."

"My God!" I leaned forward. "That means…" I thought it through. "That means that Hollander didn't commit treason after all."

"That's correct. Hollander is a patriot. At least in our eyes. Finally, someone had the—excuse the expression—balls to take on these goddamn international cyberthugs."

"Do you think Parks knew?"

"I don't know."

Knowing the strength of Parks' loyalty to the Uyghurs, I wouldn't have been surprised if Hollander and Parks were complicit. I debated whether to tell Phillips that I knew Parks was a double. I decided to keep quiet for the moment. After all, the only other person who knew that, aside from possibly the Chinese, was no longer alive. Which reminded me.

"Did you know that Parks was engaged? And that his fiancée was killed in an 'accident' on the Eisenhower?"

"So I've been told."

"Do you have any idea who might have been behind it?"

"You should ask your FBI friend. I wouldn't know."

"But if you had to speculate…"

"I wouldn't." Phillips took a breath. "We live in a dangerous world."

Was he hinting that the Chinese government might have played a role in Grace's death? I didn't know, but I did know I wasn't going to get anything further from him on that score.

"Back to Charlotte," Phillips said. "As I said, Delcroft owes her a huge debt. She saved the future of the company."

Maybe so, I thought. Though she could still be in danger if and when the Chinese found out they'd been conned. But the fact that Hollander and Parks might have been working together would explain her reaction to seeing Parks in my video. She didn't want any association between them to surface. She'd created a deep-cover operation.

But one thing didn't compute. "Wait a minute. If everything you're saying is true, why did Hollander run?"

"The way I figure it," Phillips said, "she had to know Stokes was on to her. And how dangerous he was. I'm guessing she decided it would be safer to drop off the grid than take her chances with him."

"Have you two been in contact?"

"No." He met my eyes. I sensed it was the truth. "I wish I was. I would want her to know it's safe to come back."

"You don't think she knows?"

"I don't. In her position, she couldn't risk even an Internet café."

"Because…"

"Because she doesn't know who knew what when. Stokes was probably monitoring her; the Agency and NSA too. And the Chinese. If I were her, I'd have gone as far away from an Internet connection as possible."

There was another institution he hadn't mentioned. "You forgot to add the military to your list."

He lifted his coffee cup, took another sip, then set it down. "Yes." He nodded. "Them too."

"Do they know about the adulterated files?"

"Why do you ask?"

"Because…" I paused. "They were the ones who killed Stokes, weren't they?"

"I told you I don't know who killed Stokes," Phillips said. "But, whoever it was, I can't say I'm sorry about it."

"Nice dodge, Mr. Phillips."

"What do you mean?"

"Isn't it possible that, in addition to Hollander and Parks, the military discovered that the plans were adulterated?"

"Anything is possible."

"Hollander did have an exemplary military career before she came to Delcroft."

"She did," he acknowledged.

"So how do we know *they* weren't behind the entire deception?"

He kept his mouth shut.

I'd figured Stokes planted the bomb at Dolan's office. It made sense at the time. But what if it wasn't Stokes? What if it was the Pentagon? They had a vested interest in letting the deal go through, especially if they knew DADES would turn out to be a dud.

Phillips blew out a breath. "Actually, Ellie, the government has been playing both sides against the middle for a long time."

Chapter Seventy-five

Monday

Again I was astonished at Phillips' candor. I hadn't expected it from the COO of one of the government's largest defense contractors.

"They are in a win-win situation," Phillips said after a moment's hesitation. "They can support the Chinese by selling them an antiterror system deemed critical in these unsettled days. They can even agree that terrorists of any stripe must be dealt with. Including the Uyghurs."

"So you know about them."

He smiled. "It's my job to understand all the players."

"You knew Parks was a double."

"So I have been told." He cleared his throat. "Getting back to the win-win...the US wins either way. We support China, but we sell them faulty systems."

"What about the Uyghurs?"

"They're no better or worse off than they were before."

"But if Parks knew the drone system wouldn't work, how do you know Hollander didn't give him the real thing to reward him for his complicity?"

"We don't. That's one of the reasons I want to find Charlotte and bring her in."

I tapped my index finger on the arm of the couch. "You're pretty cynical."

For the first time during our conversation, Phillips looked surprised.

"You don't see an ethical problem with all this double-dealing and duplicity?" I asked.

He smiled. "Ethics only goes so far when it comes to protection. We live in a complex world. You know that. There are—let's call them compromises we have to make along the way."

"The Deep State," I murmured.

Again, surprise flickered in his eyes. "You're an intelligent woman."

"Just for the hell of it, pretend I'm not."

"We have serious balance-of-trade issues with China. As you know, much of our debt is held by them. So it behooves us to get along where we can. Stamping out terrorism is an issue we can collaborate on."

"Even though US drones are dropping bombs on innocent people like the Uyghurs? It's happening, you know. Not just Chinese bombs, but American, too."

"I am aware of it." He leaned forward. "Would it surprise you to know I read Glenn Greenwald?"

"The liberal journalist who helped make Edward Snowden's NSA material public?"

Phillips nodded. "He said in an article that the US and, by extension, the media, do not believe human life is valuable unless it's Western. That it's easy to dehumanize non-Western victims of drone strikes, to literally just ignore them. Not even acknowledge they exist. It's only when a US citizen's life is lost that we make a fuss. Bottom line, we have been trained to view the killing of innocent people as not just an acceptable but an *inevitable* part of war. Collateral damage."

"You don't think that's screwed up?"

"It doesn't matter what I think. Ellie, this is only one tiny piece of reality. Even Charlotte's system, as advanced as it is, will become obsolete at some point. Then there will be something else we'll need to monitor and agonize over. America is too dependent on China to rock the boat unnecessarily."

I mulled it over, unwilling, in this case, to accept the ambiguity. The gray. "What happens if I go to Congress, or the press, and expose this?"

He smiled again. "You won't."

"And that's because…"

"Who did Stokes get the drive from, Ellie?"

I bit my lip.

"Even though Stokes is dead, you would be accused of espionage. Delcroft would be the victim. You would spend the rest of your life in prison. Probably in a cell next to Edward Snowden. If he ever comes back."

I felt my throat closing up.

Phillips looked at his watch. "I've enjoyed our talk, Ellie. But I need to be going now. I hope we stay in touch. I'd like you to finish that video."

Chapter Seventy-six

Two weeks later, the daffodils tentatively poked through the dirt, and the sky was that deep azure that accompanies a beautiful high-pressure system. Susan and I power walked around the village. The snow was gone, and a warm breeze danced to the rhythm of our steps. We got back to my house by four.

"You have time for a glass of wine?" I asked.

"Of course." Susan and I have concluded that wine does not cancel out exercise. The two activities work together organically to make us fit. And happy.

I opened a bottle of Chardonnay and poured us both a glass. We sat at the kitchen table. A cone of late afternoon sunlight streaked across the floor.

"You've been through hell," Susan said.

"I know." I sipped my wine. "I'm still edgy."

"Who wouldn't be? How's Rachel?"

"Probably better than me. She's sleeping through the night."

"Is she still here?"

"Just for a few more days. I want to make sure she's ready to go back."

Susan nodded. "So it's over? Everything?"

I lifted my hand and flipped it up and down. "Pretty much. There are still things I'll probably never know for sure."

"Like what?"

"For one thing, who edited the videos of the Uyghurs I watched at the library. Whoever did it obviously knew they had been viewed."

"Who do you think?"

"I think somehow the Chinese did it. They have incredible hacking skills, as you well know."

Susan nodded. "What else?"

"Remember when we were walking a few weeks ago and we saw the SUV?"

"And you wouldn't tell me what was going on?"

"Right. Well, there was a pickup there, too. Remember? It sped off when we approached."

"Oh yeah. What were they doing?"

"They were watching the watchers." I sipped my wine. "I recognized one of the guys in the pick-up at the airstrip. He was walking Rachel back to us."

"Really."

"Yeah. But now I don't know exactly who planted the bomb at Dolan's office. I thought all along it was Stokes. He seemed to take credit for it. But now I'm not so sure."

"You think it was the Chinese?"

"Chinese, the US military, who knows?" I finished my wine and poured more. "I'm still not even sure who tapped my phones or who was tailing me." I took a sip. "We know Stokes' men did, we know Grace Qasimi did, but who else? The military? The Chinese? I don't know."

"Don't you want to find out?"

I thought about it. "Actually, I don't."

"Because…?"

"I don't want to be disappointed."

"What do you mean?"

"I've learned too much about the people at the highest levels of power in our country and how they operate. I don't think I want to know any more."

Susan narrowed her eyes. We didn't say anything for a moment.

"And then there was Grace Qasimi's death."

"Gregory Parks' fiancée."

I nodded. "It was totally unnecessary. But LeJeune said he'd keep on it. Make sure someone is held accountable."

"Do you think he'll follow through?"

I ran my tongue around my lips. "Actually, yes. He turned out to be a pretty good guy." I paused. "But there's still one missing piece."

Chapter Seventy-seven

"What's that?" Susan asked.

"Charlotte Hollander. I told you how she disappeared in the middle of the mess when everyone thought she'd committed treason. Well, now she's a hero. But she hasn't come back, and people are worried."

"About what?"

"That maybe Stokes killed her, like he did Parks. Or maybe the Chinese did."

"Really?"

"The point is if she were still alive she would know it's safe for her to come back."

"Maybe she doesn't know."

"That's what Phillips said." I took another sip of wine. "But someone with her resources doesn't disappear without keeping up with developments that involve her."

"Why not?"

"She was totally plugged into Delcroft. To the military as well. At the very least, she could have gone to an Internet café and catch up on the news."

"Unless she didn't. If you want to stay hidden, you have to give up some things. You know how easy it is for the NSA to find people if they're motivated."

"Again, that's exactly what Phillips said. Do you two have a secret relationship I don't know about?" I smiled and picked up the wine bottle. Then I stopped, the bottle in midair. "Say that again."

"Say what?" Susan asked. "About Phillips' and my secret relationship?"

I shook my head. "About how easy it is to find people if you're motivated..."

"That's just it," Susan said. "It works both ways. The only way to stay completely off the grid is *not* to keep track of what's going on."

I set the wine bottle back on the table, an idea taking shape. "Hey. Do you remember a few years ago when Edward Kaiser died? And his wife, the trophy wife, ran away with all his money?"

"I do. And I remember how they caught her. You had a lot to do with it."

"Yeah, but do you remember how?"

Susan cocked her head. "Wasn't it something about your Rachel and her son emailing even though they weren't supposed to?"

"Exactly."

"I see that gleam in your eyes, Ellie. What are you thinking?"

"Hollander has a twelve-year-old son."

"So?"

"She didn't take him with her. He's living with his father in Ohio."

"And?"

"What kind of mother could give up talking to her child indefinitely? Think about it. Could you?"

"Never."

"Neither could I."

"Where are you going with this?"

"Well," I said, "we already know the NSA, the FBI, Homeland Security, military intelligence, and every other intelligence agency in the country has probably hacked the kid's computer and cell in an effort to find her, right?"

Susan tapped her wineglass on the table. "If you say so."

"And they haven't found anything. Nada. No evidence they've been in touch."

"Right…"

"But what if she found another way to communicate with him? A way that bypassed everything NSA and their minions track?"

"It would have to be something like carrier pigeon."

"Not necessarily." I jumped up from the table. "I need to talk to your husband."

"Doug? Why?"

"He's a ham radio freak, right?"

Susan sighed. "He's been that way since high school."

"Well, so is Hollander's kid."

Susan's voice rose to a squeak, which is the way I can tell she's excited. "How do you know that?"

"Hollander told me when we were having drinks at the Happ Inn."

"Do you think they're in touch by ham radio?"

"I think it's possible. Can you call Doug? Please?"

"Aye, aye, *capitaine*." She punched in a number on her cell. After a moment, she said, "Can you talk to Ellie for a minute?" A short pause. "Great. I'll put you on speaker." She pressed the "Speaker" button.

"Hi, Doug. Thanks so much for talking to me."

"No problem, Ellie."

I explained.

"So…," he said. "You want to know if—hypothetically—two people could communicate by ham radio, and the NSA or any other intelligence-gathering organization wouldn't know about it?"

"That's it."

"Of course. It's absolutely possible."

"Really?" Susan and I exchanged grins.

"I won't bore you with the technical details, but essentially, you can use the high-frequency bands on ham radio to contact anyone on the planet. All you have to do is prearrange a time and frequency. The conditions have to be right, but if you choose something in the middle of the frequency spectrum, it'll prob-ably work."

"So if you were in Barbados, and the person you wanted to talk to was in Ohio, you could, as long as both people knew the time and the frequency in advance?"

"Absolutely."

"But how do you avoid detection?"

"Anyone searching for their conversations would have to know where and when to look. They can't just monitor the entire high-frequency spectrum, as far as I know. They would need the same information as the people who want to talk to each other. In fact, that's why ham radio is so effective. It's like hunting for a needle in a haystack. It's well-known that drug runners use it all the time."

"That's it, then!" I clapped my hands.

"What's it?" Doug asked.

I told him. "I have to call Delcroft. Phillips. He needs to get someone to talk to the son and pass the all-clear signal to his mother. The kid probably won't have a clue what's been going on, but Hollander will. Thank you, Doug. You're a lifesaver!"

"Glad to help. See you later, sweetie."

They'd been married for more than twenty years, but Susan blushed. "Bye, honey."

I poured a bit more wine for us, and we clinked glasses. Then I picked up my phone to call Phillips.

Epilogue

The crowd began to assemble in Tiananmen Square well in advance. The crisp spring day, sunny and bright, was perfect for a parade. Little children waved flags. Students sunned themselves, happy to be away from the tedium of school. Even the elderly gathered to watch the festivities and gossip among themselves.

The parade, when it began, did not disappoint. Rows and rows of soldiers marched, goose-stepping in tight formation. They appeared to be younger and younger every year. But they were soon replaced by a phalanx of tanks and trucks and even airplanes rolling by. The government flexing its military muscle, reminding the world of their might. The vehicles were followed by marching bands playing patriotic music that brought cheers from the crowd. Then came more soldiers with helmets, rifles, and shiny knee-high boots; young girls in short red uniforms; and giant Chinese flags, borne proudly by eager boys and girls.

Toward the middle of the procession rolled three open limousines, German made, slowly advancing to the tempo of the bands' music. One carried the president, one bore the premier, and the third was occupied by General Gao Zhi Peng, who had recently been promoted to chairman of the Central Military Commission. There was no higher military position, and it was rumored that he might even become the next president. As he passed, cameras snapped and smartphones clicked, and the roars of approval swelled. He acknowledged the cheers with an occasional salute. He had ascended the pinnacle of Chinese power, and his beaming expression indicated he intended to stay there.

◇◇◇

While the parade consumed Beijing, the people of the Xinjiang Uyghur Autonomous Region in the Tarim Basin desert mourned their dead. The relentless drone strikes were taking their toll, and there were funerals every day. Children buried parents; parents buried children; and the sight of tiny coffins, each symbolizing a future cut short, brought anguished cries from the grieving.

One mother suppressed her sorrow and shook a threatening fist at the sky, as if daring more bombs to drop. Her husband grabbed her hand and lowered it. "There is nothing we can do. And if the soldiers see you, they will take you to prison."

"I do not care. I should be dead too; I do not want to live anymore. We mean nothing to those who destroy us. To them we are mere specks on the ground to be swept away by the fires and forgotten."

"You must not talk that way. Allah will protect us. He will vanquish the infidels."

The woman threw her husband a look that said he was crazy. "Allah? You think Allah will save us?" She spat on the ground. "That is what I think of your Allah. Unless he sends us guns and weapons that will shoot the enemy out of the sky, I have no use for your Allah."

The woman's husband blanched. "You must not talk that way. If someone hears you…"

Suddenly a man wearing the uniform of a soldier approached, attracted by their squabble. The couple said nothing as the soldier slowed, stared at them with a scowl, but then eventually passed.

"You see?" the husband said. He took her gently by the arm and led her away from the grave site.

Grace and Yusup's mother clenched her jaw. She had lost both her children to the Americans and the Chinese and their weapons. She had no more words to express her anguish. No answers. No hope. For one brief moment she had thought it would change. A bright shining light for her people would burn. Her daughter had assured her it would. But Grace had been wrong. It was not to be. It had always been thus.

It would always be so.

About the Author

Libby Fischer Hellmann left a career in broadcast news in Washington, DC and moved to Chicago thirty-five years ago, where she, naturally, began to write gritty crime fiction. Twelve novels and twenty short stories later, she claims they'll take her out of the Windy City feet-first. She has been nominated for many awards in the mystery- and crime-writing community and has even won a few.*

With the addition of *Jump Cut* in 2016, her novels include the now five-volume Ellie Foreman series, which she describes as a cross between "Desperate Housewives" and "24;" the hard-boiled four-volume Georgia Davis PI series, and three stand-alone historical thrillers that Libby calls her "Revolution Trilogy." *The Incidental Spy*, a historical novella set during the early years of the Manhattan Project at the U of Chicago was released last fall.

Her short stories have been published in a dozen anthologies, the *Saturday Evening Post*, and Ed Gorman's *25 Criminally Good Short Stories* collection. In 2005 Libby was the national president of Sisters In Crime, a 3,500-member organization dedicated to the advancement of female crime-fiction authors.

More at http://libbyhellmann.com

* She has been a finalist twice for the Anthony, twice for *Foreword Magazine*'s Book of the Year, the Agatha, the Shamus, the Daphne and has won the Lovey multiple times.

To receive a free catalog of Poisoned Pen Press titles, please provide your name, address, and email address in one of the following ways:

Phone: 1-800-421-3976
Facsimile: 1-480-949-1707
Email: info@poisonedpenpress.com
Website: www.poisonedpenpress.com

Poisoned Pen Press
6962 E. First Ave. Ste 103
Scottsdale, AZ 85251